GW00642832

The Beautiful Fall

Hugh Breakey is an award-winning and widely published philosopher. He has previously worked as a kitchen hand, editor, airport construction worker, theatre director, ethics consultant, pinball repairer, disk jockey, tennis court builder and university lecturer. Hugh lives in rural Australia with his two children and his wife, the *New York Times* bestselling novelist Kylie Scott. *The Beautiful Fall* is his first novel.

The Beautiful Fall

Hugh Breakey

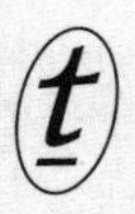

TEXT PUBLISHING MELBOURNE AUSTRALIA

textpublishing.com.au

The Text Publishing Company
Swann House, 22 William Street, Melbourne Victoria 3000, Australia

The Text Publishing Company (UK) Ltd
130 Wood Street, London EC2V 6DL, United Kingdom

Copyright © Hugh Breakey, 2021

The moral right of Hugh Breakey to be identified as the author of this work has been asserted.

All rights reserved. Without limiting the rights under copyright above, no part of this publication shall be reproduced, stored in or introduced into a retrieval system, or transmitted in any form or by any means (electronic, mechanical, photocopying, recording or otherwise), without the prior permission of both the copyright owner and the publisher of this book.

Published by The Text Publishing Company, 2021

Book design by Jessica Horrocks
Cover hand illustrations by AnMark/Creative Market
Typeset in Sabon by J&M Typesetting

Printed and bound in Australia by Griffin Press, part of Ovato, an Accredited ISO AS/NZS 14001:2004 Environmental Management System printer

ISBN: 9781922330543 (paperback)
ISBN: 9781925923957 (ebook)

A catalogue record for this book is available from the National Library of Australia.

This book is printed on paper certified against the Forest Stewardship Council® Standards. Griffin Press holds FSC chain-of-custody certification SGS-COC-005088. FSC promotes environmentally responsible, socially beneficial and economically viable management of the world's forests.

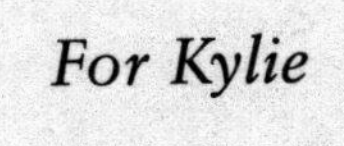

For Kylie

Read this now. Right now. Don't even think of going near that door until you know what's going on.

Your name is Robert Penfold. Age 31. The apartment you're standing in is your home: 116 Dornoch Terrace, Brisbane, Australia.

(If you're not in the apartment, you need to get there right away. *Don't speak to anyone*. This is for your own safety. Look for a street sign to find out where you are. There's a map in your back pocket. Follow it home. Your apartment is on the fifth floor, number 509. Whatever you do, don't ask for help.)

The reason you don't remember anything is because you have recurring amnesia. *The forgetting*, I call it, which means you do too.

It strikes at regular intervals: the last time was close to six months ago, and it was me standing where you are now. So believe me when I say I know you're scared.

It's OK, though. You're safe here. Your home has everything you need. There's food in the fridge. Clothes in the wardrobe. And information everywhere, about who you are and what you've done.

When you're ready, go to the kitchen. There's a cardboard box with all our paperwork and documents. The brown envelope in there contains a letter like the one you're reading now. It's the one I read when I woke up, written back when we first moved to this apartment.

There's also a manila folder where you'll find the report from our doctor, Doctor Varma. It's pretty dense, with all the talk of arterioles, limbic systems and episodic memory. The short version is: we had our first episode about two years ago. Apart from a few fragments from our early childhood, we lost all our memories. Everyone thought it was a one-off thing, maybe a stroke. Then, 179 days later, the forgetting struck again. And then it happened again, another 179 days later.

Periodic, Doctor Varma called it. A type of migraine recurring with (so far, at least) unusually precise frequency. I know you're thinking (because it's what I was thinking)—aren't migraines all terrible pain and devastating headaches? But the pain is just a symptom. The migraine itself happens when blood vessels inside the brain spasm and cut off the blood flow. If they take out the blood running to your visual centres, you get weird flashes and lights. If they take out your motor centres, half your body can feel paralysed. But I—you—got something much less common. There's a couple of little blood vessels, or maybe just a single solitary one, right in the middle of your head, running to your memory centres. And every so often—periodically—it trembles, clenches: the tiniest thing. And everything falls.

The doctor said we shouldn't be that surprised. Memory's far more fragile than people think.

The bad news is there's no cure. The good news is that these things come and go. I made it twenty-nine years without an episode. For all we know the forgetting might never strike again. Or it may carry on for the next ten years.

Since you're reading this, I guess things haven't improved yet. If the timing is the same as previous episodes, then the forgetting will have struck exactly 157 days after the day I wrote this, making it Sunday, 25 September.

You are about to have a very bad few days. Without memory, everything can seem meaningless. You'll be filled with despair: I was.

But we're actually lucky. Most people with recurring amnesia don't have this long between episodes. Sometimes they have a few hours, or a few minutes. We have almost six months between each forgetting. Enough time to come up with plans, work on them and see them through. Just like a normal person.

You'll see what I've done when you look through the apartment. When I first woke up and read the letter, I felt like I had no history at all. You'll see that you've done something special. A project planned by my past, achieved by my present, and passed on to you, my future. That's why I can talk about 'us'—because we're one and the same person. Through the work we go on. We endure, no matter what the forgetting does to us.

The letter that set me the task said I was doing something no one else had done. Like a kind of record, I suppose. To be honest, I don't really care about records. But I hope you'll be able to see the beauty in what I've done, and know that it came from your hands: our hands.

OK: some practicalities. Make sure you spend these first few days at home—preferably a week or more. Get your bearings. Go through the records. There's a mementoes box as well, full of treasures from our distant past.

Don't go outside until you're ready. A year ago, after the third forgetting, the police found us out on the streets, lost and wandering. Any repeat of that and Doctor Varma says the government will have to put us in a home—because it has a 'duty of care'—and if that happened we might never get out. So stay safe at home. Take as much time as you need. A grocery delivery comes every Tuesday. It's all organised, and it's paid for out of our pension along with the rent and utilities. Just smile and nod and sign the receipt they give you. You'll be fine.

Whatever you do, never let anyone know your condition. *Keep to yourself to keep your self.* That's what my letter said, and you'll see it was right. Memories are like armour—without them, you have no control, nothing to hold your shape. You'll become whatever anyone tells you to be. That's why you have to be on your guard from the very first moments.

Our life may be solitary, but at least it's *our* life, and not someone else's. It's all anyone gets. Keeping it—that's the real fight.

Robert Penfold, 21 April

Day Twelve

Twelve days to go. So much work to do—now more than ever. I'd set my alarm for 6.00 a.m. but the reason for the early start, the accident yesterday, was also what made me want to stay in bed. I dreaded having to face the enormity of what had happened. Take things one step at a time, I told myself. You don't have to deal with it straight away. Just work through the morning routine.

I PULLED myself to my feet. My workout proceeded like any other day, except that I kept my eyes averted from the archway between the kitchen and the living-room—and the wreckage lying there. I focused on the exercises, pushing myself harder than normal through the reps. The burn in my muscles took my mind off anything else.

But when I started my stretch-down and my pulse stopped hammering in my ears, my thoughts went straight back to yesterday's accident. *How many hours did I lose? Have I got enough time left to fix it?*

I couldn't face up to it, despite the sense of urgency. I dawdled through my shower and breakfast. Did some tidying; cleaned the toilet. *It doesn't count as procrastination if you're being productive.*

Finally the jobs ran out and I slumped down at the kitchen table. *Fine. Now I'm officially procrastinating.*

I could feel the minutes crawling by. Twelve days. The sum total of all I had left. About two hundred waking hours which was—a scribble on the nearby notepad—around twelve thousand minutes. Minus the three I'd just spent doodling.

'Delivery,' a voice called, with a sharp *rat-tat-tat* on the apartment door.

I sat up straight. Tuesday: grocery delivery day. *Perfect.* I'd have to go through the livingroom archway to get to the apartment door. The problem of facing up to the wreckage had been taken out of my hands.

As I rose from the chair, it struck me that the voice

was different: it wasn't Mr Lester, who usually brought the groceries. Then I remembered about his holiday, the cruise he'd organised for his wife's sixtieth. He'd been going on about it for weeks but, with the accident yesterday, it had fallen off my radar. Somehow Mr Lester had failed to mention that the new delivery person might be a young woman.

It was months since someone new had crossed my threshold. I ran my hand through my hair and realised how long and scruffy it had grown. I set my shoulders and took the central path through the livingroom to the door, trying to avoid looking at the chaos on my left.

'Delivery,' the voice called again. *Rat-tat-tat*.

Deep breath. Shoulders back. All I had to do was act normal. Remember to breathe. I slipped the chain off its latch. With one final wish that at least she wouldn't be pretty, I swung the door inward.

I peered out into the dimly lit hallway. Green eyes shone out of the shadows, matching the flicker of two earrings and a jewelled piercing above her lip. She had jet black hair, cropped short with a fringe falling over one side of her forehead.

Dammit. She'd look good wearing a sack.

I could tell because she was wearing a sack. Her uniform top, in the familiar blue of the delivery company, looked at least three sizes too big. Perhaps the company didn't have any uniforms for someone of her slim build.

A white earbud sat in one ear, the other hanging loose over her shoulder. Tinny music squeaked from it. My heart thumped against my chest. I hadn't been this close to a woman under fifty in months, much less an attractive one.

'Robert, right?'

I was staring.

'Robert Penfold?' Wide eyes looked up at mine, thin dark eyebrows arching. She flashed a polite, tight-lipped smile.

I tried to nod, and for a crazy moment it felt like I'd forgotten how to do that as well—as if an amateur puppeteer was making a hash of tilting my head.

But she seemed satisfied. 'Julie.' She held out her hand. 'Hi.'

I stuck out my hand, and her delicate fingers folded around it. Did I have a memory of touching a young woman? Maybe once. A shop assistant's fingers grazing my palm as she took my money.

I swallowed. The trick was just to plough through. No way they were paying her enough to deal with my awkwardness.

'Come in...' Hell. I'd been so busy taking in everything else that I'd already forgotten her name.

'Julie.'

'Julie, right. Sorry.' *Julie-Julie-Julie*. I pressed the name on to my mind. If I could keep it in my head until she left, I could write it down. Then it would be fixed, ready for next time.

Julie produced the chock of wood the deliverers always had handy and wedged the door open. She loaded herself up with groceries from the trolley. I stepped back, making room for her to enter.

'Careful with the, um...' I smiled weakly. 'Well, you'll see.'

Julie stopped short. A central path ran straight through the middle of the room, like the parting of a strange sea. On each side, an ocean of dominoes covered the entire floor and stretched up several thin bridges to raised platforms: rectangular wooden boards fixed to the wall with metal brackets.

'Hmph.' Julie looked the dominoes up and down, side to side.

Reluctantly, I looked with her. It was every bit as bad as I'd imagined. On one side of the room the dominoes stood neatly on end where they had been so carefully placed. On the other they lay toppled over, thousands of them, like a forest levelled by a meteor strike. If I had to guess—and I really didn't want to guess—about fifteen thousand dominoes had fallen.

At least all my raised platforms were untouched. The stepped ramps to each platform were only wide enough for a single line of dominoes. I'd been able to snatch a handful of those linking dominoes and halt the spread of the damage, but I couldn't contain the damage on the ground. The collapse there spiralled out in every direction. Days of work destroyed. Days I did not have left.

Beside me, Julie looked this way and that. 'Neat.' Her eyes flashed towards mine, and it felt like she was seeing me for the first time. Actually taking an interest.

A little tug of pride warmed my chest. Then another pang: of regret that she hadn't been able to see the work the day before, with all its thousands of tiles still standing poised, ready to unleash at a touch on its hair-trigger, charged with life and energy.

Julie pointed towards a group of collapsed dominoes at the centre of the wreckage. 'I like the whirling patterns.'

'Thanks,' I said. 'But that's what caused all the destruction. Once that part went, I couldn't stop it.'

'Oh.' Her eyebrows arched. 'Oops.'

'Yeah. Oops.'

'Just through here with the bags?' Julie turned and motioned towards the kitchen. I nodded, and she left me standing alone in the room, a flicker of hope in my heart. Yesterday, all I could see was the days of work ruined. But the delivery woman had seen the work still standing, and was impressed. Maybe things weren't so bad after all.

'Cold bags on the table?' Julie's voice carried from the kitchen.

'Thank you. I'll grab the rest.'

On the trip back to the kitchen, I had to step around her. Our eyes met for a moment. She really was beautiful.

Her polite smile returned and she stepped away to let me pass.

Back in the livingroom, I found Julie looking at the dominoes again. In one hand she held a small bunch of papers; the other twirled the cord running from her earbud, coiling it along her finger. 'So you accidentally bumped them and they just…?'

'Yeah.' I nodded. 'Those spirals are the worst. The damage corkscrews out in all directions. It's impossible to stop.'

'Hmph.' Her finger paused its coiling. 'You need a way of containing the damage. Like firebreaks, you know? Some kind of barrier thin enough to fit in the gaps.'

'It would interfere with the patterns.'

'Hmph.' She shrugged. 'This one's for you to sign.' She handed over papers and a pen. Once I'd returned them to her, she gave me a shiny blue card. 'That's our info, with the number to call if there's any problems.' Under the company logo, Julie's details stood out in dark blue lettering. I ran my thumb along the smooth surface with a sense of satisfaction. Documentation: tangible. This was going straight in the records box. And now I wouldn't need to write her name down as soon as she left.

'Any problems, my number's on the back,' Julie said. 'Don't call the old number, he's on holidays.' She pushed the loose earbud into her free ear. 'See you next time.' Her voice was louder as she spoke over the music in her ears.

'Next Tuesday.' I nodded.

Almost out the door, she stopped as if struck by a thought. 'Can I just ask?' Her fingers pointed at my work with a neat flick. 'Why dominoes?'

'Well,' I stumbled, 'because they're there, I guess.' Stupid answer.

But Julie seemed satisfied. 'Right,' she said. 'Like Everest.' A quick nod and she was gone.

I shut the door behind her. With the security chain

and deadlock snapped home, I was safe at last from pretty women and disturbing questions.

Why dominoes?

Standing in the middle of weeks of ruined work, it felt like a reasonable question. The answer I'd given was partly true, but normally when people say it about climbing mountains, they mean they're out there somewhere on the horizon. My own particular mountain—a stack of heavy cartons filled with boxes of dominoes—had been left for me, piled up in the centre of my livingroom. A bit harder to ignore.

Early on, I'd started work on the project for the reason set out in the letter: to have some kind of mission that spanned the forgettings. My past self had handed me the task, and all the required materials and tools, leaving the design and assembly to me. And then, when the final hour arrived, it would be my future self who would see what we had achieved, who would witness its final wonderful fall. In this way, we would show that we still had a life and could achieve things. Maybe even things no one else ever had.

The forgetting might take our memories, but our choices, plans and work could still control our lives.

Why exactly my past self had chosen *dominoes* for this purpose, I didn't know. It made sense for the work to be done alone and in private. The letter had hammered home that lesson: *For someone with our condition, solitude is the best defence. Keep to yourself to keep your self.* But still…why not card towers or a scale model of the Taj Mahal made of matchsticks, or poetry? And why not something more productive, or less costly? These thousands of dominoes—83,790 of them, by my count—couldn't have come cheap. I didn't know. Maybe someday I would.

Anyway, none of that explained why I felt physically sick at the thought it wouldn't be finished on time. Not the weight of expectations from the mountain in my livingroom. Not the need for projects that extended past the forgetting's assaults on my mind. Not even the investment of so much of my very short life into all I'd done so far.

My concern was something else again. It hadn't taken much fooling around with the little tiles to see the strange beauty they had when they were falling. With forethought, it was possible to really choreograph things, to have the cascading dominoes fall in unison, or chase each other playfully or race towards each other. The letter had never mentioned the beauty in the work, but it was that feeling of creation, almost art, that had driven me each day.

And now it might not be finished in time and the thought was intolerable. If the fall was to happen as I'd designed it, every part had to be finished. All of it. Otherwise it would be like a classical sculpture with rough, unfinished patches all over it. Like trying to dance when the music keeps cutting out.

I would not let that happen. Come what may, I would get this thing done, and my new self would see the final fall exactly as I'd created it.

Time to get back to work. First things first, though. There were still some unopened domino cartons stacked against the kitchen wall. On top of them were the two open cartons I used to store my records and my memen-toes. I wrote down the date on the business card Julie had given me—*Tuesday 13 September. Day 12*—and added it to the records box.

I put the groceries away, set my shoulders, gritted my teeth, and strode into the livingroom. I'd learnt from previous small accidents that although it was tempting to begin with the easiest areas—fix as much of the dam-age as fast as possible—the better strategy was to start at the hardest spots, in the corners.

That was why I'd placed stepping stones, flat heavy circles of wood the size of my feet, in between the dom-ino runs. It still took balance and flexibility to get to the corners, but the morning stretches paid off as I teetered and loomed and held myself suspended over the delicate work underneath me.

After about twenty minutes I looked around. Before last night's accident, I'd been enthusiastic, charging ahead of schedule: closing in on a goal of fifty thousand.

Now I was way behind. Working at top speed, I could lay down about a thousand dominoes every hour and a half. On a rough survey the accident had cost me more than three days' work—time I didn't have unless I put in longer days. But I'd already been planning to work seven and a half hours on the project each day, so the disaster meant that—

I quashed the line of thought. Better to wait and see what it looked like this evening.

At noon I sat cross-legged in the middle of the living-room, ate a sandwich and planned the rest of the rebuild. The good news was that rebuilding was faster than building. If I could get my speed up towards one thousand per hour, then perhaps it wouldn't be so bad...

My thoughts drifted to Mr Lester with a sense of regret. Seeing him last week, I hadn't processed that it was for the last time. He was the closest thing I had to a friend, the only person in my life to tell me I looked too pale, that I should go outside and get some sun. By the time he returned from his holidays all my memories of him would be gone, and only my future self would be here to greet him. It seemed a shame.

Still, I probably should be pleased he was away. *Keep to yourself to keep your self*, after all. My past self had been so insistent about the importance of being on my own that the letter put a positive spin on telling me that I had no family still living. Apparently my parents had died in an accident years ago. Given that the only memories that survived the forgetting were a handful of happy ones from childhood, the news had been hard to take.

But the letter said it was a good thing. In those first moments after the forgetting even parents—maybe particularly parents—could not be trusted. No way they would miss the opportunity to make some improvements. To leave out all the past problems and mistakes that made me who I was. And in the end, I'd be remade into something new. Something I had no control or choice over. Solitude was my best defence. Which was presumably also why I'd been left with no television, radio or internet.

If all that was true of parents, it was probably a bit true of Mr Lester as well. Maybe it was no bad thing he'd be in the middle of the ocean when the forgetting struck. But it was hard to feel thankful. He'd witnessed the whole domino process from its humblest beginnings. He would have commiserated with me about yesterday's disaster; unlike Julie, he would have been able to see what I'd lost. I sighed and finished the sandwich, and there was no excuse not to return to the work.

It was frustratingly slow. As the late afternoon sun began to shine through the kitchen windows, I could feel my concentration flagging. My back and thighs ached and I knew this was when mistakes could happen. But I pushed on, setting to work on another line of fallen dominoes.

Resentment gnawed at me. The rebuilding wasn't satisfying in the same way as new construction. It lacked any sense of breaking new ground. Actually, it was worse than that. Once it was done, the work became invisible. No one looking at the completed product could know its history, the sweat and toil of failures overcome. You had to know the history to see the person behind the work. Even the delivery person would know what had happened here—perhaps when she next arrived, Julie would mention how far I'd come in putting them all up again. Then in twelve days only she would know the history that I had forgotten. A complete stranger.

The whole point of the dominoes was to show my history. To *be* my history: a baton held out to me by my past self and ultimately passed on to the future's waiting grasp.

Rebuilding—work that papered over a crack in history as if it never happened—seemed wrong. The dominoes fell, or they didn't. Either way they couldn't communicate the full story of what had happened and what I'd done. Taking the trials and pitfalls into the future required the very thing I didn't have. Memory.

The idea hit me with the shock of the obvious. *I could write it down.* A history. Not just the emergency note that I carried with me everywhere. I was talking about *memory*: a journal recording my final twelve days.

My heart thumped at the idea. I would need to buy a new notebook. My telephone notepad wouldn't cut it. The corner store had a stationery shelf with nice ball-point pens and—I felt certain of it—hardcover notebooks. Perhaps a little fancier than I needed, but probably still within my budget.

Once the idea took hold, there was no stopping it. The dominoes were done for the day anyway. If I kept pushing on, I'd probably just make another mistake and be back where I started.

I rubbed my hands together with new-found resolve.

~

Any trip outside—no matter how brief—required preparation. While there were good reasons to expect the forgetting to follow the regular path it had tracked so far—and so strike in precisely twelve days' time—there was no guarantee. I'd phoned Doctor Varma in my first week, and she'd stressed the imprudence of expecting the condition to follow a neat timetable. So I needed to be prepared, with enough information to get me back home and safe. I gathered together the necessary equipment and stuffed it into my backpack. Keys, wallet, map, letter.

The door to my apartment sported two locks, an ordinary old door lock and a shiny new deadlock. Probably my past self had added the new one in the run-up to the last forgetting. He'd left the key in the envelope with the letter—making sure I couldn't venture outside without reading its contents and discovering why leaving might be such a bad idea.

Deep breath. It must be a few weeks since I'd been out. I swallowed, turned the key and stepped through the doorway.

Outside, tall buildings and high ground blocked the setting sun. The yellow streetlights were beginning to come on as dusk set in. The evening air smelled fresh and alive, a warm breeze gusting through the wide streets. The weather felt hotter than I remembered. My apartment had heating and air-con, making me oblivious to the changing seasons. The last time I'd been out there had been a breath of chill in the air, but no more. The world had changed.

The corner store turned out to stock a suitable kind of notebook at a very reasonable price—just $4.95, plus a dollar for the pen. I splurged on a meat pie and can of soft drink and sat at one of the little tables outside the shop. To any passer-by I would have looked completely normal. Just a guy grabbing a quick snack from the local store.

Those who did pass were mostly commuters heading home. I was connected to them in a way, though they could never know. When I'd asked Doctor Varma on the phone about where the money from my pension came from, I heard a shrug in her voice. 'The government,' she said. 'Taxpayers.' She seemed amused. 'You want to do the right thing by all those taxpayers? Keep your good self out of an institution. Hospital beds cost more in a day than your pension does in a month.' Still, I was grateful to the faceless crowds. They were paying for my sickness and would continue until it finally disappeared which, the doctor thought, might be years.

By the time I got back home it was almost seven o'clock but the last of the orange light still tinged the western sky. The days had grown longer as well as hotter. Once inside, I sat down at the kitchen table, took up the pen, and opened the book to its first page. Clean white paper. Thin blue lines.

I would make a journal entry for each of my last twelve days.

A memory bubbled up in my mind. Like all my surviving memories, it was buried so far back in childhood that my condition couldn't dislodge it. In my grade four classroom, a teacher who then seemed impossibly ancient asked the class to name the single book we would take to a desert island. A forest of hands; all sorts of titles called out. A quick-witted girl had won the day by suggesting a book on how to survive on a desert island.

But it had taken me all this time to see there was only ever one answer.

What book do you take to a desert island?

A blank one. And a pen.

At 6.38 p.m. on 13 September, I wrote four short words—and memory began.

Day Eleven

The morning alarm punched me out of bed.
Wednesday. Nothing special about it to anyone
looking on but today, behind every breath,
minding every misstep, was the journal. Now I
had a way for memories to leapfrog the forgetting,
every moment seemed to have new meaning.

TODAY, I could live and learn.

Wearing just pyjama shorts, I threw myself into my morning exercises, warming up my muscles in the air-conditioning. Until yesterday the exercises had seemed my best way of impacting on my future self. The forgetting might destroy all my memories, but it could not touch flesh and bone, tendon and muscle. And tendon could be stretched. Muscle could be built. The exercises I did now could reach through the forgetting into the future me.

Working out the exercises had actually been a lot of fun. The letter had only briefly referred to doing 'morning exercises'. With no gear or equipment in the flat, it was left to me to get more detailed information from my body itself. Across the mornings of the first fortnight, I felt my way to each new stretch or strengthening exercise: push-ups (palms and knuckles), planks (side and standard), squats, crunches, lunges. Then the cardio: star jumps, burpees. And on it went. Somehow, my body knew what came next, and how it should be done. Each day I teased out a new part of the morning routine, like a musician whose fingers remember the notes of a song the conscious mind has forgotten. Whose fingers *want* to remember—a will to move burned into flesh and nerve itself.

Chin-ups were the last exercise I uncovered, almost a month later than the others. That morning, exercises complete, I was heading into the bedroom when I reached up to the architraves above the doorway. There was no thought involved. It was as if a puppeteer above me tugged invisible strings running to my wrists. My biceps clenched and up I went—to come face to face with tangible evidence of my past self's exercising. Dust and grime lined the top of the architrave. But there were two patches where the dirt was light, recent: right where my hands were. History might be hidden from my mind, but evidence was everywhere, if you only knew where to look.

I could sense that history now, as my muscles warmed into the movement, a feeling of familiarity taking hold, my body starting to find its rhythm. I pushed through each of the reps in turn, and then cycled through them again, before turning, breathless and sweating, to the stretches. In what it could do, and what it couldn't do, my body held as many clues as a crime scene. And not just the body, but the mind as well. There were also hints of past history in the words I knew. I could name all the muscle groups as I stretched them, one by one: quads, traps, glutes, lats, hammies, adductors and the rest. Who would know such terms? Everyone? No one? Just people like me?

And who might *they* be?

Done at last, I hit the shower. My body tingled from the exercise and the stretching and the shower, and I felt ready to face the challenge I'd avoided yesterday. It was time to crunch the numbers, to find out how far

Monday's accident had set back the dominoes task. Maybe the numbers would be awful. But at least today I had the journal. By writing it all down and passing it on, it felt as if something positive might come out of it. As if I had a chance, for once, of learning from my mistakes.

Eating my cornflakes at the kitchen table, I braced myself and started the calculations.

Monday: Day 13. Early evening, and everything was on track. Around forty-seven thousand dominoes—well over half the total—were in their places. Eight of the seventeen platforms were up, along with their interconnecting bridges. That was a real achievement: putting up the platforms took a lot of time.

Then the accident. Almost half of the total floor dominoes were lost: something in the order of fifteen thousand fallen. Days of work gone in seconds. Somehow I had to cram the necessary work into my remaining hours. Yesterday had shown that rebuilding dominoes was faster than laying them from scratch, but I'd still have to work nine hours a day for the next eleven days. I didn't know if a nine-hour day was possible. If my concentration flagged near the day's end—as it had on Monday—then the final hours of work weren't merely ineffective, they were dangerous.

Still, I could only do what I could do. Sitting here feeling daunted wouldn't help. I squared my shoulders and strode into the livingroom. The trick would be in dividing the mammoth project into smaller, more manageable sections.

In retrospect, if I'd started full-time work earlier, it would have left more breathing space for the inevitable setbacks. But it had taken a lot of preliminary work to build up skill in laying the dominoes, and to get the placement design properly sorted out.

And anyway, part of me was excited that the project was coming down to the wire. The idea that I'd still be working feverishly on Day Zero as the final moment approached, racing against time to see the last tile put in place. What else would there be to do on that day but while away the dwindling hours, waiting for the end? I might be devastated—furious—at the prospect of failing to achieve the one task set down for me, but at least I wouldn't have time to myself at the end, alone with my thoughts.

I snapped together another row of dominoes, my hands moving faster, the dominoes almost leaping to attention in my fingers.

The corner was done: great. I moved to a more central area. Stopped short.

Here was the source of Monday's collapse: the intricate pattern with the whorls that made it impossible to prevent wholesale collapse once a single domino fell. I could redesign the whole section, but the spiral pattern was the centrepiece—it controlled the timing of the entire fall. Tearing it out would be like ripping its heart out. I gritted my teeth and began rebuilding, reaching out to scoop up one of the spiral arms.

And my fingers bumped a standing domino.

My breath stuck in my throat. As if moving in slow motion, the tile tilted, then wobbled. My hands were full of the dominoes I'd just picked up and there was nothing I could do as it toppled, finally, and fell into its neighbour and…

Nothing happened.

Miraculously, the neighbouring tile stood firm. The curve of the dominoes was at its tightest near the spiral's centre. The angle, combined with the first domino's tentative fall, saw it stand firm. Moving as if handling crystal, not daring to breathe, I reached out to the fallen piece and lifted it to safety.

Okay.

Breath rushed back into my lungs. I backed away to the central path and reached down to touch my toes, fingers, knuckles, palms to the floor. Gradually the stretch began to release the surge of panic. Disaster averted.

Still, it was a warning: something had to give. I couldn't work fast on complex patterns without an element of risk, but I couldn't afford risk. Julie's words echoed in my mind: 'You need a way of containing the damage. Some kind of barrier.' She'd only looked at the wreckage for a minute, but she'd nailed it. I looked around the room for inspiration. Living such a spartan existence meant there wasn't much spare stuff lying around the apartment, just the store of plastic bags from my deliveries and the packaging from the dominoes: a dozen or so empty cardboard cartons.

I peered at them.

Yes. The cardboard was sturdy, but thin enough to slip between the existing gaps in the dominoes. I went to work with a box cutter until I had a pile of rectangular barriers and then, one by one, the barriers went in. Slowly, carefully; until I'd imposed a strange cardboard grid over the whorls and curves of the standing dominoes. Then I got back to the real work. By the time I turned to lunch, the rebuilding was going quicker than ever and it was clear that laying the barriers had been time well spent.

I got the tomato, cheese and ham out of the fridge,

reached for a new loaf of sliced multigrain—and found that what I had was raisin bread. All three of the loaves Julie had delivered, enough to last me the week, were the same.

The frustrating thing about these mistakes was that my order never changed. Like everything else in my life—rent, electricity, the postal service—the grocery order had been set up by my predecessor, and was paid automatically out of my account. As far as possible I'd tried to keep things as he'd left them, to feel some continuity with my past. It was only a little thing. But little things were all I had.

In any case raisin bread for lunch wasn't an option. I pulled Julie's card out of the records box, dialled the number and explained the situation. She didn't seem very enthusiastic about doing an extra delivery, and couldn't fit it in today anyway. Eventually we settled on tomorrow before lunchtime, and I made myself a breadless sandwich, which tasted about as satisfying as it sounds.

The afternoon's work went well, but by three o'clock I found myself checking the clock. Despite my flagging concentration, I trusted the barriers to prevent the fallout from any accidents, and persevered. Four o'clock inched past, then at last four-thirty, marking the completion of my first nine-hour day.

I sank back on my haunches and surveyed the day's work. The best part of Monday's disaster stood behind me: from the look of it, I'd recovered more than three-quarters of the fallen tiles. Only two or three thousand remained, but they'd have to wait until tomorrow.

I made a simple dinner and headed out onto the balcony to eat. It was a while since I'd been out here. After a full day's hard work, crouched and contorted to lay the dominoes, the relief at just sitting made me feel almost light-headed.

I sat for a long while after dinner and watched the sun set over the mountains beyond the city. A soft breeze tugged at my shirt and ruffled my hair as the city lights flickered on and the day's light faded into night.

Tomorrow the last of the disaster would be erased; the only record remaining would be the one in my journal. That would be something.

Day Ten

6.00 alarm. My third early start in a row.

I ROLLED out of bed, still half-asleep as I stumbled through the start of my exercises. On the best mornings—mornings like this—I felt like a sculptor chipping away at a block of marble. Every moment of exertion, every drop of sweat running down my neck, was carving out my future self.

After a shower and breakfast, I washed the dishes and tidied the kitchen. Odd; I'd never tidied up for Mr Lester.

Not that odd, perhaps. Until yesterday I had no memory of ever even talking to a young woman, far less inviting one into my home. My one actual encounter (if you could call it that) was about eight or nine weeks after my memory rebooted. I'd developed enough confidence to face the outside world and looked forward to a long walk each evening at sunset, down the winding path through the parklands to the boardwalk. When the sun disappeared and lights began to twinkle along the river, I'd turn and retrace my steps back home.

I liked to watch the joggers. While the rest of the world trudged and stomped, the joggers skimmed over the track, vivid and full of energy.

On that night, I'd only just set out when a jogger approached from the opposite direction. Over the weeks, I'd worked out the road rules used by the various recreational path-users and it wasn't usually too difficult keeping out of the way, but that evening I must have been distracted. By the time I realised what was happening, we were about to collide.

I registered a quick impression—skin glistening with sweat, slick strands of dark hair escaped from a ponytail to frame the face, sleek black runner's sunglasses—and jerked out of her way at the same instant she tried to dodge me. We moved in the same direction. She veered sharply, her foot caught the edge of the path and in an instant, all her gracefulness disappeared. She fell forward, her ankle turning sideways under her.

Almost without thinking, I moved to catch her. I could see it was possible. She was close enough and I was quick enough. But the sudden image of my hands grabbing her body to halt her fall pulled me to a shuddering stop.

How would she react? Was it okay—permissible—to touch a woman you didn't know? I hesitated and she tumbled, crying out, and her ankle caved and she crashed on to the grass.

Mortified, I looked down at her crumpled figure. I wanted to help her, I did, but the sense of shame overwhelmed me. I backed away, praying with each step she wouldn't look up to see me fleeing the scene. At the last moment, I turned on my heel and walked on, disappearing from her view behind a clump of jacaranda trees.

Guilt nagged me about the whole thing for weeks afterward. I lay awake at night wondering if she had sprained the ankle or just twisted it. I stopped my evening walks altogether.

No wonder I felt nervous now. There was nothing to be done but to soldier on. Julie would remain beautiful, and I would remain awkward. At least I could take some solace in her dismissive attitude and her one-earbud indifference.

I turned my attention to something I could actually control in the world, and went into the livingroom to scoop up a new line of dominoes.

By the time the knock on the door and cry of 'Delivery' echoed through the apartment it was late morning. Monday's accident lay buried in the past. There was not a single fallen domino to be seen. If not for my journal record of the event, no one would ever know it had occurred. Apart from Julie, of course.

I unlocked the door and pulled it open. One earbud, like before.

'Hey,' she said, smiling politely.

'Thanks for coming back.'

'No worries.' She passed me two grocery bags. 'Three loaves of multigrain.'

'Thanks.'

'Sorry about the mistake.' She produced a clipboard and a pen. 'Can I just get you to run through everything on your order form, to make sure we're working off the right list? It doesn't look like it's been checked in a while.'

'Yeah, no problem.' My hands were full with the bags. 'Um. Do you want to come in?'

I carried the bags through into the kitchen. Julie waited in the livingroom. When I arrived back, she was looking from side to side and nodding.

'Yeah,' I said. 'The barriers were a good plan.'

'Hmph.' She handed me the folder and the pen. I began to make my way through the list, ticking each item in turn. It all looked fine.

'You're using twice as many as you need to. That's why you have those larger gaps.'

I followed her gaze to the cardboard barriers.

'See?' With a tug, she popped the earbud out of her ear. 'You've given every section its own barrier. So you've got all those double walls, taking up unnecessary space. If you just put down half as many rectangles, leaving a space in between each one,' she pointed, 'you'd get the same protection.'

'Oh, I see.' Relief flooded me as realisation dawned. Most of the dominoes could be protected by the barrier guarding the neighbouring groups. It was obvious now she'd pointed it out. 'Thanks. That's helpful.'

'Hmph.' She tapped her forehead modestly with the pen. 'When I need to, I have a very strat—' An electronic shriek drowned out the rest of her words, reverberating off the walls with heart-pounding urgency.

'What is that?' Julie yelled with her hands over her ears. 'A fire alarm? Do you have a drill today?'

'Not sure.' My voice went missing in the din. I tried

again, louder. 'I don't think so.' I followed Julie in clamping my hands over my ears, but the sound was unrelenting.

The dominoes seemed to be standing okay, but they wouldn't hold for long if the vibration belting my ears carried through the floor. My heart squeezed. The barriers could stop a single mistake cascading through the entire structure, but they could do nothing in the face of a system-wide assault.

I wrenched my right hand from my ear and placed it flat on the nearest wall.

Nothing.

Despite the racket, relief washed over me. Julie looked at me and then dropped into a neat crouch and placed her hand flat against the floor. She smiled up at me and nodded. It was a nice thing for her to do. I couldn't help feeling a tug of appreciation. She had to be right about the noise. A fire alarm. It was coming from inside the building. It couldn't be anything else.

'We should probably get out.' Julie had to lean forward and yell to make herself heard. 'Do you need a hand grabbing anything?'

She was right—the noise wasn't the threat: the noise was meant to alert us to the threat.

Fire.

The whole building could be alight. Forget my dominoes collapsing, the apartment itself might be gutted. I stood there gaping, struggling to get my head around the idea. The apartment contained my whole life. Every memory I had, every clue to my past, everything I'd built for the future, it was all within these walls. I shook myself. What should I take with me? I charged into the kitchen, Julie following in my wake.

I snatched up my backpack and rushed to the records box. Ignoring everything else, I grabbed the letter from my past self and the doctor's certificate. Both went straight into the bag, pressed up against its hard back so they wouldn't be crushed. Then I emptied the contents of my mementoes box into the backpack. Even in the rush, I checked to see I'd got them all: the little elephant made of dark wood, the beaded bracelet, the short but chunky crystal vase, the amethyst geode, the engraved copper medallion and...where was the key? I'd almost missed the filthy old thing half-hidden in a corner of the box, camouflaged by its grubby colour. Okay: wallet with my carefully saved hundred and forty bucks in twenties; apartment keys...and of course the new journal. I couldn't forget about that.

Done. My life in a bag. And barely full.

I turned back to Julie. She was facing away from

me, staring at the open apartment door, all the blood drained from her chalk-white face.

She was saying something—or at least her mouth moved as if forming words. One word, over and over. But no sound made it through the siren's squeal.

Smoke.

The smell tickled my nostrils at the same instant my mind recognised the word on Julie's lips. As we watched, a thin dark cloud oozed through the open door, pulsing like a live thing.

'I can't—' Julie shook her head. Her eyes flashed at me and then back to the intruding smoke. She looked petrified.

A sheen of sweat glistened on her too-white skin. Raw fear washed out of her, although if anything, it seemed to me that I should be the one panicking. It was my home being threatened. Julie reached out and grabbed a handful of my shirt, her eyes still on the smoke pouring through the door.

'It's okay.' I tried to sound calm while shouting: not easy. 'The fire escape is right outside. It'll be fine.'

'Ro—Robert.' She stumbled out my name. 'I can't go out there. I was in a fire.' Wide eyes turned to mine, and she pulled me towards her. 'It was the smoke,' she said, as if that explained anything.

I reached out and wrapped my arm around her shoulders. Her body pressed hard into mine. My heart started thumping.

'It's okay.' I leaned in so she could hear me. 'We'll go down together. We'll be fine.'

With her face so close, I could almost breathe her panic. But she took a deep deliberate breath, her shoulders rising and falling. 'Okay.'

I wrapped my arm tighter around her and pulled her towards the apartment door and the writhing smoke. The clear path through the dominoes hadn't been designed for two people walking side by side. I felt a bit guilty as I edged Julie in front of me. She was panicked, and I was worried about keeping her feet clear of my cardboard barriers. But we managed to cross the room without incident and squeeze through the door.

Out in the corridor the smoke was thicker, stinging my eyes and throat. The heat was nowhere near as bad as I'd feared—maybe the fire was on the other side of the building (and please let that be true)—but I couldn't see the green exit light on the door to the stairs. It couldn't be more than a couple of dozen steps away. If I tracked along the wall there was no way I could stumble past the exit.

Julie planted her feet, however, coming to such an

abrupt stop I almost fell over her. Dammit. Maybe I would have to carry her out, fireman-style.

'Shut the door.' Her voice was a hard whisper. 'Slow the fire…'

I nodded and pushed the door behind us further open, loosening the wooden chock from the doorjamb. It tumbled to the floor, and the apartment door swung shut. We were plunged into darkness with smoke churning around us. It wasn't hard to see how a previous fire could have left such a mark on Julie.

There was still no heat in it, though, and my eyes were stinging less. 'This way.' Step followed step, further into the darkness. Fear started to bubble in my veins. Too many steps without reaching the door. My blood hammered through my neck, sounding in my ears, despite the alarm's clamour.

At last my hand glanced against a doorjamb, and the neon exit sign above it came into view. A cold flush of relief. The door opened without fuss, I pushed through it with Julie in tow and it clanged shut behind us, leaving us in a bright oasis of clean, fresh air and fluorescent lighting. Pale grey concrete stairs and whitewashed walls. I took a deep breath. Not a hint of heat. Not a sniff of smoke. The alarm still wailed, but the solid walls of the fire escape muted it.

Julie laughed. A sound of pure relief, echoing in the stairwell. She released the front of my shirt. Her body straightened up, and a tiny invisible layer of distance appeared between us. I loosened my arm from around her shoulders; she shifted away.

'Thanks.' Julie looked down at her feet. 'Sorry.'

'It's fine. I was scared too.' A weird feeling of emptiness remained in the space where she'd been a moment earlier. 'We should probably keep going down.'

Five floors up meant ten flights of stairs to get down—enough time for me to go back to worrying about my apartment. What would I do if the fire gutted my home? The hundred and forty dollars in my wallet was a lot of money normally; nothing if I had to find a new home. And the forgetting was only ten days away.

We arrived outside, squinting in the bright midday sun. A cool breeze freshened the air, keeping the heat at bay. I looked back at the apartment block. It seemed fine. The alarm was audible, just, but there was no hint of smoke or fire.

A few other tenants milled on the lawn in front of us. I followed Julie over to them. Some were smiling and chatting, the others just tapping at their phones. They seemed incredibly relaxed about it all.

Julie plonked herself down on the grass. 'First week

on the job and there's a fire. I should ask for danger money.'

No one else was sitting down. But I couldn't really stand towering above her. I shifted on my feet, then squatted beside her.

Julie pulled out a pair of dark glasses and put them on. I wished I could have done the same. The sun blazed down ferociously. My eyes watered, still irritated from the smoke. I cupped my hands across my forehead and shaded my eyes as best I could.

Julie rummaged briefly in her pockets, coming up with a pack of cigarettes and a lighter.

I didn't want to seem rude, but I had to ask. 'You have a fear of fires, and you smoke?'

Her mouth creased into a crooked smile as she held the cigarette between her lips. 'The two are not unrelated.' A deep breath, and it flared to life. She took a long drag, looking for all the world like someone taking their first breath of pure air after being trapped down a coalmine. 'You know how they always warn people not to smoke in bed in case you drift off with a lit cigarette in your hand?'

'I guess, yeah. Of course.'

She grinned. 'Well, they're not kidding.' She took another long drag and slumped backwards, half-sitting, half-lying on the lawn. 'By the time the fire alarm woke me up, half the room was alight, but I could barely see the flames through the smoke. I got my butt outside pronto, but I lost all my gear. Scared the life out of me.'

'So that's what set the fire? Your own cigarette? You didn't think to give up smoking after that?'

''Course I did.' She took a final puff and stubbed out the cigarette on the grass. 'Turns out thinking and doing are rather different. But I did give up smoking in bed.'

I squinted upwards into the blazing blue sky. Not a hint of smoke. 'I hope my place will be okay.'

'We didn't see any flames. Sometimes when there's a lot of smoke, it's actually because there isn't an open fire.'

I pursed my lips. That sounded like the sort of thing you would say just to reassure someone.

'Did anyone see any flames?' Julie raised her voice in the direction of the group. 'Does anyone know what floor it's on?'

The group turned to her. One of the tenants—a woman from the first floor, I think—spoke up, and then the rest chimed in. It turned out no one had seen anything burning. It sounded as if the smoke was confined to the fifth floor. My floor. My insides clenched at the thought.

One of the older men said idiot kids sometimes lit fires in rubbish bins for kicks. Lots of smoke, but only a tiny fire. It felt weird to hope all this havoc had been caused deliberately, but if that would mean it wasn't a full-scale inferno tearing through my apartment, then I wished it with all my heart.

Julie and a few of the tenants were still talking when a siren wailing down the street cut off their conversation. A fire truck appeared, its engines roaring and lights flashing red as it mounted the kerb and bounced its way to a halt on the grass. Massively built men in helmets and bulky coats streamed out from the vehicle. Our little crowd hurried out of their way. We settled in the shade of a large fig tree that overhung the front lawn. Barking sharp orders, and splitting into smaller squads, one group headed straight for the building's front entrance. They had this.

'I wonder how long they'll be,' Julie scowled. 'My trolley's still up there.' She looked at me, and the scowl disappeared in a flash. 'Oh, sorry. You're worried about your place and I'm bitching about waiting for my trolley. Really, I'm sure it'll be okay.' She smiled sympathetically and then frowned. 'Is that Mrs Davis?'

'Who?' I followed Julie's gaze. A slightly built older woman stood on the footpath beside a box almost as tall as her. She was wringing her hands and looking about.

'Second floor.' Julie bounced to attention. 'You're not the only person in the building we deliver to, you know.' She hailed my distant neighbour as I scrambled to my feet.

From what I could gather from their conversation, Mrs Davis had organised the delivery of a new piece of flat-pack furniture: that was the box. The delivery people had left it on the footpath because of the fire alarm, and now she was stuck there with it.

'Well, let's at least get you out of the sun,' Julie said. 'We'll carry it over there under the tree with everyone else.' She turned to me as she tipped the box towards her. 'Come on, muscles. Let's put those guns to use. Grab an end.'

I hurried around to the other side. Nobody had ever called me 'muscles' before, to my knowledge. Hard to know how to feel about it. Squatting down with one knee, I edged my fingers under the box and lifted it up. Not too bad for me, but Julie's lithe arms corded under the weight. Still, she seemed unconcerned, twisting her upper body around as she walked backwards. I followed, keeping up my end. My neighbours parted to let us through.

We arrived under the tree and Julie started to lower her side. As she bent, the box's centre of gravity shifted suddenly towards her, and she tipped forward. 'Whoa. Crap.'

There was nothing I could do. As the weight slipped away and down, with it went my control over the box. Julie began to topple forward, her fingers effectively trapped under the bottom edge.

'Drop your weight!' I yelled. 'Widen your stance.'

Julie snapped her back foot further out, dropping at the knees. Her centre of gravity lowered, she braced her arms and shoulders against the box, halting its momentum. 'There you go. You've got it now.'

She did have it. Better positioned, she lowered the carton gently.

'There, all done.' I smiled at Julie, but she was looking away, not paying attention to me, or to Mrs Davis' thanks.

'Jeez, that smoke.' Her face flushed from the momentary exertion, Julie wiped at her eyes. 'I should go. I've got four more deliveries before lunch.'

I bit my lip. Had something changed? Was it me? I had *snapped* at her. *Drop your weight. Widen your stance.* Where had those words come from? They'd just tumbled out.

No wonder she was annoyed. No one likes being bossed about, especially by a weird hermit like me.

Julie hitched her bag over her shoulder. 'Can you help Mrs Davis get this up to her place later?' She pointed with her chin towards the large box.

'Sure. No problem.'

'And could you just wheel the trolley inside for me? I could come by tomorrow and pick it up.'

'Yes. Absolutely.'

'Great. And, you know. Thanks.' She reached out as if to clasp my arm, but stopped halfway. The moment passed. She stuck her earbud back in one ear, flashed me her polite smile, and headed for the street.

Maybe she wasn't so upset after all. Just eager to get on with her work day. She strode off with a quick step. The sunlight glinted off her short dark hair, picking up a red highlight running through the black. Reaching the footpath, she glanced back over her shoulder.

I only realised I'd been staring when her gaze met mine. A surge of guilt gripped my gut. For all the world it felt like I'd been caught doing something wrong. Creepy. But she didn't seem put out. Her expression was completely neutral. Then she turned back in the direction she'd been going and disappeared from view.

My heart was hammering. That split-second glance

was scarier than the whole fire episode. One of the problems with having no adult memories was that social interactions could be hard to understand. Meaningless events—two people looking at each other for perhaps two seconds—could so easily get blown out of all proportion.

I took a deep breath. Returned my attention to more pressing matters—like the state of my apartment. As the minutes passed, the firemen's air of urgency faded. Their movements slowed and their barked communications gave way to chatter. A good sign, surely. Perhaps the entire affair really was all smoke and no flame.

Still, it didn't look like we'd be getting back into our apartments any time soon. The only productive thing to be done right now was to relax and recharge as best I could, so I'd be able to make up for lost time tonight.

I slumped down on the ground, as Julie had done, and went through my backpack, hoping I hadn't damaged any of the mementoes in my rush to stuff them in.

One by one I checked them. The carved wooden elephant rested heavily in my palm—it always felt denser than it looked—as I laid it out beside the bracelet with its midnight-blue gemstone beads, the crystal vase, the geode, the copper disk with the strange lettering engraved on its face and the key. They were all fine. Relieved, I put them away and lay back on the soft grass, fingers knotted behind my head.

One of the firemen came over to address our little crowd. Good news. They'd put out the fire—it sounded like the older tenant might have been right, and it had just been kids lighting up one of the big rubbish bins. The smoke had almost cleared; we'd be able to return soon.

Hopefully the firemen hadn't needed to enter my apartment. I didn't want to think about a posse of thick-set men in heavy boots tromping, half-blind in the smoke-filled chaos, through my dominoes.

But frankly, after all the morning's fears crowding in on each other, I didn't have the mental space for more. Besides, the fire seemed to have been contained in the area near the bins, which sat near the lift on each level. My apartment was at the opposite end of the floor, so with a little luck they hadn't gone near my door.

It took another thirty minutes before we received the go-ahead to return to our apartments. The group surged back through the front door. I was itching to get upstairs to check on things, but I could hardly leave an old lady in the lurch. We waited for the crowd to go in, then I hoisted the flat-pack box up onto one shoulder.

Carrying it by myself was unwieldy, but I could manage. *Muscles*, Julie had called me. Maybe my long-sleeved shirts didn't hide as much as I'd thought.

We took the elevator to the second floor, and I deposited the box in Mrs Davis' tidy front room. Her niece was coming over later to help her put it together, she said, so I figured I'd done enough. I left as soon as politely possible, bounding up the fire escape stairs two at a time.

My apartment door was still closed; Julie's hand-trolley stood nearby. The door handle slipped in my hand, a thin layer of soot smearing my palm, but inside everything was just as I'd left it. Even the smoke that had roiled in before I shut the door had disappeared without leaving a smell. I let out a burst of relieved laughter.

It didn't take long to get everything sorted. The letter, the doctor's certificate and the mementoes went back into their box and I wheeled Julie's trolley into the kitchen.

The rest of the day continued without a hitch. I kept up a solid pace of work, and it felt good to be moving forward again. Julie turned out to be right when she said I could get away with putting down half as many barriers, and it was saving me time. It also meant the dominoes on either side of the barriers could be placed closer together: perfectly positioned for the final fall.

By late afternoon I began to tire, my brain weary and hands cramping. The frenzy of early-morning activity had taken its toll. Maybe in my remaining nine days I'd cram in a spare hour somewhere, but not today.

Anyway, I'd just got to the end of a carton of dominoes. It was time to break open another full one from the stack in the kitchen, and that meant I could gauge my progress exactly. A few quick calculations revealed I'd just crossed the fateful fifty-thousand mark. A warm feeling of achievement rose in my chest—only slightly spoiled by the knowledge that I'd been on track to get here two days earlier.

I made a quick dinner and ate sitting outside again, watching the sun set over the city's west. I took my journal and pen outside after I finished eating, and used the last of the light to detail the day's events.

The longer I stayed out, the more my mind went to the moment when Julie turned back to look at me. The stillness of her expression, as if a mask had fallen. In the back of my mind, I'd assumed she had a boyfriend, or a significant other of some sort. Not that she wore a ring or anything, but she was smart and beautiful and confident, so why wouldn't she?

Now I wondered. Something in that final moment...

It unnerved me, even as it squeezed my chest with a strange pleasure.

Idle thoughts from a tired mind. I emptied my water glass into a pot plant and took myself off to bed.

Day Nine

Nine days to go and more than thirty thousand dominoes still to be placed. But even that enormous number didn't properly express the difficulty of the task before me. The problem wasn't the sheer amount of dominoes remaining, but where they needed to go.

UP.

Onto the elevated platforms and bridges. Some of them I'd already constructed, but most were yet to be done. And unfortunately, setting those up took serious time.

I raced through my morning exercises, sweat dripping

from every pore by the time I hit the shower. I ate my morning toast sitting cross-legged in the livingroom, working out a plan of attack and looking at my design sketches. By day's end I wanted to have two more platforms up, and at least one of them filled with dominoes.

But things didn't move quickly. It was almost a week since I'd put up the last platform. I'd been in a groove with it, and now I wasn't: remembering all the steps slowed me down. Just getting used to handling all the little tools again took time, and by mid-morning the first platform was only half done. I'd just finished screwing in the base when the familiar *rat-tat-tat* echoed from the door. Julie, of course, come to pick up her trolley.

She wore a slim-fitting white top, open at the shoulders, and a pale blue skirt fell loose around her legs. This time everything matched. The pixie-cut hair, the green eyes and matching earrings, the simple top and fluttering skirt; even the sturdy black boots.

My heart pounded.

'Hey.' This time her smile looked a bit more genuine. Things had changed since the fire. I just didn't understand how or why.

'Hi.' I grinned back. 'You look...' I searched for the right word. 'Different.'

Different. Really?

'Oh.' Julie looked down at herself. 'I have Fridays off, so.'

So she transformed into this fearsome creature.

'Come in. The trolley's in the kitchen.' I ushered her in. Her skirt swished above her knees as she walked, its loose hem fluttering alarmingly up and down. I'd supposed her legs would be lithe, like her arms. Not that I'd really given the matter much thought. But solid muscle rippled from the legs under the skirt's dance.

Eyes forward. The kitchen. The trolley.

The best plan seemed just to get her out of my place as fast as politely possible. 'Here it is.' I strode over to the trolley in the corner. 'A little soot got on it, but I wiped it down.'

'Wow. You have a nice view.' Julie was looking out the back windows. 'Can you see the river from your balcony?'

'You have to lean out a little.'

'Nice.' Her left hand started curling around her earbud lead.

'Do you want to see?'

'Sure.' The earbud popped out into her hand.

I opened the door and followed her outside.

'That breeze is divine.' She went straight to the rail. 'You can almost smell the storm season coming.'

The wind whipped her skirt. Sent it flapping up her legs, and a quick jolt of adrenaline through my body.

'Look,' Julie said. 'I thought so.' She pointed into the distance, not in the direction of the river but south. 'You see that red building there?'

I joined her at the rail and squinted into the morning sunlight. Julie shifted closer, one arm resting on my shoulder, the other still pointing out, her flank pressed against the side of my chest.

Focus, Robbie. 'See the building there—next to the tall blue one?' She leaned closer and a hint of sharp, sweet scent washed over me. I doubted if I could have seen a nuclear explosion where she was pointing, but I nodded anyway.

Julie carried on talking. 'That's my place. I just moved there two weeks ago. Third floor, so no views, I'm afraid. Not like this.'

Then she leaned away and out over the balcony, craning her head in the opposite direction. 'Ha. River views indeed.'

I smiled. Her appreciation of the view made me feel almost proud, though I could hardly take responsibility.

'Well. My trolley and I should get out of your hair.' Julie faced me with a smile. 'Thanks for sharing your view.'

She turned back to go indoors, the wind taking a final tug at her skirt. I followed her inside, fixing my gaze resolutely beyond her. All I had to do was survive a few more moments and I'd never have to see her like this again. Next week it would all be back to baggy uniforms.

The thought made me both relieved and a bit sad. It wasn't Julie's fault, of course. The problem was my limited history with women. And my even more limited future.

Back in the livingroom, Julie was surveying my morning's work as she plugged the earbud back in. 'Do you ever need help on this? The dominoes, I mean.' Her words came out fast, almost blurted. 'Tomorrow's Saturday. I'm off work. If you like, I could come over and help you out a bit. It looks like fun.'

My mouth went dry. Had Julie just asked me if I'd like her to come and visit? And not as a grocery deliverer, but as something else, something more like a friend?

'Thanks, that's very kind of you to offer,' I fumbled. It was unthinkable, of course. Company was dangerous at the best of times—let alone just nine days before the forgetting. The very time I was meant to be barricading my doors against the outside world, not flinging them open. And in any case, these last five minutes had shown how much I struggled with social situations.

'The thing is…I'm trying to reach a sort of record. The dominoes have to be assembled just by me. It's an individual sort of thing.' In its way, that was all true enough. 'Sorry.'

'Oh. Is it like a world record?'

'I know it might seem a bit silly, but—'

'Not at all. That's kind of cool.'

Silence fell. Awkward as hell, but I couldn't for the life of me think how to break it.

Julie said: 'Does the rule just apply to setting up the dominoes themselves? Would it apply to building the platforms and bridges? I spent the best part of two years doing set construction, so I'm pretty good with power tools.'

Panic surged again. My chest tightened till it felt like my ribs were squashing my lungs. There had to be a way of saying no without hurting her feelings.

'We could add some better supports to the platforms you've already got up.' She pointed with her chin. 'The way they are right now I worry the dominoes aren't the only thing set up for collapse.'

'It's not a good idea.' My voice cut over hers.

'Oh.'

You jerk, I mentally hissed at myself. *You utter jerk*.

Her polite smile didn't reach anywhere near her eyes. It didn't even seem to reach her mouth. 'Okay. Whatever.' She plugged in her second earbud. 'Probably for the best. I work fast, and it'd be a shame to rush it.'

She turned her trolley to the door, then paused. 'I'm sorry if that seemed…' She shook her head, cutting off her own sentence. 'It's just, it's my birthday tomorrow and I'm new here, that's all. So that's why. Sorry. Bye.'

The door clicked shut behind her.

How had it all gone so wrong so fast? One moment she was admiring the view, the next she was slamming the door in what looked for all the world like embarrassed rejection.

Jerk. Pain pinched deep in my gut, and my mouth tasted bitter. I hadn't meant to hurt her feelings. Up until a few minutes ago, I hadn't thought of myself as having the power to hurt anyone's feelings.

This was the problem of having a condition that everyone around you didn't—*couldn't*—know about. What had it looked like to Julie? She'd reached out to me, and I had cut her down.

A thought flashed across my mind—Julie's card was in the box of records. And her number. I could phone her back. Rescue the situation. Maybe I could say I'd checked the rules for domino records and found it was okay for her to help with the platforms.

She might say no, of course. Maybe she'd still be upset that I'd cut her off. But at least she wouldn't feel rejected. If I called her quickly enough, she wouldn't have time to feel upset about it. Chances were she hadn't left the building yet.

I made it as far as the records box before sanity returned.

What was I thinking? I'd been so mortified at Julie's embarrassment I'd forgotten everything else. The whole point of the dominoes was to do a project created by my past, done by my present, and given to my future. It *had* to come from me. Letting anyone else into that moment was like a sculptor handing his chisel to a stranger for a couple of taps.

Besides, I'd just struggled to manage a five-minute visit. Someone with a bit more experience might have been able to deal with her offer without leaving her feeling rejected, but not me. Imagine the trouble I might get into if she came over for a whole afternoon.

I put Julie's card back in its place and returned to the livingroom. Actually, scratch that—at some point the tide of dominoes swelling across the floor had taken over. It had become the dominoes room.

The day's work still stood before me. I hadn't

finished the first platform. It was almost a relief to focus on the work. Putting up the platforms left little mental space for anything else since I had to hold the screw in place with one hand while twisting the screwdriver with the other and balancing the wooden board itself on whatever body part was at the right level—shoulders, elbows, knees. Sometimes even my head. It was tough work, the contortions a weird mirror of my early-morning stretches.

A second set of hands would make things go a lot faster. I didn't know what set construction was, but it sounded impressive. Julie said she'd done it for two years. For all I knew she might be an expert at this sort of thing...My gaze drifted towards the telephone.

I dragged it back again. Reminded myself how much I struggled to concentrate around Julie. Far from moving me forward, having her 'help'—no matter her skill-set—would probably see me reeling backwards.

I parked the next two screws between my lips. I had to wedge this platform against the side of my neck to pin it in place against the wall; then I twisted until I could get both hands in position and sank the screws into the wall. The solid wood held fast. In a moment I'd have to buttress it with some more brackets, but for now I could step back and massage my aching neck.

Never mind the aches and pains; I smiled to myself. Even without the dominoes, the platform looked impressive. It sat a little above hip height, with a long ramp running down the wall to link it with the dominoes on the floor.

There was now a sense of being inside a larger construction, as if a blueprint had sprung to three-dimensional life. It would look better again once a few other platforms were connected to it, all populated with standing lines of dominoes.

I worked and lunched and worked some more. It was slow going, especially in comparison with the recent days, but by the time the sunlight through the back windows had dimmed, two platforms extended out from the right-hand wall.

Finally, I could start setting up some dominoes—and at least this involved a little creativity. I'd pencil-marked the walls and measured up the platforms weeks ago; now I was just screwing them into place.

That got me thinking. In a way, it wouldn't be an intrusion on the achievement to have help with this. The thing that mattered in the work was the creativity and skill in designing and laying out the dominoes. The choreography, not the construction. If the help I got from Julie was just menial work on the scaffolding rather than on the dominoes themselves, it wouldn't stop them fulfilling their purpose...

But none of that changed the deeper reality. With only nine days—soon to be eight—left before the forgetting, now was not the time to start making friends.

I returned to setting up the dominoes on the first platform, trying to enjoy being freed from the boring work and able to turn to decisions about creation, flow and timing.

By the end of the day, dominoes filled the first platform and all the intersecting ramps, standing in ranks like an invading army spreading out from the floor and advancing to the higher ground.

Enough. My neck and shoulders were aching. I went through my evening chores, and dropped into bed exhausted.

Day Eight

Last night I tossed and turned, sleepless. Julie's words replayed over and over in my head.

'I'm new here.'

THEY SHOULD be my words, not Julie's. It was my curse, after all. To be forever new.

Of course, Julie just meant she was new to the city: a new job and a new apartment. But every six months, my whole self was new. New to everything.

I couldn't do much more about *my* situation. My 'birthday' would happen in eight days, and it was not the kind of thing you could share.

I'd have to hope that the dominoes, the exercises and

the journal would get me through it.

But I could do something about Julie's. She was alone in a new city, with no one to spend her birthday with. She probably didn't know anyone else. After all, most of her other grocery deliveries would be to elderly people with mobility challenges, not young shut-ins like me. So I could mean the difference between her spending her birthday alone or with someone. It wasn't like she was inviting me to be her best friend. Just to be company.

I pushed the tangle of sheets away and sat up. Calling her was still an option. I could say it took me overnight to check up on the rules for setting domino records. It was tempting. As I stripped off my pyjamas and pulled on exercise shorts, I considered the possibilities. The kitchen clock had the time at 6.47. I fished her card out of the records box and placed it beside the telephone.

Then I dropped to the floor and into my push-ups, weighing up my options. People remembered birthdays. I could still recall candle-glow and sugary cake from my childhood. If I did this thing—or if I refused it—the memory might live on for years in Julie's mind, long after my own memory was gone.

I pressed harder into the push-ups. Faster. The kitchen floor zoomed in and out of focus. Julie's invitation presented something new. An opportunity to change the outside world. In eight days, my time would be over, the baton passed to my next self. But here was something that would endure beyond me, outside the reach of my four walls.

Push-ups spun into crunches, stomach muscles beginning their slow burn. Today it just felt like fuel for the fire. I increased the pace. I couldn't be a proper friend to anyone—not ever, and certainly not with a mere eight days left before the forgetting. But I could do this one thing.

My torso wrenched with each rep. I bounced to my feet, and over to the doorway for the chin-ups. With just eight days to the forgetting, accepting the invitation was risky. I couldn't ignore that. Suppose she showed up unannounced in eight days' time, when I was stripped clean of memories, before I had read the journal or anything: still just so much mental plasticine. She'd be able to shape me into whatever she wanted.

I paused, shaken by the thought. To have someone else with me at the time of the forgetting would be the ultimate loss of control. The surrender of everything I was working so hard to build.

From chin-ups to burpees, and then on to lunges, squats, calf-lifts, planks. Still the temptation itched at my mind. To reach out into the world and make it change in this one, tiny way. To make it better.

Heat radiated through my chest and shoulders; sweat ran down my arms. The pain felt right. Deserved. A just punishment for being so inept yesterday handling Julie's invitation.

The risk could be managed. I could leave instructions on the door the day before the forgetting, if it came to that. *Don't open! Don't let anyone in*. I could do this.

Bathed in sweat, I made the call.

'Hi, Julie. It's Robbie here. Robert Penfold. From your delivery yesterday.'

A pause. 'Hi, Robbie.'

'You were right yesterday. I checked on the rules and it's okay to have help on the platforms. Just not the dominoes themselves. I had that wrong. Sorry.'

'Okay.'

'So if you'd still like to come over and help, if you haven't planned anything in the meantime, then that would be great. No problem.'

'Sure. I haven't planned anything.'

'How about after lunch?' I figured if we worked through the afternoon, that would be enough time for a proper birthday event, without totally destroying my schedule.

'That's fine. I'll see you then. Thanks.'

'Great. Oh—and happy birthday.'

Satisfied I'd done the right thing, I headed off to shower my sweat away.

It had been a tough workout, and I could still feel my body humming with energy as I left the shower, the muscles of my shoulders and torso clenching as I towelled myself off. In the bathroom mirror, my body shone, muscles and veins carving the skin.

Was it just vanity, this self-scrutiny? There was certainly a sense of exhilaration in observing the way my body was changing as I stepped up the morning exercises. The body fat shaving away; the muscles gaining size and definition. I looked forward each day to some little improvement. A subtle curve; a shadowed indentation.

At first I'd revelled in the knowledge that these changes would survive into the future, beyond the next forgetting. Then, as the months passed, it felt like I was uncovering something deeper. What had looked like a body—any old body—was more like a sheet of skin covering a secret design: an ancient blueprint hidden beneath. Every day I'd look, and remind myself about the parts of me buried so deep that the forgetting could never touch them.

If that was vanity, fine. I would take my victories where I could get them.

Anyway, normally all this was safely tucked away under my shirt. Except Julie had seen. *Muscles*, she'd called me. Was it possible Julie looked at me as something more than a potential friend? And if she did, was it a problem? I'd been trying to ignore any desires Julie aroused in me—they were useless at best—but if she had any similar feelings, she would have no reason to push them away.

The worry seemed silly, arrogant. But I replayed that strange moment on the day of the fire when she looked back at me. I still didn't know what to make of that. If there was any possibility Julie's feelings went beyond a wish for a brief, friendly visit, then I would be crazy to risk inviting her over. The whole point of my solitary life was to make sure I stayed in control at that critical moment just eight days away. Panic gripped my chest. What had I done?

I took a deep, steadying breath and studied my reflection from top to bottom. It wasn't easy to know what another person might find attractive. There were some obvious positives. Tall. Fit. Solid across the shoulders and chest, lean from the waist down. Nice posture. But my hair wasn't great: too long, and untidy. I'd started off cutting it myself to save some money and the result had led me to stop cutting it at all. My clothes—old jeans and shirts, worn sneakers—were unlikely to fan the flames of anyone's desire and my material prospects, as an unemployed recluse, were underwhelming. Then there was my talent for sparkling conversation.

Okay, so much for that. I turned away from the mirror and went to find a clean shirt and jeans.

~

I was halfway through laying down the dominoes for the remaining platform when it occurred to me I didn't have anything for Julie's birthday. I couldn't invite someone over for their birthday and not have a gift.

I had no idea what she would want or where to get it. I didn't have time to wander the shops looking for inspiration; I couldn't afford much anyway. But there was a bottle shop at the end of the block. I'd passed it every day when I used to take afternoon walks. I even wandered in one evening, looked over the shelves, ticking the mental boxes where I recognised the names, and found I knew a chardonnay from a shiraz. My tongue almost tingled with the tastes as I rolled the terms over in my mind.

A bottle of champagne, then. I tried not to worry about the cost. If Julie didn't know anyone else here, then it might be the only present she would get. It seemed a shame there wouldn't be a cake, but the kitchen clock kept ticking away, counting down the hours, and I had to get back to the dominoes.

~

I ate a sandwich for lunch, tidied the kitchen and brought in the chair from the balcony so there were two at the kitchen table. The outside chair had seen better days. A lot of them, by the look. As well as general wearing from the weather, it suffered from one leg bent out of shape. Even after I brushed away the dust, the rusty metal and faded paint still looked drab. I didn't have time to deal with the problem, so I just draped an old pillowcase over the back of it and propped up its dodgy leg with a folded piece of cardboard.

Next I sorted out all the equipment my past self had left me. One corner of the kitchen floor soon housed square wooden boards, long thin bridges, buttresses and piles of screws. And my tools: the cordless drill and drill bits; spirit level, screwdrivers.

It was almost time. Having been working and walking around all morning, I needed to change my shirt. I tossed the old one in my laundry box and picked my newest-looking shirt off the wardrobe hangers. Well, not my *newest*-looking shirt. My eyes strayed to the far side of the wardrobe. Perhaps a birthday celebration demanded something special. I pushed all the faded cream shirts to the side, revealing one that looked altogether out of place. The shirt was a soft satin, almost slippery to the touch, with black press-studs instead of buttons. At first glance, the fabric appeared purple, but wherever the material folded, it seemed to turn a dark crimson. It looked like it cost more than the rest of my wardrobe combined. Hell, it looked as if it cost more than my apartment. Why did I own this? Had I bought it for some special occasion? There was nothing about it in the letter or the mementoes.

Rat-tat-tat!

Julie's knock echoed through the apartment. The shirt slipped from my fingers like quicksilver and fell back into place.

Some other day, some other life. I pulled on the best of the others and buttoned it up on my way to the door.

Julie met me with a smile, a sunny greeting matched by a bright summer dress with a yellow print.

'Happy birthday!' I returned her smile with my own best effort and held open the door.

'Thanks. And thanks for inviting me over. I come prepared.'

She did indeed. In one hand she held a professional-looking toolbox made of hard scuffed plastic and big enough to carry my little collection of tools twice over. Her other hand held a paper bag: something from one of the nearby bakeries.

She bounced in with a spring in her step—it must be nice to think of birthdays as a time to celebrate rather than an obstacle to be survived—and I showed her into the kitchen. Her dress splashed colour and curves as she strode through my black-and-white world. She put her handbag and the paper bag on the bench, saying we'd get to it when we broke for afternoon tea. Excellent. The break would provide the perfect opportunity to present my little gift.

Julie set her toolbox down next to my spread-eagled pile of equipment and tools. She kicked off her shoes and crouched down, her naked feet pressing against the floor.

Not naked. Bare. Bare feet.

'All right.' Julie rubbed her hands together. If I'd had any worries she'd been just using the set-construction line as an excuse to get invited over, they were soon put to rest. She looked the very picture of enthusiasm, nodding with an air of expertise as she took in each piece of equipment.

Maybe this would work out okay. The more we focused on the dominoes, the more we might get something worthwhile done. And the less I'd need to struggle with small talk.

'That's a shiny new piece of machinery.' She reached out and picked up my cordless drill. My predecessor had bought it for me, but so far as I could tell had never used it himself. 'We can keep the drill bits in yours and the screw bits in mine.'

'Yes, good.'

She put the drill down and opened her toolbox. The top folded out to reveal two neat plastic shelves with little compartments sitting above a wider space. Its scars and grime gave it an air of long use. The way a real toolbox should look. Julie rummaged through the compartments, coming out with a set of short screwdriver heads that could fit into the drill. I wondered why my past self hadn't thought to get them. You could put a screw into a wall stud in seconds with that set-up.

Julie hauled out a bulky leather tool-belt with a pocket like a holster for her cordless drill and strapped it around her cotton dress. My heart pounded with a sudden surge of naked desire. I coveted that belt.

Duly decked out, we went back into the dominoes room. I explained where the platforms were meant to go, and how the bridges would connect them. She prodded me with questions at every point.

I'd thought an extra hand might make things go easier; I hadn't counted on getting skilled guidance. I picked an easy, low-lying platform to begin the work but Julie turned out to be quite the expert. She taught me the trick of lubricating the screws by spitting on them before you put them in, how to space out the fixtures buttressing the platforms, and to keep my elbow raised as I used the drill, so the hole went in square.

'How do you know all this stuff?' I stood holding the platform and Julie's old drill. She sat crouched on the other side, working underneath the platform where we were attaching the struts. 'You said set construction?'

A half-nod. She had two screws stuck in the corner of her mouth and the long line of her neck was exposed as she tilted her head to see under the platform. Her stance was deep and low, her bare feet splayed wide across two of the stepping stones. It made putting up the platforms a minor exercise in contortion. The yellow dress stretched against her body as she hunched and twisted herself around to drill in the screws under the platform. She plucked one of the two screws from between her lips and pressed it against the pre-drilled hole. The drill buzzed.

'Right,' she mumbled with the screw held between her lips. 'For theatre shows. I still do a bit of set design and construction for stage. I have a BA in it.'

'So what exactly does that qualify you for?'

She plucked the second screw from her mouth and set it into position. 'Helping clueless strangers assemble domino platforms, smartass. Hand me some more screws.'

I fished them meekly out of my pocket. She plucked them from my palm and the drill whizzed to life once more. Party dresses and power tools. There was no rational reason for that combination to jumble my thoughts.

'So you can imagine my excitement when I saw an opportunity to use my expertise in the real world,' she continued, her voice muffled under the platform. 'Unless some passer-by experiences a sudden need to block a Shakespearean soliloquy, this is as good as it gets for me.' Her drill whined once, twice, and she unfolded herself from her position. 'Moment of truth.' She released the platform and stepped back.

My hands held the platform for a moment longer. They seemed almost glued to it—as if the concern for the dominoes had taken over the muscles themselves. After all, I hadn't checked the final fastenings myself on this one. And the earlier ones had been buttressed in the corners, which made them more solid.

Julie looked across at me, eyebrows raised. One deep breath; I pried my hands off the platform. It held fast. Not so much as a wobble. Okay. Relief flooded my chest, and an involuntary smile spread across my face. Julie grinned back at me. Probably she saw my smile as one of achievement, rather than relief.

As we moved on to the second platform, the work began to fly by. This time we had a bit of a system: a knowledge of who did what and when. As soon as we were done, my hands released in time with Julie's. Again, the platform held fast.

I checked the kitchen clock and blinked. The first platform had taken only a little over an hour, once we were all set up. But that couldn't be right. It would mean the second platform had taken barely thirty minutes.

Thirty minutes for an entire platform! Impossible. I checked the time twice. If this rate could be sustained for the next couple of hours, I would—

'Can I put some music on?' Julie held up her phone.

'Sure.' I tried not to sound too unenthusiastic. Music obviously wasn't my thing, otherwise I would have left myself some record of it, or equipment for it, like I had with the exercises and the dominoes. But part of me was curious to know what music Julie had semi-permanently belting into her ears.

She placed her phone on the first of the empty platforms we'd already constructed. A quick tap or two on its surface, and the murmurs of a song began. It sounded nothing like the half-heard disharmonies that twanged through the weekend night air from the cafes below. There was a soft synthesizer melody, but beneath it a driving rock beat with drums building. A strange feeling washed over me, like being sucked up skyward and forward. I placed the drill back on its platform and turned to face the little device. My chest felt buoyed but my feet stayed anchored, grounding me against the sensation.

I could sense Julie's eyes on me. She must think me a complete weirdo. But the sense of possession held me transfixed. My fingertips itched and my core buzzed.

Julie spoke up, as I leaned in towards the phone. 'It's a Sydney band. You may not have—'

I stabbed at the screen and the music halted. Silence fell, and a wave of freedom flooded through me. Breath flowed back into my body; my limbs felt like my own again.

I felt Julie's eyes boring into the back of my head. The quiet shifted in a heartbeat from blissful to awkward.

The overwhelming urge to remove the source of the seasick feeling had bypassed my brain and run straight to my hands. Any concerns about whether it would be rude to cut off Julie's music, or to touch her phone at all, hadn't had a chance to register.

'Sorry,' I stumbled an apology, turning to her and trying to summon up a remorseful smile. 'I'm feeling a little unwell and the music…it's hard to concentrate with it on.'

It wasn't a lie. The music really had made me feel sick.

'Oh. I didn't realise. And I foisted myself on you today.' She pulled away. 'Should I go?'

A tiny pang of guilt twisted inside me. 'It's nothing really. Just a headache—just enough not to want any noise.'

'It doesn't sound right without a proper sound system anyway.' She scooped the phone up and slipped it back into a pocket.

I nodded supportively. Not too supportively—she might pop over some time with a sound system.

We got back into the groove of work without too much awkwardness. At least now it was clear why my past self hadn't left me a stereo. Though some sort of warning might have been nice.

A third platform—this one higher and more difficult—was complete before we stopped at four o'clock. I could hardly credit how much we'd accomplished. This day did deserve celebration. The champagne would be perfect.

I got the table ready while Julie busied herself with the paper bag from the bakery, which turned out to contain two thickly iced cupcakes large enough to be miniature cakes. All my food came from the same grocery lists set up before the last forgetting: plain and healthy fare. Yet my mouth remembered food like this. It was already salivating.

We'd just started peeling back the wrapping from the cupcakes when I realised what was missing. 'Wait! We have to do the song.'

It felt a bit weird starting up 'Happy Birthday' by myself, but Julie went with the flow. 'Happy birthday to me,' she chimed in. She plucked out her lighter, sparked it to life and held it over her cupcake like a candle; when we got to the end of the song she blew it out and I laughed.

We bit into our cupcakes and sweetness exploded in my mouth. 'Wow. That's *good*.'

'I only found this bakery last week. Dangerous stuff.'

I nodded. Best not to include anything like this on my grocery list.

'So,' Julie said between mouthfuls, 'I have to ask. How much did all those dominoes cost you? It must have been thousands of dollars.'

I coughed, almost choking on my cupcake. '*Thousands?*'

'Well, yeah. Each of the little packs holds about fifty, don't they? Even at wholesale they'd have to be at least two dollars a pack.'

I swallowed. 'That sounds about right.'

'So for eighty thousand-odd dominoes that's, what, three or four thousand dollars?'

I struggled for breath. I'd never actually thought to do the maths. How on earth had my past self ever had that kind of money?

'They were actually bought for me by someone else, so I don't know exactly.'

'Oh.' Julie smiled. 'What an amazing gift.'

Amazing indeed. I hopped up from my chair and retrieved the wine from the fridge. 'I didn't get you a cake. But I did grab a bottle of bubbly.'

My previous worries were forgotten. The champagne fitted perfectly with the celebratory atmosphere.

But Julie drew back in her chair. Her eyes skipped from me to the bottle. 'Sorry.' She winced. 'That's such a nice thought. You didn't have to. At the last minute and everything.' She shook her head. 'But I don't drink, I'm afraid. At all.'

'Oh.' This possibility hadn't crossed my mind. What a stupid blunder. 'Sorry.' I turned back to the fridge.

'You weren't to know.'

It was nice of her to say, but part of me stung as if I'd been rebuffed along with the gift. I thrust the bottle to the back of the top shelf and busied myself for a moment shoving jars and cans in front of it as if I could bury the whole event.

'I did promise I wasn't going to take up too much of your day.' Julie stood, picking up her handbag. Maybe she felt my discomfort. Her gaze lowered as she rummaged for something in the bag. 'Before I go, I wonder if I could just get you to take a picture of me in front of the platforms we did?' She produced her mobile phone and offered it to me. 'It'd just be nice to remember.'

'Sure.' I perked up at the proposal. From my perspective, this was the point of the whole visit—for it to be marked and carried forward.

'Great! So you just...' She gestured towards the camera icon and led me into the dominoes room, tidying her fringe.

'Yeah, I've got it. No worries.' And I did have it. The phone nestled easily in my hand, my thumb perched above the little button. I knew how to work this, or at least some of it. Just like earlier I'd known how to stop the music.

Julie was standing in front of three of the newly constructed platforms, bare feet astride the stepping stones. Butterflies stirred in my stomach. Posing for a photograph allowed you to look directly and unapologetically at someone.

I positioned the phone firmly between us, like a safety barrier, and moved forward until I had a good shot. Rule of thirds: the vertical line of her body one-third across the picture frame, the domino platforms behind her on either side, and her smiling face two-thirds high—

I blinked. Where had that come from? What second nature had powered that movement? Julie's visit had unearthed more questions than a month of searching the corners of my apartment.

One tap of the button: the shutter clicked. She looked happy. Even proud. Years later, she could point to this photo and tell her friends of something strange and half-beautiful she did on her first birthday in a new city.

'Great, thanks.'

'One more.' I framed a closer shot, just her head and shoulders, and the platforms unfocused behind her, like a strange backdrop. The shutter clicked again.

Beautiful. 'Done,' I announced, quashing the instinct to continue. To move in closer again.

A pity I didn't have a copy of the photo myself, for my own records. A memento.

Julie thanked me, reaching out to take her mobile back. 'You want me to take one for you? Do you have a smartphone?'

'No.'

'Hmph,' Julie huffed. 'That's sort of cool really.'

'That's me.' Probably no one in the history of the world had called me cool before. 'Still, it must be nice always having the camera with you.' Such a perfect form of memory, the photograph.

Julie shrugged. 'It's the music I'd miss. Wherever you go, it's right there.'

Just for a second, our eyes met. I swallowed.

'Do you want a hand tidying up the tools before I go?' she said.

'Sure.' A warm flush of success spread through my chest. There had been more than a few blunders, yet here we were at the end of it all, smiling away as we packed up together.

Much of it was a credit to her, of course, and the sunny mood that matched her dress. Still, I'd entertained a visitor who had stayed at my house for hours.

Hours. And at some point—I'd been too preoccupied to notice when exactly—it had stopped being awkward and started being something else.

I stood up at the thought. Julie stayed on her knees beside me, putting the last of the tools away. Perhaps I was actually getting better at being around other people. Even beautiful women like Julie.

But that made no sense. My social awkwardness followed from the forgetting. It stripped me of all knowledge of what was normal, expected. So how could I be doing better? My memory was still as empty as before. Maybe this was not about conscious memory after all, but something deeper. Faster. Snap judgments honed by practice until they became instinct. Not memory but...mental muscle. Developed over time, just like biceps and triceps.

Just like biceps and triceps.

And if so, then open to training. To practice. And able to be recorded in a form—unconscious instinct—that could survive the forgetting.

Julie had stopped tidying up, and was looking up at me. 'This was fun,' I said, my heart in my mouth. 'Thank you. If you've ever got any spare time in the next week, and want to help me out again, let me know.'

She lifted herself to her feet. 'I think I've got an old

phone. Maybe three years old. The camera probably still works. I'd be happy to see it go to a good home.'

I looked at her blankly, unsure what she was proposing.

'Would you like to have it?' she asked. 'Tomorrow's Sunday. I'm free. I could bring it over.'

'Okay. Yeah. Definitely. That would be great.'

'Do you want anything left on it? Music? Games?'

'No, thanks. Just having the camera would be fantastic.' Her birthday and she was offering me a present. My own camera. It would be like the journal on steroids.

Julie packed away the rest of her stuff, and we said our goodbyes with cheery see-you-tomorrows.

I tried to rein in my excitement. In my earliest moments, full of fear after reading the letter, the future forgetting had loomed in my mind as a mental wrecking ball. It was almost a death sentence, at least as far as my consciousness—my awareness of myself—was concerned. But in the past few days I'd unearthed some ways of skipping stones through time. First the journal. Tomorrow the camera. Now this new idea of training the mind through new experiences, building skills and habits until they became second nature. And after all, aren't those the instincts that really make the person who they are?

My condition had never seemed less terminal. For the first time, I felt like I could build something capable of holding together through time. A great mass of instincts and skills and muscles, journal pages and camera shots and dominoes, that would see me ride out the forgetting. Survive it.

The exhilaration sustained me through the next domino session, and by late afternoon I'd filled one more of the three platforms Julie had helped me set up. In a single day, the entire shape of the room had transformed. With thirteen platforms now complete—*thirteen*—the dominoes seemed to be swarming upward.

I switched out the light. In the glow from the kitchen, shadows leapt to life in the strange sculpture surrounding me. The pale platforms were nodes floating in space, linked by a complex web of neurons. With only their black angles and white dots showing, the dominoes seemed like an electrical current streaming through all this crazy circuitry, motionless but humming with poised energy. I could start to see how it might look when it was complete.

It was late. Dinner time had come and gone, but I still didn't feel hungry. I poked around the fridge. The champagne bottle glowered out at me, lurking shamefaced behind the milk. The urge gripped me to pour it down the drain and bin the bottle—thirty-six dollars and ninety-nine cents be damned—but in the end I decided to keep it. The work was going well and, with Julie's help tomorrow, perhaps the project would be done in time. On Day One, there might be cause for a quiet celebration of my own.

I fixed myself a quick sandwich before starting on the maths. Since the Day Thirteen accident, the evening calculation of remaining work had served only to hammer into my brain the prospect that I couldn't make it.

Now things had changed. Today's numbers surpassed anything I'd previously thought possible. As I scribbled them down on my notepad, the work hours remaining shrank back before my eyes. I drew a line through the calculations and rechecked them from scratch.

Back on target. No more nine-hour days. With ordinary work times for the last seven days, the task would be complete—even without factoring in Julie's help tomorrow. A few hours with her on the platforms, and I would be cruising.

I finished up the last of the day's chores, a smile pasted on my face. It was safe once again to imagine my new self, mind rinsed clean, awakening to something beautiful, basking in the pride of an extraordinary achievement. And tomorrow, sometime, there would be Julie, presenting me with another opportunity to train myself for society, and a new avenue to muscle my way past the forgetting and into the future.

Day Seven

My body groaned as I wrenched it out of bed, pecs, lats and abs aching after yesterday's workout. I let myself go easy today. No point passing a muscle strain to my future self.

IRONICALLY, the fact that Julie and I had worked so fast yesterday meant hard decisions would soon have to be made about the final dominoes.

One carton remained in the kitchen. Sometime today, all going well, that one would be used up. It would then be necessary to break into the remaining dozen unopened cartons. But they made up the base of my bed. A thick yellow ratchet strap ran around the perimeter to hold the cartons together, and a double-bed mattress lay over the lot, fitting almost perfectly on the strange base. It wasn't a fancy bed, or a large one. But with the strap ratcheted tight, the whole thing held together surprisingly well.

Raiding those cartons for their contents meant that the mattress would have to lie on the floor. I sighed. Having a proper bed gave the bedroom an air of permanence. Without it, the whole apartment would seem more transient, as if I was just passing through the place. Not a pleasant reminder of my situation.

Maybe I could keep the bed for a little while longer. If one row of cartons was removed the mattress would overlap the edges, but it would still feel like a bed. I released the ratchet strap, split off four cartons and re-tightened the strap around the remaining eight.

Armed now with a healthy pile of dominoes, I got to work on two long ramps that had to run upwards along each of the side walls. The brackets needed to be fixed to the wall, then the ramps screwed on. If I got them both done this morning, Julie and I could tackle something more challenging later.

She hadn't mentioned what time I should expect her, so I kept waiting for a knock on the door. I drilled the holes expecting a knock; attached the brackets to the walls and fitted the two completed ramps expecting a knock. I ate my lunch expecting a knock. By the time the smart *rat-tat-tat* finally echoed through the apartment in the early afternoon, I'd been rolling the sound around in my head for so long the actual knock took a moment to register.

Julie bustled in, a mess of movement and colour. Today she wore neat shorts and a trim sleeveless top, yellow again. She carried several large bags, including some more baked goods, but the real prize lay elsewhere. As promised, she had brought the phone.

'It's an old one.' She handed it over. 'But the camera works okay. I checked it this morning.'

The phone may have seemed old to her, but it looked new to me. I sat down at the table, bowled over. I now held in my palm a new type of memory. Another way to reach across time and pass knowledge to my waiting self on the other side.

A strange sense of pride—or maybe something like a sense of belonging—gripped me. What if I passed this object on to my future self? Would this same feeling pass from me to my future, as if I could hand down personality along with my possessions?

The phone nestled comfortably into my hand and my thumb hovered above the screen. The whole thing felt intuitive, just as it had yesterday.

And why shouldn't it? I had probably owned such a device in my earlier life. Before the condition struck, I would have had some sort of job, presumably. Money. Friends and contacts, just like everyone else.

But if so, why didn't I still have the phone? Perhaps it had broken or just worn out, and I hadn't thought it was important enough to preserve as a memento. Perhaps my missing phone represented another one of those perplexing gaps in my life where an absence spoke louder than any one of my existing mementoes.

'It's vanilla.' Julie's voice returned me from my reflections.

An odd thing to say. The phone was silver and black.

'Nothing on it,' she explained. 'It's wiped completely clean.'

'Vanilla.' I nodded. She meant nondescript. Blank.

'We can fix that right now, if you like.' She grinned and took the phone back from me, her fingertips brushing my palm. Then she was crouching, bringing herself down to my height. Her shoulders leaned back, pushing so far into my space that her hair brushed the side of my face, tickling it. The smell of her perfume rushed in.

For a moment, I had no idea what was happening,

but I followed her line of sight to the phone. Its screen showed Julie's gorgeous face tilting towards mine. I knew what this was called. A selfie. The shutter clicked, capturing my cautious smile alongside Julie's dazzling grin.

'Now we just make that your home screen.' With a few deft swipes, the photograph appeared on the screen again. My tumble of feelings in that instant were now frozen forever. She handed it back to me. 'Done. Vanilla no more.'

With the phone came the charger. Julie gave me a quick demonstration but again, the whole thing felt intuitive.

Then we got down to the business of the day, Julie kicking off her shoes and strapping on her tool belt as she surveyed the long ramps I'd attached to the two opposing walls, remarking on the single-file line of dominoes standing one to each little step. The two platforms in the far corners were bound to present the toughest challenge: we'd leave them until later and tackle the easier ones first.

It didn't take long before we fell into a routine. Within an hour we had two more platforms up. Then, before embarking on the fiddly job of setting up the connecting ramps, Julie proposed a break for afternoon tea.

'I'm dying for a smoke,' she said. 'Why don't we sit outside?'

Declining my offer to bring out the chairs from the kitchen, she parked herself on the floor by the balcony railing. The summer sun sat low in the sky, but it had lost little of its force. A breeze tried vainly to stir some life into the stifling heat. Julie lit up, and blew a stream of smoke out at the view. Summer clearly didn't bother her. I shrank back in the shade.

She smiled up at me. 'What?'

I'd been caught staring. 'Nothing.' I shook my head, embarrassed, and busied myself unwrapping the muffin she'd brought over.

She lowered the cigarette to the saucer she was using as an ashtray. 'Sorry. The smoke bothers you.'

'No, it's not that.'

Julie held me fixed in her gaze, hard eyes under arched brows.

'I just wondered about the smoking. Given you're so strict about not drinking, I mean.' I almost bit off my words at the sound of them. Spoken out loud, they sounded judgmental. 'Sorry. Silly thought.'

'No. Quite sensible really.' She brought the cigarette to her lips. 'One vice at a time. That's all.'

I nodded, but it struck me as a weird set of priorities. If

she was a regular smoker, that had to be more damaging than the occasional drink.

Unless.

Unless it wasn't the occasional drink. Unless for her the drinking had been a real problem. But that seemed unlikely. Julie was only a little younger than me—too young, surely, to be an alcoholic?

'Knock off the worst vice first?' I ventured.

'Three hundred and fifty-one days.' She flashed a crooked smile. 'But who's counting, right?'

She fished through her bag and produced a thick metal medallion attached to a jangling set of keys. A puff of pride in the way she held it out for me. My hand dipped with the unexpected weight of the thing. Six months, it proclaimed, with the date engraved into the matt-grey metal. Six months dry.

'I'm almost up to the twelve-month trophy. Exciting stuff.' Again the mix of pride and irony, as if she was mocking her own sense of achievement.

'That's great.'

Julie shrugged. She reached to take the medal back from me and stuffed it unceremoniously in her handbag. Despite her lightness with the subject, as if she could blow it away on a puff of cigarette smoke, I still felt a little honoured. Like she'd let me in on a secret.

Truth be told, it fitted somehow. Since the minute she'd appeared on my doorstep, I'd struggled with seeing someone so vivid, so charismatic, in such a mundane job. Perhaps I was just naive, but the picture made more sense to me if she was a recovering alcoholic and this delivery job was her way of getting back on her feet. A new occupation. A new apartment in a new city. Rebuilding her life, piece by piece. A surge of warmth flared in my chest.

'Again: what?' Her eyes narrowed.

Dammit. Caught staring. Again. I needed to improve my poker face. But then, improvement was the whole point here. To make these mistakes and get better around people. 'Sorry. I just thought that you seem a bit young to be overcoming serious vices.'

Her eyes narrowed further. 'I'm not sure whether that's a compliment.'

'Oh, definitely a compliment. I just meant that I haven't lived as much. You have a real history.'

'Alcoholism isn't really an achievement.'

'No, I see that. But facing up to it, overcoming it, that's something.'

'Hmm.' Her mouth tilted upwards in the hint of a smile. 'Well, by that logic, I'm highly accomplished. I must have given up drinking about a dozen times already.'

I smiled, taking her point: eleven failed attempts. Still, I envied her that history. Her smoking, not-drinking, myriad piercings, hard boots and fluttering dress: all of those layers announced a life lived, for better or worse. So much more than mine.

I'd fallen into staring again, but this time Julie didn't call me out. She turned towards the view and took another drag on her cigarette. For a time, I could just look at her, the bright sun beaming down on her black hair and bringing a touch of red to her cheeks. A web of thin smile lines radiated out from the corner of her eyes, and a narrow white scar ran from her temple into her hairline: traces, perhaps, of the drinking she had given up. None of it detracted from her beauty. The sinews and scars of history—a survivor's beauty, hard won.

She stubbed out her cigarette and tossed the butt in my kitchen garbage as the apartment's cool air welcomed us back inside.

I explained the new task confronting us. Putting up the next platform, nestled in a high corner, was going to be difficult, and it soon became apparent that it required a certain amount of contortion. Julie's right foot and my left one had to share a single stepping stone—the outside edges of my sneaker lined up alongside her bare skin like ill-fitting jigsaw pieces.

Ignoring such distractions, I set about getting the platform positioned, using one hand to hold it in place. With my free hand I held whichever drill Julie wasn't using, while she busied herself with the actual work. This left my face a few inches from hers, side-on. Her eyes fixed in concentration on aligning the fastenings on the platform. I could see the faint dusting of freckles across the bridge of her nose and the top of her cheeks, lending a blush of colour to her pale skin.

The quiet of the room and our closeness seemed like the humming before an explosion. An urge to speak seized me; anything to break the quiet.

'I read about their history this morning,' Julie said, mercifully. 'I came across it this morning, googling for videos of how other people had done dominoes.'

'The history of dominoes? I didn't know they had a history.'

'Everything has a history.' She dropped her weight a little as she drilled the holes under the platform. As her knee tipped forward, it bumped into my lower calf and stayed there, using me as a handy bulwark. 'I don't remember all the details. It started in a Middle Eastern town somewhere. Apparently, the place went crazy for the game, and used to play all day long.'

I tried to focus on her voice. But the closeness of her

skin and the soft whisper of the breaths between her words seemed to saturate my attention. It was only willpower that kept my attention fixed on her words.

'Then they wound up getting invaded and pillaged by some warlord. In the wake of the invasion, the town elders blamed the game...' She paused as the drill surged to life in her hands, once, twice. 'And fair enough. If the townsfolk had all been watching their borders instead of playing dominoes, and probably gambling on them, they mightn't have been invaded at all.'

Up this close, I could make out the individual muscles in her forearms, tensing in rhythm with the drill's intermittent whine, driving the bit forward into the wood. I dragged my attention back to the dominoes and their blood-soaked history.

'So the elders decreed that no one ever mention the game again. And it would have disappeared forever. But the story goes that one of the young villagers went travelling, and told a stranger about the game.' She took the screwdriver drill from my free hand and replaced it with the one she'd been using. 'This is where it gets weird.'

She glanced back at me. 'For no obvious reason, this stranger got it into his head to write down all the game's rules on stone tablets. Then he put them in clay pots and buried them. All in different places. A field here, beside a pathway there. Then it all disappears from history. There's no more record of him, or the town or dominoes. But the pots remained there, hidden away. Can you imagine?'

'No. I mean, yes, I can imagine.' Of course I could. The pots lying deep within the earth, lost from memory and history, but with all the information still there on the tablets. Not dead. Just lost.

'You fixed in this side, didn't you?' Julie started manipulating the platform into place.

I nodded, turning to pick up our next lot of screws from the pile. 'The one on the right, yes.' I stopped. The mental picture in my head didn't quite gel with what I'd said. Julie was facing the opposite way, meaning that her right would actually be—

'That's funny. It feels a bit...Oh!' She lurched forward, her arm scooping underneath the platform as it tilted and dipped away from her. But its weight pulled her forward and down.

The platform blocked Julie's view of the floor: she couldn't see where the stepping stones were. Her feet stayed glued in position, unable to step forward into the unknown and halt her fall. There was nowhere to go but down. Nothing to break her fall except the thousands of dominoes below.

For a split second, her body's crazy tilt forward stayed fixed, as if by sheer willpower she could resist gravity. A vision of the jogger incident flashed through my mind. The feel of my hand on her slick, muscled body felt as real as true memory.

'Shit! Little help!' Julie tumbled forward.

Her voice sparked me into action. I went in fast and low, one hand catching the platform, the other pushing forward, trying to meet Julie's torso with a soft palm. Tight muscle met my hand, and her momentum pushed me back and down. My knees and arms flexed, stiff-ened, held. Julie, the platform and I rocked to a halt.

Silence. No sound of streams of dominoes cascad-ing out from under us. Nothing but Julie's shuddering breath.

'Fuck,' she said. 'Nice catch.'

'I'm going to push you back up.' My voice sounded surprisingly authoritative. Like someone was actually in control.

At first, I could hardly move, the taut muscle behind the soft cotton pressing down on my hand with all her weight. Slowly, I pushed my shoulder forward and Julie backwards, until her weight returned over her centre of gravity to balance on her own two feet. Limb by limb we disentangled, each keeping our precious hold on the platform until we had it fixed firmly in place.

'It's good now,' I said, and we each let go. The platform held fast, but heat burned my cheeks. The whole thing was my fault. 'My bad.' I turned a little sheepishly to face her. 'I meant left. My right but your left. That can happen. When you're facing the other way. I mean, everyone knows that. Obviously.'

When you're in a hole, stop digging. I clamped my mouth shut.

'No worries.' Julie shrugged. 'Pretty good catch, in the end.' Her hand smoothed over her top where I'd caught her, pressing out the crumples. She looked around the room, resetting her feet on the stepping stones, and turned to face me. 'I'm going to explode if I don't ask the obvious question.'

I bit back my apprehension. What obvious question? Had I made some sort of blunder that gave away something about my condition? Or—maybe worse still—was it something about how I'd put my hands on her?

She raised an eyebrow. 'You didn't think to do all the platforms first?'

I blinked.

'If you'd done all the elevated stuff first,' she said, 'we wouldn't have to balance as we rigged the platforms and almost topple over and ruin everything.' She grinned. 'I mean, I like the challenge of three-dimensional Twister as much as the next person, but wouldn't it have been ten times easier to do the platforms first and the floor second?'

'Oh, I see what you're saying.' I nodded. 'No, I had to do it this way. Until all the dominoes are in place on the floor, it's hard to get any idea of the overall timing.'

'Timing?'

'It's all about the timing. The spirals you liked, the—' I fumbled for the words she had used. 'The whirling patterns. They're not there to look nice. The way the domino flow spirals outwards alters the timing of their fall.' I pointed to one of the larger patterns. 'Longer arms take more time to fall, so the lines flow differently, moving in tides, and then in waves, chasing and overtaking each other. But the platforms are too small to contain large patterns. It's the dominoes on the floor that shape how it happens. So I had to do the floor first, so that I'd know how the platforms would feed into and out of it.'

I took a deep breath. That had to be the longest speech I'd ever given to another person. As far as I knew.

'Hmph,' Julie said. 'That hadn't even crossed my mind.'

'Well, it took a lot of practice to get a feel for the timing. I spent weeks setting them up on the kitchen table and then watching how the different shapes and curves and set-ups accelerate as they tumble down.'

'How did you get the idea to look for that? Did you see it online or something?'

'No. That's just what it was always all about.' Sometimes the simplest things seemed hardest to explain. 'It's not just that one moment you've got eighty-three thousand dominoes all standing and the next you've got the same number lying flat. It's about how it happens. The flow and waves.' I'd never had to put it into words, not even in my own thoughts. It just seemed self-evident. 'The beautiful fall.'

'Oh.' She looked away. Down and to the side. 'Okay.'

I bit my lip. Having heard it out loud, the idea did sound a bit weird. The letter that set me the task hadn't mentioned a word about the beauty of what I was meant to create. But the more I toyed with the dominoes in my first weeks, the more I'd begun to play with the possibilities. Now it felt like the most natural thing in the world.

'I should be going.' Julie shook herself a little. 'We've got that platform fixed properly now, so you should be right with it.'

'Sure, of course. You've been such a wonderful help.' It felt like I'd said too much.

Julie busied herself collecting her handbag from the kitchen. I tried to tell myself this was the reason I'd wanted her to visit—for me to make mistakes and learn some lessons. But all I felt was stupid and embarrassed.

She turned back at the door. 'Thanks for letting me come over.'

'You didn't finish your story,' I said. 'The history of dominoes.'

'Oh, right.' She smiled and leaned back against the doorframe. 'Where were we?'

'The dominoes buried in the ground.'

'Right.' She nodded. 'Centuries passed. Empires rose and fell. Until a traveller heard a rumour of a buried treasure in the local fields. He set about digging them up, searching for weeks. It upset the locals who were trying to work the fields, but lo and behold, he found one of the pots.' She spread her arms. 'And here we are.'

'That's amazing.'

She grinned. 'Think of all the things that had to go right for that to happen. The guy from the town blabbing about it. This random stranger who decides to conserve it all for posterity. The treasure hunter who hears the ancient rumour.'

I smiled. Half in agreement, and half because things had returned to normal.

'I'm delivering to Mrs Davis tomorrow,' she said. 'How about I pop up and see how you're going with it?'

'Sure.' I nodded. 'Definitely.'

She opened the door, but just before she stepped across the threshold, turned back towards me.

'I liked what you said before.' With that, she gave a nod, and was gone.

She liked what I said about what? The more I ran over our conversation, the surer I became that she was referring to my little speech about the timing of the dominoes. No other answer made sense. She didn't find it weird; she liked it.

Julie, with all her complicated history, with all her other-worldly beauty, had seen me, and heard me. And, just for the merest moment, she had understood and responded. A warm glow seized my chest, clamping its hold around me as fast as the rush from any drug.

The rest of the afternoon passed in a haze. Enough time remained in the day for me to fill one of the new platforms. The work went slowly. My left hand still tingled where it had caught the flat of Julie's stomach. The nerves in my fingers and palm seemed to have their own memory. Replaying the interaction, revelling in the feeling of Julie's top as it shifted beneath my hand, and the hard press of muscle under it.

At last, despite all the distractions, the day's work was finished. Like yesterday, I switched off the main light and took a moment to look around at the growing edifice before me. I breathed it in, wishing I could capture this feeling for all time.

The camera.

For once, this image could be fixed: given a concrete form that could be passed on to my future.

I took several snaps and then a panorama, taking in the entire structure. I had no trouble using the camera—clearly I had previously owned such a device. The shots couldn't capture all the details in the failing light, but I didn't mind. In the deep shadows, mystery seemed to swirl about the strange sculpture.

The day's work recorded, I eased my way through the evening chores. Dinner finished without me tasting a bite. Instead, my fingers kept straying to the phone next to my plate, and the photo on its home screen. Julie's cotton top touching my shoulder as she leaned in towards me. History captured. Memory of that moment nailed down; ready to pass on.

I tidied away the dishes on autopilot, my mind elsewhere, my attention flagging. But writing the journal could not be done on autopilot. This type of memory took effort.

I opened the notebook to a fresh blank page and scrawled the first words. Concentration slipped through my fingers like warm honey. The phone beside me kept pulling me back, the picture fading to black after about thirty seconds so that I needed to keep reaching out and touching it. I didn't mind.

I wrenched my eyes back to the short words written at the top of the page. *Day Seven.*

One week. Seven days meant one week.

That couldn't be right. I flipped back through past pages until I found the beginning of yesterday's entry. Day Eight. That made today Day Seven. Basic maths.

Yet it just didn't feel right. I strode over to the wall calendar. As I did every evening, I drew a diagonal line through today. Directly under it was a day marked with a red star. That day had been marked almost six months ago. I'd counted it out twice to be sure. Back then, my remaining time spanned before me like a vast emptiness, heading off to a distant horizon.

It didn't seem distant now.

Today was Sunday. By the time next Sunday evening came around, it would not be me marking off its passing. Not the 'me' that remembered marking the day with a red star. Not the 'me' that remembered drawing a blue diagonal on the box above. My heart tightened. This was my last Sunday night.

Stupid thought. Of course it would still be me next Sunday. It just wouldn't be remembered with the same mind that had lived through this Sunday. The two memories would never be filed away side by side, and the memory of this moment, of this very thought, would be gone. Except to the extent my journal managed to carry a sense of it through to the other side.

I pressed the heel of my hand against my forehead, hard, pushing back against the rising panic.

Deep breath. The mind that reclaimed those memories, that read through the journal pages, would still be me. The letter, the dominoes, the mementoes, the exercises and the locks on my door—all of them ensured the man who came out the other side would share my thoughts and practices. He would be like me, created by my choices and actions. After all, I'd been preparing for this final week since my first days.

Yet now the week had arrived. And what was I doing? My gaze went to the phone on the table. Julie's phone. My hand still tingled from the touch of her body. My mind still echoed her parting words.

I'd been distracted. That was the truth of it. And at

the worst possible time. This was the time when I most needed to be in control, my every effort focused on surviving the week, of coming out the other side the same man I am now.

I scooped up the smartphone and tapped the screen. Two smiling faces shone up at me.

It had been a nice idea to open my door to Julie. But with just seven days to go, the risks were too great to continue. It was not only that if the friendship continued, Julie might visit unannounced next Sunday or Monday, and I would lose all control over what I became. There was something deeper. A threat I hadn't anticipated. The way my heart thumped around her. The fascination with the picture we took, and the strange pleasure in seeing Julie respond to my words. She made me forget myself.

This was what addiction must be like. This was why people didn't want to be free of it.

Tomorrow, I wrote, *I take back control.*

Day Six

It had to be today.

I SNAPPED my eyes open.

Only six days left. I needed a plan to cut Julie from my life. For once the job wasn't to build, but to take something apart.

Her role delivering my groceries complicated things. I couldn't get away with using some little white lie about going away on holidays for the next couple of weeks. But the thought of any sort of direct confrontation made sweat spring cold from my skin.

I tossed aside my sheet and pushed myself into my morning exercise. Soon, physical exhaustion started to burn away the anxiety twisting my insides. I pushed harder, until only fatigue and habit remained, and the only conscious thoughts were of ticking off the numbers, one by one. Healthy, hot perspiration washed away the night's clammy sweat.

After the exercises, the stretches. I breathed slowly into each new posture, helping clear my mind. No need to over-complicate things. I could ask Julie about getting a double grocery order tomorrow, enough for me to skip next week's delivery. Then I could just say I'd be out of touch for a little while. If she asked me about it, I could say it's something private I'm dealing with. She'd respect that.

Then in the future, I could let our friendship—or whatever it was we had started—dissolve of its own accord. Mr Lester would be back from his holidays. If I wanted to continue my attempts at being sociable, perhaps I could invite him over for dinner sometime. Julie had shown me that it was possible to do that: simply invite someone out of the blue.

A plan. Relief swelled in my chest. I practised my lines as I twisted through the last of the stretches, and then in the shower. 'Listen, Julie, I've got some things to do...' I tried it in front of the mirror, with a smile sort of friendly but rueful.

I turned to the dominoes work with a glad heart, though I knew I'd miss the excitement of Julie's visits. I couldn't help looking forlornly at the empty space where the final platform would go. The plan was for it to span high above the kitchen entry, linking the two structures on either side. I'd left it until last because its height made it a real challenge to build; now I kicked myself for not getting it done when I had help at hand. Oh well, I'd just have to get it done myself. Everything would seem easier once I'd freed myself from Julie's company.

She arrived just after lunch, greeted me with a warm smile and nodded as she looked over my recent work. 'It's really coming together, isn't it?' she said. 'You've done so much just in the last week.' She swivelled about, taking it all in.

My mouth opened in readiness, rueful smile poised on my lips.

Julie glanced at her watch and said, 'I'm due back at base by two o'clock—I can spare exactly thirty-eight minutes. We could probably get the platform over the doorway up.'

I closed my mouth. It would be fantastic to get the difficult platform done. Thirty-eight minutes sounded about right. It would also give me ample opportunity to say my piece.

Once we started, though, I decided it would seem more natural just to tell her when she was leaving. Apart from anything else, the work took all my concentration: it was hard. Being an old apartment, the room had a tall ceiling and though the doorways were quite low, only a little above my own height, the platform was still at least fifty centimetres higher than any of the others. I had to work with my hands above my head and, despite all my exercising, holding unwieldy objects above head height turned out to be surprisingly demanding. I soon felt the burn of lactic acid in my traps and triceps.

For Julie it was worse, though at least she could stand on the central pathway, while I had to balance on the stepping stones to one side. Even with her arms fully extended, she had to be up on tiptoes to do the drilling. 'Thanks, Mum—knew those ballet classes would pay off eventually,' she said. 'Are you right to hold that position?'

'Oh, you know my thing for three-dimensional Twister.'

Julie grinned back, her eyes scanning me from top to bottom. I probably was a little ridiculous with my low, wide stance and upstretched arms.

Fixing the platform in place, Julie shifted into position. She had to stand almost inside my stance, up on her tiptoes with her hands high above her head. I focused on holding up the platform. Julie's body tensed as she tried to press forward with the drill, struggling to get enough force out of her upraised arms. The effort pushed her backwards, the long line of her neck within inches of my face. It was worse than yesterday. I took a deep breath, and a subtle waft of vanilla and salt scent twisted itself into me.

This close, I could see the tiny chain links in her thin gold necklace as it swooped around the base of her neck and then curved forward and down, disappearing under her top. Higher up, her hair was brushed forward from behind her ears into the pixie cut that framed her face. The hair lost its inky blackness at its roots, revealing hints of amber. I could feel my pulse thumping through my ears.

With all her attention on the work above her eye-line, Julie seemed not to notice how close we were. She moved to the next set of pencilled marks on the wall, and her body tilted back hard as she pushed the drill into the wood. An inch more and we would be touching, the tip of my nose grazing the back of her neck, the hairline behind her ear.

There was nowhere to go. I couldn't budge an inch without releasing my hold on the platform. Panic seized me but I was trapped, frozen in position, my senses overwhelmed by her closeness and scent.

This had been a mistake. Letting her help again had been a mistake. Hell, letting her through the door had been a mistake. How had I ever imagined I could control this? It seemed impossible she couldn't feel my breath on her neck or hear the pounding of my heart.

No more waiting. As soon as we secured the platform, I would have to say my piece and finish this.

'And done!' The whine of the drill trailed off. 'The last platform is up.' Julie turned towards me with a flourish. 'Oh.'

She hadn't realised how close we were. She drew back a touch. Her lips parted in a half-smile, and her hand flitted to my right shoulder, as if to gently guard her space.

If I'd been determined to bring this closeness to an end before, the wide eyes and the crooked half-smile filling my vision settled the question. It had to be finished now. Right now.

I took a deep breath. Her eyes met mine and she jutted her chin upwards a millimetre—the tiniest, most trivial movement—and I kissed her.

It happened without thought. Just a sudden, insane urge, the movement towards her as natural as gravity, as effortless as walking. Our mouths met in a soft crush. If there had been resistance—some fleeting flinch or tiny tension—that might have been enough to snap me from my madness, but the lips meeting mine betrayed no hint of hesitation. They yielded to my press and then kissed back hard. Her mouth opened and—

I tore myself away. 'Sorry.' I released my hands from the platform above and raised them helplessly. 'I'm sorry.'

'It's okay.' She smiled and shook her head a little in surprise. Her cheeks and lips had blushed red. Even in my horror, she looked more beautiful than ever. 'Really, it's fine.' She reached out a hand towards my face, as if to cup it.

I lurched backwards out of her reach, stumbling over the stepping stones to the safety of the central pathway. 'No, it's not.' I shook my head vigorously. 'I'm so sorry. I shouldn't have done that. It was a mistake. A crazy stupid mistake.'

'It didn't feel like a mistake. It felt quite deliberate.'

If anything, she seemed bemused by my apology. Perhaps that was understandable. I must appear mad to her. Kissing her without warning, and then reneging on the whole thing.

'You don't understand. There's no way we—' I bit off

the word. There was no 'we'. There never could be. The concept didn't apply. 'I'm so sorry.'

If the kiss hadn't taken Julie aback, my blundering apology seemed to do the trick. A frown replaced her smile. 'All right. We'll call it a mistake, then.' She spread her hands, palms out. Pacifying. 'No harm done. Everybody makes mistakes. Let's just stay calm.'

The situation called for anything but calmness. I felt like my lips and body had betrayed me. And in doing so, poor Julie had become collateral damage in the battle for myself. The battle against myself.

I had to get her out of the apartment. Out of my life. I didn't know what scared me more—that I had kissed her or that she had kissed me back. 'No,' I said. 'We have to finish this. All this. You coming over and helping me. You have to go.'

'Okay.' She kept her hands raised. 'If that's what you want, I'll go.'

'That's what I want.'

She looked at me for a moment longer. My reaction must have seemed bizarre. What kind of crazy person kisses someone and then turfs them out? 'I'll get my purse.' She turned towards the kitchen, her head a little bowed.

Guilt clutched at me. What an awful thing I'd

done—acting as if I had feelings for her, then instantly denying it. I pushed the guilt away. This had to be finished right now. I couldn't trust myself around her. Keeping my distance from her as she walked by, I moved from the pathway and out onto the stepping stones.

She turned around as she passed me. 'So...' she began. 'Just friends, right? Let's say it never happened.'

'No.' She still didn't understand the stakes. How could she? 'I cannot see you again. Ever. It's all over.'

She stopped short. 'What are you saying?' Her arms folded across her chest. 'Why are you being like this?'

'I'll call your work. I'll explain to them. I'll say—'

'You can't call my work. I need this job. I just started.'

'I won't get you in trouble. I'll tell them it's all my fault. I'll say I have a problem.' That would be true enough. I reached out towards her, not trying to make contact but just to shepherd her towards the door. All I could think was to get her out of the room as fast as possible.

'No!' she cried, her arm swatting aside my hand. 'You can't do this. It's not fair.'

'This is the way it has to be. I'm sorry.'

'No!' She was almost shouting.

I stopped short. 'What do you mean "no"?' I

attempted the remote ushering again. 'You have to go now. I'm sorry, but there's no other way. You have to leave.'

She stood her ground. 'Why are you punishing me?' Julie demanded. '*You* kissed *me*.'

I shook my head. It wasn't hard to understand her anger. It just seemed to me she should have angrily stormed out, not angrily stood her ground. 'I'm sorry. It was a moment of weakness.'

'Or strength—and this now is the weakness.'

Her response knocked me off-kilter. 'I know this is hard to understand,' I pleaded. 'But I can't be around you. Not even for the deliveries. It's not safe for me.'

'Why don't you just tell me what's wrong?' Her voice softened and she advanced towards me. 'I can tell you like me. You kissed me.'

'You don't understand.' My voice rose in volume and pitch, more in panic than anything else. I backed away but the dominoes at my feet and the platforms around my head hemmed me in.

'Well, explain it, then.' She advanced as I stepped back, her feet finding each stone with the precision of a stalking panther. 'You can't just throw me out. Tell me what's going on.'

'*You have to go*.' My voice cracked. I'd reached the

corner platform. Nowhere left to go. Yet still she came at me.

'You don't have to be frightened.'

'I'm not frightened of you. I'm frightened of...' I broke off.

'Sunday.'

My mind stumbled over her word. 'What?'

She gazed back at me, silent, eyes burning. She took a couple of calm, deliberate steps backward, as if giving me the space to appreciate what she'd said.

Sunday.

Six days away.

The day of the forgetting.

'You saw the date marked on my calendar,' I said, pointing at her. 'You've been spying.' The calendar had been up in full view in the kitchen, the red cross straight through the Sunday. She might have linked it with my urgency to get the dominoes done.

'I know what happens on Sunday. I've always known.'

The reality hit me. 'You've been through my journal!' She'd had opportunity. I'd left it out every day. I couldn't be by her side at every moment. 'What have you been doing? Spying on me?' I advanced towards her, pointing her to the door. 'You should leave right now.'

She didn't budge. Or speak. My dominoes milled at her feet like thousands of tiny hostages.

Enough was enough. Julie had revealed herself to be some sort of crazy person worming her way into my world. 'Whatever you're playing at, it's over.' I drew myself up to my full height, my voice loud and firm. 'If you don't get out right now, so help me I will carry your crazy—'

She knocked my outreached hands aside and struck me in the chest.

'*I'm your wife, Robbie!*'

Air whooshed out of my lungs. I struggled for breath and stumbled backwards. My foot missed its stepping stone, crumpling onto one of the cardboard barriers and skittering a little copse of dominoes, but I hardly noticed.

'What did you say?'

'We're married, you dumb jerk.' She wiped at the corners of her eyes, but they seemed to be shining with anger more than glistening with tears.

I managed to get control of my knees before I toppled over onto the sea of dominoes under me. Barriers or not, there was no coming back from such a fall.

'We. Are. Married.' With each word a push. 'Robert. Phillip. Penfold.'

I didn't know my middle name—just that there was a P on the medical certificate—but something about the way she said it smacked of truth. I recoiled against the very possibility. She had to be lying. Crazy.

'You're not married. You're not wearing a ring.' Nothing else came into my mind to say. I was drowning, and this looked like a straw.

Julie scoffed. She fished along her neck, teasing out the gold necklace she always wore, exposing an elegant ring of gleaming white metal and green jewels. Emeralds, presumably. It matched her earrings and her eyes. It matched her.

I scowled defiantly. It didn't prove anything.

Julie's fingers closed hard around the ring and with one swift, violent tug, she snapped the chain. It slithered from her neck. She went to shove the ring on to the fourth finger of her left hand, but stopped.

'Hmph.' She looked at her hand with a half-laugh. 'You never really stop wearing a wedding ring anyway.' She held her left hand up, palm towards me and fingers splayed. 'If you wear a ring long enough, your hand grows around it. It wears the flesh itself.'

On her ring finger, just below the knuckle, an undeniable indentation curved into the skin. My throat clamped shut.

Before I had a moment to register her movement, her fingers snapped around my wrist. She wrenched it up before my eyes.

'Wear a ring long enough,' she repeated. 'And it wears the flesh itself.'

There it was. Just below the knuckle on my fourth finger, the flesh curved inward. Little wonder I'd never noticed it. Just the smallest indentation. A missing piece of me.

'No,' I whispered, denying the mark, denying its history, denying what it might mean.

'Yes.'

'It's impossible. I would know.'

'You *do* know. You kissed me.'

My head kept shaking. I didn't know what to believe. Except that I needed some space to think this through. 'You have to go.' My voice trembled on the final word. It sounded weak. Pathetic. 'Please.'

Julie took a step backward, as if unnerved by the desperation in my voice. The anger left her face. Her hand went to her mouth. 'I'm sorry. You're upset. This wasn't at all how I'd planned it. I know this must be hard.'

'Hard?'

'You're right. It's not your fault, and it's not fair to you. I should have prepared better for this possibility.'

This possibility? Me kissing her? Me throwing her out? Both?

'Can you please just go?' I wasn't thinking of the future, or that I needed time to get my head around this. I just needed a moment to breathe.

Her eyes searched mine. 'I'll go. If that's what you want.'

'Yes. It is what I want.' My voice stammered in relief. 'That's exactly what I want.'

'Okay, then.' Slowly, she nodded. 'But this isn't over, Robbie. It won't be over until all of this is finally fixed.' She waved expansively with her hand as she spoke. The gesture seemed to encompass everything. Me. Her. The room. The dominoes.

My mouth stayed shut. She had agreed to leave. Nothing else mattered. I summoned up all my strength just to meet her gaze. Her eyes glinted with determination. All I had was desperation.

A sigh escaped her in one loud huff of breath. 'Fuck.'

Before I had a chance to gather myself, she turned away and strode towards the door.

'Wait.' As much as I wanted this to end, I had to know. Julie looked back, and my question blurted out. 'Why did you lie to me? Why not just tell me the truth from the very beginning?'

Her face darkened. 'Right.' She scoffed. 'Like last time.'

She gave a final shake of her head and left, slamming the door behind her.

In one last effort, my legs carried me to the central pathway, and then to the door. I slammed the locks back one after the other.

Alone at last, safe at last, I made it out of the dominoes room and slumped down at the kitchen table. All the while, her final words bounced around inside my head like a pinball.

Last time?

Breathe.

I was shaking as I sucked in air and buried my head in my hands.

Married.

My gut instinct was to recoil from the very thought, but it burrowed into my mind like a screw twisting into soft wood. Julie's claim wasn't impossible. The fact was I didn't know that much about my past life before I moved to this apartment a year ago, except that I'd come from Melbourne, where my doctor still was. Julie had said she came from down south, so maybe I had lived with her back then. Been married to her, even. It would explain why she knew about me and my condition.

And it would explain the mark on my ring finger. I sat up in my chair and forced myself to look at it. The indentation looked ugly and unnatural, like a tree-trunk grown around a loop of fence-wire. Years later, the wire long since rusted and snapped, the tree still bore the marks of its captivity. I glared at the thing, as if it had betrayed me. The one piece of really tangible evidence that Julie had been able to provide.

No; there had to be some other explanation. Julie's story had too many loose ends. If we had been married, why weren't we still together? Why had I moved thousands of kilometres away from her and set up on my own? And then, if she had followed me up here—'last time', like she'd said—then why wouldn't I have accepted her claim? Why the need for this elaborate ruse to inveigle herself into my life?

And, come to think of it, why hadn't any of this information been passed down to me? There was no wedding ring matching Julie's in my collection of mementoes. No matter what I thought of her, no matter how it might have ended, I surely couldn't have just thrown such a thing away. Not in my state. Marriage is about as important as it gets, and I didn't have enough links to my history to be casting any aside like that.

What's more, the letter hadn't mentioned her. To make

sure I hadn't missed anything, I went to the records box and pulled it out. I pored through every sentence, word by word, though I knew the thing almost off by heart.

There was nothing. *Maybe* the bits stressing the importance of solitude and keeping to myself alluded to a past where I hadn't done that. Where I had tried being with someone through it all. But, equally, those sentences might have been meant to warn me about strangers trying to insinuate themselves into my life. Either way, there was no direct reference to being married, which is hardly the sort of thing you'd forget to mention.

My mouth felt like parchment. Something like a lifetime had passed in the last moments of Julie's visit. I forced my way to the fridge and got myself a glass of water; pressed the cold glass up to the side of my temple. Slowly, clarity returned, seeping through my skull with the chill. I didn't know what game she was playing, or how she knew what she knew, but Julie's story just didn't add up.

The outside chair was still in here, beside the table. I carried it back out to the veranda. The mid-afternoon heat radiated up from the street below and prickled at my shirt. I looked out at the city, and for the first time it felt like the city might be looking back. Was it possible

Julie had been spying on me? Could she still be spying on me now? From what I'd learnt in the last hour, I couldn't put it past her.

I went back inside and shut the door to the balcony. The lock mechanism felt rusty as I turned the bolt. Up here on the fifth floor there was usually no need to lock it, but now it felt like I needed every barricade I could get my hands on. I checked the front-door locks again, unnecessarily. No reason to feel afraid. This place was home. I was safe.

Whatever Julie's game was, she was locked outside. With the dominoes work proceeding well, everything was on track. Nothing else mattered. The forgetting still lay five days away. The letter's warnings against others endured, more relevant now than ever.

So be it. I set my jaw in determination and shut it all out: Julie, the ring, her crazy story, everything. I would focus on the dominoes.

But even there, in the dominoes themselves, it seemed to me that Julie's touch ran through it all, like a gold vein through dark rock. Everywhere I looked some mark of hers seemed to blaze out at me, from the barriers carving up the room into neat symmetrical lines to the platforms arching above it. Even the whirling patterns I'd invented now looked stained by her appreciation. I may have got Julie out of the apartment, but she'd left traces everywhere.

No matter. I pushed myself mercilessly back to the task, starting with the two little rectangles of dominoes I'd clattered over earlier as I backed my way into the corner. With each new phalanx of tiles set upright, each piece set straight, I felt like I could erase her touch. Holding on to that thought, I worked my way tile by tile through the rest of the day.

But by the time evening came around, it became harder to discipline my thoughts. They kept drifting back to Julie. I gave up on the dominoes, fixed myself a sandwich as an early dinner and ate it at the kitchen table. I didn't want to go outside, given the possibility of prying eyes.

The phone sat next to my plate. Idle fingers reached out to press the home button: a pair of smiling friends stared back at me.

Not friends. Nothing but a ruse. A lie.

Anger swelled in my gut. She didn't deserve to be in my life, and certainly not smiling her way into it, her innocent-seeming grin beaming out into my world. I stabbed at the phone until I'd deleted the offending picture from the home screen. An urge to get rid of it entirely flashed through the back of my mind, but I couldn't. I didn't have enough history to let any of it go.

I folded the letter back up and returned it to its place. If its aim had been to warn me about Julie, it had only done so indirectly. I could do better for my future self. I opened the journal at the next blank page and began to write. Forewarned would be forearmed.

As the shadows deepened, I used the phone's home screen to shed a little pool of light. Its bland blue face shone out in the evening's dimness.

Vanilla once more.

But inside it, filed away, the photo of Julie and me remained. That memory, at least, would pass through my hands and into the future.

Day Five

Five days to go, and for the first time in ages, no morning exercises. Freedom from Julie should have left me feeling released. Instead, I felt lethargic. I dragged myself to the kitchen table and ate some toast. I couldn't even muster the willpower to feel bad about slacking off.

IT WAS almost as if I missed her. As if the promise of Julie had bounced me out of bed these last few mornings. And now that she was gone, all motivation had fled my body.

All I could do was focus on getting through the day; getting the dominoes done. I gave up on breakfast, binning the last of the flavourless toast. Despite my listlessness, things had to be done. Decisions made.

For one thing, I'd need to deal with the issue of supplies—namely food. My future self needed to get through his first few days on his own without any intrusions into his crucial formative period. So I needed to sort out my deliveries. I'd have to ring the supermarket, something I'd never done before, and organise a new delivery person, at least until Mr Lester returned. I thought briefly that this would all be easier with the internet on, then found the number, set it down on the table and reached for the apartment's old landline handset.

As I did so, it started to ring.

I snapped my hand away from it as if it were a live thing. It was so long since the phone had rung, I'd almost forgotten the sound now crashing around the quiet apartment. Julie. It had to be. No one else had any reason to call. And she'd said it wasn't over.

The phone rang on. I stood my ground. It could scream all it wanted, but it couldn't make me answer. At last—after an eternity—the ringing stopped. Then, with barely a pause to let me gather my thoughts, it started up again. She was determined, if nothing else. And if her story was true, and I really was her lost love, why wouldn't she be?

I couldn't deny that part of me was drawn to the idea that it might be true. And not just because she was so attractive. Given the last twenty-four hours, I could probably add resourceful and determined as well. I shut my eyes, and for a moment I surrendered to the fantasy that she knew me—really knew me—and could be trusted completely.

It would be such a perfect solution to my condition. Julie would know all my hopes and dreams. All my work and plans. We would build a life together, and when the forgetting struck that life would still be there, and I could just fall back into it. It would be like pressing soft clay into a hard mould. Everything that I used to try and push myself beyond the forgetting—the exercises, the dominoes, the journal—she could be all of that and more.

If it was all true. And if she could be trusted.

The phone stopped ringing, then started up again. I opened my eyes and looked at it. I had to concentrate on evidence, and not on what I wanted to be true. The stakes were too high to fall for that mistake. There was no new evidence here. She had said it wasn't over, and now she had tried again.

I pulled the phone out of its socket. The ring cut off, mid-peal. Done. Hopefully now she'd start to realise how pointless her efforts were: that I would defend myself against her.

I pushed all my wishful thinking away and got on with the work. Soon enough, I was engrossed in the job and the hours passed quickly. I started to attack the remaining unpopulated area of floor. This called for some creative decision-making, the perfect thing to take my mind off—

Rat-tat-tat!

The room echoed with the knock. Her knock. Panic gripped my insides. Idiot! I should have foreseen this possibility. I couldn't let her in, that much was clear. The memory of being trapped in my own room yesterday when she refused to leave still burned in my brain.

Rat-tat-tat-*tat*.

'Hey.' Julie's voice carried through into the room, as dangerous as a siren's call. 'It's me.'

I went to answer, just to tell her I knew she was lying and to order her away, but my voice caught in my throat.

Julie's voice broke the silence. 'Come on, open up. I want to apologise for yesterday. It was wrong to spring it all on you. I owe you an explanation.'

My mouth clamped shut. A pulse ran through my jaw, grinding my teeth together. I stared at the door in a stupid panic, unmoving and wordless. Maybe it was better this way. If I didn't speak, then we wouldn't be able to communicate. She wouldn't be able to talk me into opening the door, and then to letting her into the apartment. Give her an inch and she'd take a mile.

'Look, I've got your grocery order out here,' she said. 'It's Tuesday, in case you've forgotten. You'll have to come out and get it eventually or it'll spoil.'

Damn, she was right. My legs freed up enough to move, and I made it over to the door.

The knock came again, louder this time, and I could almost feel it quiver through me physically, from my feet welded to the floor all the way to the rigid neck at the top of my spine.

'I know you're in there, Robbie.' Her voice sounded frustrated. 'Please open up.'

Absolutely not. I didn't trust her around me. I didn't trust myself around her much, either. Eventually she would have to give up and go away.

'Are you seriously doing this?' Now her voice bore an edge of annoyance. 'Are you actually going to just cower in there in silence?'

I crossed my arms on my chest. Not cowering at all.

Rat-a-tat-a-tat-a-tat. 'Robbie?' Despair was replacing frustration.

I reached out to the door. Maybe part of me still wanted to see her. Despite everything. What would it feel like to just give in? I didn't have to ask. I knew exactly how it would feel. As sweet as a kiss. I planted my palm against the door, my weight holding it there, safely away from the locks.

'Okay, fine,' came Julie's voice. 'I'm talking to the door. I'll just stand here and talk to the bloody door. Like an idiot. Hope your neighbours don't mind.'

A pause followed. Maybe seeing whether I would have mercy on her.

She sighed. I could barely hear it through the door. 'I'm sorry I couldn't just tell you the truth about everything. Or about anything. But I had no choice.'

I wished I could see her. Whatever emotion was on her face, whatever thoughts were visible in those eyes, they were lost to me. I stood my ground, listening to a voice through the door.

Like an idiot.

'I'd lost you, the third time it happened,' she continued. 'The forgetting.'

She used my term for it. *The forgetting*. Was that evidence of our past together? Or just evidence that she'd read my journal, or the letter?

'You were left out on your own. That was how we

were separated. It took months before I finally tracked you down and found you living here, all alone. I was so excited. I knew it must've been hard on you, being lost and alone. But I didn't realise how hard. It hadn't occurred to me how you'd react when I just appeared out of nowhere. I threw myself at you, so happy and stupid.'

I turned my back to the door and slumped against it. My weight slid down its smooth surface until I was left with my butt on the floor. Maybe I'd been wrong to not believe her.

'You threw me out,' she went on. 'You were scared and angry. You didn't want anything to do with me. You even…' Her voice trailed off. 'Anyway, I should have been smarter about it. You didn't want to know me, so I had to try a different approach.'

I shook my head, rolling it back against the door. Every answer she gave just opened up a dozen more questions I didn't have the strength to ask. I just sat there, silent and pathetic.

'I'm sorry for lying to you. But I'd tried the truth. This isn't the first time I've been left hammering on this door. When the last forgetting happened, I knew that you'd forget my face, and that I could use that opportunity.' Her voice quickened. 'I knew there would still be a piece of you in there that would remember us together, if only we'd give it a chance. And there is. I saw how you looked at me. I felt how you kissed me, Robbie.'

I shut my eyes tight against her words. I'd felt it too.

'Don't leave me without choices, Robbie.' Her voice dropped and I needed to strain to hear her words. 'I know you're lost and alone, but you are my responsibility. That's what we agreed. Us. Together. Don't leave me with no other option.'

No other option apart from what?

'You do believe me, don't you?' she said. 'I've got all the photos of us on my phone. I can show you, if you just open up.'

A pause, and then Julie hammered on the door again. The shudders quivered down the wood and into my shoulders.

The hammering stopped abruptly. Maybe she'd worked out that my body was pressed up against the door.

'Robbie?'

After a moment, the door shifted behind my back. A subtle movement, as if Julie had seated herself down on the opposite side, directly behind me. So there we sat, back to back, facing out in opposite directions. Little more than a couple of inches of timber between us.

Silence.

I could feel time passing, measured through the beat of blood pulsing through my neck. But I didn't want to move. This was as close as I could be to her and still feel safe.

I don't know how long we sat there. It may have been minutes or hours. Then she spoke. 'Well, starving you out wasn't really my plan. I'll unload your food out here and leave it for you. I'm going to leave my licence here too, in case this is all a bit hard to believe. I faked the name on the business card, but my licence has my real name. You'll see.' There was a pause, and then her voice came through softly. Barely audible. 'Don't keep your back against the wall too long, babe. You never know what some crazy bitch might resort to doing.'

A series of soft bumps and rustles followed, and I got the sense she'd given up at last.

I rocked my head back against the door, feeling wrung out. I let the minutes trickle past. Silence. Surely she must have gone now. I pulled myself up from the floor, snapped back the locks, and opened the door.

Coast clear. My groceries sat in a neat pile beside the door. There was a pale green plastic card on top. Julie's licence. She looked different in the photo. Long red hair tumbled about her shoulders, framing her face.

The colour, the pixie cut, were new. She'd darkened her eyebrows and lashes too. Under the photo her name was laid out in black and white. Julie Penfold, I read. *Penfold*. And beneath it, a Melbourne address.

Evidence.

I tried to think it all through as I put the groceries away. Her story was making more sense now. It did seem possible I'd been so angry with her for leaving me on my own that I'd refused to reunite with her. The licence showed not only that we shared a surname, but also that she'd originally lived in Melbourne. And that wasn't all. Her final words had rung with confidence, as if she had options that she hadn't used yet. They'd almost sounded like a threat.

That was a worrying thought. What if she was my wife—and that *wasn't* a good thing? She might have all sorts of legal powers over me, especially in the period just after the forgetting. What if she arrived outside my door that day with her lawyer by her side? If I called the police, who would they believe? The hysterical guy with no memory? Or his loving wife, doing her best to help her poor confused husband?

I shivered, my skin prickling into goosebumps under my shirt. Even if everything she'd said were true—*especially* if everything she said were true—then she was a stranger to me. Everything I'd seen of her so far was part of a ruse. Apart from her willingness to lie, I knew nothing about her for certain. Yet she held enormous power over me.

No more cowering behind doors. I had to act. I had to fix this.

~

'How were we separated?'

'Robbie. Hi.' The smile in her voice was audible even over the telephone line. 'I'm glad you called.'

'You said we were apart when it happened.'

'Can't we do this face to face?'

'No. Right now. I want to hear it.' I didn't want to give her time to make up a story.

She sighed. 'Okay, well, this was back before we realised about the timing, so we didn't know when it would strike. I would never have left you for a moment if we'd known.'

I nodded to myself. That was possible, at least. It would have been the third forgetting when we were separated. That was the one where the pattern became clear. 'But why didn't you come find me as soon as you found out? It doesn't make sense.'

'I was out of touch. Away in the country.'

'Why?'

'I was off helping someone. Ironic, given how my own life was about to explode.'

'Who were you helping?'

'Jacinta. Jazi.' A sigh. 'I'd been doing well at AA. Over a year dry, and I was a sponsor, if you can believe that. You thought *I* looked too young to be an alcoholic; Jazi wasn't even twenty. I went on a trip with her to help her sort her life out. After the forgetting happened, it took ages for them to contact me. Then once I finally got back, finding where you were in the hospital system turned out to be bureaucratic hell.' I could hear her shudder. 'By the time I'd tracked down where you were, you'd been working it all out without me. It was hard for you. I think the horror of those first hours when you were lost and alone affected you. And maybe you blamed me for us being separated. I can't argue with that. I blame myself.'

'You're my wife. Wouldn't you have had some legal right to make me come back or something?'

'I did see a lawyer. But the problem was your doctor. We'd been upfront about my drinking problems, and she didn't think I was reliable enough. Without Doctor Varma on my side, there was nothing I could do.' Her voice became more urgent. 'But, Robbie, you have to remember we didn't know about the date. I would never for a moment have left you if we'd known. Not for Jazi. Not for anything. That's why I'm being smarter now. To make up for us not being smarter then.'

'Okay.'

'Okay, you'll come back to me?' The rush of hopefulness in her voice was almost unbearable.

'Okay, I believe you. That you were my wife.'

She paused. 'So what now? Can I come over?'

'Not here.' I wouldn't be trapped in my own home like I was yesterday.

'I could take you out to dinner tonight, then. How about that? I know a place.'

'No, not today, not tonight.' I didn't want to give her any strategic advantage. 'Tomorrow.'

'In the morning then. First thing. Breakfast'.

I hesitated. Early morning seemed wrong. Too intimate, too...domestic. To my mind, the only people who had breakfast together were...

Married people.

'We're on a clock, Robbie,' she said. 'I don't think you want this still unresolved come Sunday.'

'Okay. Not over here, though. You said you lived locally. You pointed out your apartment.'

'Yes.'

'Was it true? Or just part of the act?'

She sighed. 'It's true.'

'I'll come to you.'

She gave me the street address and some directions.

'Eight a.m.,' she said. 'See you for breakfast.'

I bit down on my lip. Was I just falling further into another trap?

'Do you want this sorted out or not?' She sounded as if she'd read the doubt from my silence. And why wouldn't she? This was my wife. She would know my mannerisms better than anyone. Better than me.

'More than anything.'

'Then tomorrow.'

'Tomorrow.' I hung up the phone. Exhaustion washed over me, though it was only early afternoon. But I refused to let it slow me down. I prepared for tomorrow's trip as best I could, packing my backpack with everything I could think of. But I could hardly wrap my head around it. I paused and stood there, looking at the little wooden elephant in my hand. Looking beyond it.

I'd been married.

No. Wrong. She'd spoken in the present tense. I *was* married. I was married to *Julie*. I'd known, met, touched, kissed, courted, caressed, fallen for, loved, argued, proposed, laughed, married, yelled, carried, apologised, commiserated, shared...and left her. In that order, or pretty close. I'd done all of those things with her. By her. To her. Against her. And I'd forgotten, re-met and rejected her, and then forgotten again.

I had history.

Part of me wanted to feel pride in it. To have once won the affections of a woman as beautiful and determined as Julie. But I may as well have been learning the achievements of a stranger. I felt no connection to the man who had married her.

Too bad. I stuffed the last of the mementoes in the backpack and buckled it up. There was enough time left in the day to get in some more hours on the dominoes.

Work went slowly. Today my focus was on the floor, and over the course of the afternoon, almost five thousand new tiles spanned out. I raided the bed again, emptying another two large cartons. I had to rework some of the dominoes I'd already laid down on some of the earlier platforms, to get the overall timing of the collapse to flow through to the newer platforms and bridges.

This was the first platform Julie and I had put up, on the afternoon of her birthday. Except it wasn't, of course. Her birthday. That claim had obviously been part of the whole ruse. *I'm new here. It's my birthday*. No wonder she'd sucked me in. It was all part of her plan...

I stopped work and put the dominoes down. It wasn't the birthday that first changed things between us. That happened earlier. The fire; her reaction to it.

I felt my back straighten. *Surely not.*

Julie hadn't been scared at first. When the alarm went off, she was the one who realised it was the fire alarm and prompted me to gather up my things. The moment replayed over and over in my mind's eye. I'd just complimented her on her idea about the barriers. She smiled and said something, her words all but drowned out by the alarm. Not completely drowned out, though. I could still recall something of them.

'When I need to, I have a very strat—'

I could recall her lips moving around the last words as those eyes sparkled with intelligence.

Strategic mind.

My stomach tightened, and my mouth became thick with liquid. She had faked her fear to pull us together. Who does that? Who even thinks to do that?

And I had agreed to meet up with her tomorrow. What had I got myself into?

Day Four

> In the end, I slept well. Surprisingly. With the showdown with Julie looming today, I'd feared another restless night. But when the alarm woke me I felt refreshed and alert.

THE MORNING routine zipped by: exercise, shower, shave. No breakfast, of course. A few pangs of hunger gnawed at my belly as I tossed the backpack over my shoulder and set out.

Outside, the familiar heat settled in and I squinted into the sun's brightness. At this hour on a Wednesday morning the streets were busy, and the footpaths too. I flowed with the crowd across intersections and down laneways. It took less than ten minutes to get to Julie's solid red-brick building. Into the lift, down a long hallway—then I was standing outside her third-floor apartment. It felt weird. Usually I stood on the other side, with the door and locks defending my space.

I checked my watch. It gave the time as a few minutes to eight. I took a deep breath and knocked.

The door opened within moments. Julie smiled in welcome; we said our hellos. She was wearing a dark blue cotton dress with leggings beneath. Bare feet. She looked relaxed, and at home. Maybe for the first time I was truly seeing her. Or perhaps it was just another mask.

Either way, she was beautiful. Her little apartment was too, filled with life and energy, posters, patterned wall-hangings and a warm rug by the couch.

'I'll make us breakfast soon.' Julie ushered me towards the sofa. 'Can I get you a coffee?

'I don't drink coffee.'

'Right.' I got the impression she meant 'wrong'. 'Juice, then?'

I nodded, sinking uncomfortably deep into the couch's too-soft cushions.

A stick of incense burned on the coffee table, filling the air with a sweet, exotic scent. Nearby lay a picture frame, face-down. Beside them stood Julie's phone, upright in a little wooden box. Music came from it, and the box seemed to amplify the sound. The music wasn't at all like the driving rock Julie had put on at my apartment. It was melodic and instrumental. Relaxing. I wondered if that was the intended effect, and if so, who it was meant to relax.

Julie returned with my orange juice, and one for herself. For a panicked moment, I thought she might sit down next to me, but she settled in the armchair on the other side of the coffee table. She folded her legs under her with an easy flexibility.

'So...' Julie began. 'Husband.' She smiled. Curled up as she was, she looked almost playful.

'Wife.'

'Sorry again for springing it all on you on Tuesday. 'That wasn't part of the plan.'

'I'm sorry for shouting. For overreacting.'

'I'm not sure what counts as an overreaction in a situation like that.' She leaned forward. 'You must have questions.'

About a billion, yes. 'How much of what you said over the first few days did you make up?'

'Let's run with the premise that absolutely everything I said to you back then was part of the ruse, then if it turns out any honesty slipped in we can treat that as a bonus.'

Well, at least it sounded like she'd be honest about her dishonesty. That was something. 'True or false? You've just moved here?'

'False. I've been here for months. It took me ages to find a way into your life.'

'Last Saturday wasn't your birthday.'

'Correct. My birthday's April eight. You might want to write that down. You completely forgot my last one, so I'm expecting something impressive this time around.'

A joke. She was teasing me. Part of me, some strange instinct, wanted to smile too.

'You deliberately placed an error in my first grocery delivery so you had a reason to come over again.'

'True. Well spotted. I'll make a strategist of you yet.'

'We're married?'

'Of course!' Julie snapped up in her chair. 'That's completely true.'

'We're *still* married? I mean right now?'

'Sure.' Her eyes flickered to the right. 'True.'

'You don't seem certain.'

'I am certain.' In a flash, her composure returned. She fixed her eyes back on me. 'We're married. Right now.

Legal fact. You don't need to take my word for it. It's a matter of public record.'

'You went to all that trouble to get back inside my life, but you didn't seem to like me at first. Or even notice me.'

'Well, I couldn't be too obvious. You might have suspected something, and then I'd be back at square one.'

'Suspected something?'

'I was pretty sure you didn't have any photos of me, so you would have forgotten my face. But you'd still know you had a wife out there somewhere, so you could have suspected.'

'But I didn't know.' I shook my head. 'I wrote myself a letter. But I didn't mention you.'

'You wrote yourself a letter and you didn't think to mention you have a wife? Great. So I cut and dyed my hair for nothing.'

'I saw that you'd changed your look.' I pulled her licence from my pocket and set it down on the coffee table. 'You looked nice. With the long hair I mean, and without the colouring.' I realised the compliment may not have come across exactly as I'd meant. 'Not that you don't look nice now.'

Julie gazed at me levelly for a moment. 'I have thousands of photos, of course.' She nodded to the picture frame lying face-down on the coffee table. 'But I wasn't sure what you wanted to see. I didn't want this to be...' She sighed. 'Intimidating for you.'

My fingers itched to turn the frame face-up. But instead I spoke. 'How is your name different on the business card you gave me?'

'Please.' Julie rocked back in the chair. 'That was the easy part. Nobody checks identification when you're getting business cards made. But I did have to pay for a hundred cards to be printed. That was the smallest order they'd let me do. Unless we're going to keep playing this game for the next fifty years, that's money down the drain.' She grinned at me with her crooked smile.

Again with the joking about my condition. Or our condition. Was this the real Julie? Perhaps she could be herself now. If so, she had an acid sense of humour.

'So you changed your name and acted uninterested just in case I'd told myself to be on the lookout for a wife?'

Julie nodded, lifting herself from the chair and taking back her licence. 'I suppose I would have had to change my name anyway. Even without being on the lookout for a lost wife, you might have twigged if we had the same surname.'

I nodded slowly. I liked that Julie would think I might

be clever like that. But in truth I doubted the idea would ever have occurred to me.

'Why don't I get breakfast?' Julie went to the kitchen.

The warm smells of cooking soon began to fill the room. I looked around. The stars and swirls on the posters on the walls tickled my memory. Perhaps they were famous. Or perhaps they were from our home in Melbourne, and that was why they seemed familiar.

The more I looked around, the more it felt like memory was tugging at me from every direction. The incense burner. The rolled-up yoga mat in the corner. Even the polished wood bowl on the kitchen counter.

Julie was cooking omelettes, and she already had the mixture ready. I set the table as she finished up.

'This smells good,' I said, as she put a plate in front of me. 'What's in it?'

'I should give you the recipe.' She smiled and tossed a forkful of omelette into her mouth. 'Back.'

'I used to cook?' The breakfast in front of me wouldn't have seemed out of place in the hip-looking cafes along the river. A lot more appetizing than the dull toast I ate every morning. 'I used to cook these?'

'Every morning.' Julie nodded. 'I missed having omelettes for breakfast, without you here, but it turned out I'd picked up a few practical life skills from you. So

I started making them myself.' She looked away from me and down at her meal. 'It's nice to have you here.'

I picked up my juice. 'Cheers to that.' I held up my glass.

'Cheers.' She clinked my glass with her own. Her eyes shone with hope.

It was long past my usual breakfast time, and the omelette was good. Warm cheese melted with mushrooms. Perhaps tastebuds possess their own memories. Or maybe this had always been my favourite breakfast. Julie knew what I liked because I'd known what I liked.

'When did you decide to pick up everything and come after me?' I asked.

'Decide?'

'After you met me here the first time, you went back home.'

Julie nodded. 'I rushed off as soon as I found out where you were. Grabbed the first flight here, not even packing a toothbrush. I'd had this fantasy I would just swoop in and rescue you, and we'd be home together in a flash.' She sighed and skewered the omelette with her fork.

'But then after you'd gone back home, what happened to make you decide to leave everything behind and move up here?'

'Nothing happened. There was no *decision*. I would never just leave you behind.'

'Oh.'

The rest of the meal passed politely, and Julie took the dishes away.

'I was wondering if you wanted to go for a walk?' she asked as she piled the dishes into the sink. 'It's a lovely day.'

'Could I have that coffee?'

'Sure. Absolutely.' She turned back to the kitchen bench and flipped the switch on the kettle.

'The timing must have been tight if you wanted us back together before the next forgetting. You had less than two weeks.'

'I know, right? Twelve days. Not a lot of time for a girl to play hard to get.'

She had her back to me, adding instant coffee to two mugs. I stood up and moved to the end of the table, watching her carefully. 'You faked your fear on the day of the fire.'

'What?' Julie turned.

'Your panic drove us together. Without your reaction to the smoke that day, things wouldn't have changed between us. You made it all up. The whole story about you smoking in bed. It was all just an act.'

'An act?' She scoffed. 'Please.'

I pulled up short, a twinge of hope flaring in my chest. Maybe I'd been wrong. Perhaps the whole fire thing had just been dumb luck, and not some clever subterfuge.

She shrugged. 'That was the whole point, after all.'

'The point?'

She gazed evenly at me.

Her words made no sense. She spoke as if—

'*You lit the fire*,' I breathed, almost a whisper. 'To push us together.'

'Well, not fire exactly, but yeah.' Julie shrugged again, and turned back to making the coffees. 'Full disclosure. I did a trial run first, here in the sink.' She nodded to the basin as she made her way to the fridge. 'I had to make sure I'd get the right amount of smoke.'

My legs wobbled. I backed up to the table, feeling its welcome stability against the back of my thigh. 'You could have burnt the whole place down. Killed somebody.'

'No, no.' Julie turned to me in alarm. 'I used a smoke bomb. Not an actual fire. I got the recipe online.' She waved her hand in a placating way. 'No fire. No flames. Just smoke. Totally harmless.'

'No, smoke is dangerous.' My primary school

memories recorded that fact. *Smoke kills more than fire. All walls lead to a door. Get down low and go, go, go.*

Julie sat the milk on the bench and strode over to stand in front of me, hard eyes fixed on mine.

'Ordinary smoke is dangerous. That smoke couldn't hurt a fly. It's not even hot. I held the thing in my hands.'

'No, it's not right. It's still...' Words failed me. 'It's still—'

'Still what? You're worried someone else on your floor might have got scared by the smoke?' I'd hardly started to nod, when she cut me off: 'But everyone else had already left for the day. The last person was the lady in 14B, who left around ten o'clock. Like she does every Thursday. The only people on your floor were the two of us.'

Had she been staking out my apartment every day? 'You mean—'

'Or maybe you're worried about sprinkler damage, right? All those alarms going off? Water damage.' This time I kept my mouth shut. 'Except sprinklers hook up to heat detectors, not smoke detectors. And there was no heat, because there was no fire.' She glared at me. 'Well? Have I missed anything?'

'How do you know all this?' I shook my head in

disbelief. 'About alarms and sprinklers and making smoke bombs?'

'It's all public information. Online. Right there for anyone who has the time to look for it. And what have I had except time?' She put her hands on her hips. 'I worked it out. And I got it right.'

'This is madness.' My voice cracked. 'Building smoke bombs, staking out my apartment, infiltrating my life. Who does all this?'

'Your wife! I love you! That's what I do. That's what we agreed.'

'Love isn't about being strategic.' My voice rose to meet hers. 'We're not at war.'

She ignored the kettle's shrill whistle and strode towards me. 'This is my war. This is life or death for me.' Somehow, despite my size, she seemed to tower over me. 'Wake up! The important things in life aren't what you should be romantic about. They are what you should be *smart* about.'

'It's one thing to be smart,' I protested. 'It's another thing to lie, and…and break the law. This isn't normal, what you've done. It's stalking.'

'You're *my husband*. You let me fall for you. You fell too.'

'You don't think this is all a bit extreme?'

Julie's lips jammed shut, white with rage.

She held up her free hand, as if placating, but I got the impression she was trying to calm herself more than me. 'Okay.' She backed away a little, her steps jolting and clunky. She turned back to the kitchen. 'So tell me. What would you have done? If you loved someone, made promises to them, and they were struck down by some awful accident? What wouldn't you do to rescue them?'

'That's not the point.'

'It *is* the point. You say it's not normal. Fine.' She turned back towards me. 'So put yourself in my position. When would you have decided it was too much? Too hard? Too crazy?'

'I wouldn't lie. I wouldn't spy and light fires. Or smoke bombs. Whatever.'

'So you would have just left me there, alone and scared? The person you'd sworn to support and love, in sickness and health?'

'I didn't say that.' I folded my arms. 'I would have tried something else.'

'I did try something else! I tried *everything* else.' She threw her arms up. 'I tried getting a lawyer. When that didn't work, I moved to the next "something else". Like trying to get a room on your floor, or at least in your building. No luck. So I moved to the next something else. And the next. And here we are. Is there something I missed?' She spread her arms wide. 'What else could I do? Tell me!'

My insides squirmed. 'I don't know.'

'You don't know?' Her hands went to her hips and she looked me in the eye. 'That's the talk of a man who knows *exactly* when he'll give up. When it gets too hard. Too crazy. Too lonely.'

'I just wouldn't have done anything so over the top.'

'*Over the top?*' Her cheeks burned red with anger. 'This is what we promised each other we'd do. This thing has destroyed my life. It has torn the best friend I ever had away from me, and thrown him lost into the world. I'd tell a thousand lies, light a thousand fires, break a thousand fucking laws if it would get you back.'

Julie snapped her hand to her mouth and took a step back. 'Dammit. I promised myself I wouldn't lose my temper today. Or swear.'

She raised one palm in what looked like some sort of apology. 'Shit,' she added, which seemed ironic, considering. She went to the kettle and turned it off. The piercing whistle continued a moment longer, and then quieted. 'I know I swear too much. You've told me before.'

'I didn't used to swear?' I kept my voice mild, trying to turn down the anger in the room.

'Not much, no. You always said the best words shouldn't be worn down by overuse.'

I nodded. That sounded sensible. 'And what did you say then?'

Julie shrugged. 'Fuck that.'

I burst into laughter. I don't know why. It was just so easy to imagine some world where someone quite a bit like Julie would say that to someone quite a bit like me. And both of them would laugh.

But Julie just looked sad. 'I'm sorry, babe. But you have to see.' She went to the coffee table and picked up the framed photo. Then she stood in front of me, cradling it in her hands, its back still towards me.

I took it from her, and turned it around. A black and white wedding photo. More proof of our togetherness. Julie was leaning back into me, my arms around her. From what I could see of it, she wasn't wearing a traditional wedding dress. Just something long and elegant. Even so, the photo had a ceremonial feel.

She looked beautiful.

I looked happy.

My hands trembled. But I ignored them, ignored everything, and held my gaze on the photo. Every inch of it held some clue of difference or sameness. My sharp, stylish haircut. The press of my shoulder against the suit jacket where my arm curled around Julie, betraying the muscles beneath. The easy way the formal suit sat across my shoulders. And above all, overwhelming every other detail, shone out the togetherness of Julie and me. Of *us*.

I looked at her. Wide eyes searched my face, and for a moment she didn't look clever or fierce. Just small. 'Tell me,' she said, her voice little more than a breath. 'Tell me that's not worth fighting for.'

'I can't.' The photo seemed to draw me in, as if it were a window into another world. For me, forgotten. For Julie, lost.

'What wouldn't you do, to protect that? To save it?'

'If that was me, there's nothing I wouldn't do.'

She let out a deep shuddering breath. Then she smiled and squeezed my arm. 'Thank you for saying that. It's easy to go a bit crazy when you're on your own, you know? Without someone there to keep you grounded.'

'No. You were right to fight. To be smart.' I remembered her words as the fire alarm sparked into life. 'Strategic.'

'Well, these are matters of the heart. "Strategic" sounds a bit clinical.'

'What word do you prefer?'

'Conniving.'

My smile mirrored her grin, her sense of humour growing on me. Or maybe I was getting re-used to it.

Her hand lingered on my arm for a moment. 'Coffee.' She turned to the kitchen bench, and busied herself.

I sat, putting the photo on the table. Not face down, but sitting up. Like a real photo.

Cutlery jangled against the crockery as Julie stirred the two cups. She walked over to my side of the table and put my coffee down. For a moment I just stared at it. Some step in the process had gone missing. 'Aren't you meant to ask me how I have it?'

Her eyebrows arched.

'Oh. Okay.' I sipped it. Apparently I have my coffee white, with no sugar. Who knew?

Julie leaned against the kitchen bench. Quiet, looking at her coffee.

'So what did I used to do?' I asked. 'As a job?'

She pursed her lips. 'We need to talk about the future. There's only four days left, and then we all return to Go.'

I nodded, wondering what she had in mind.

'Four days is enough time to really fix things. I could book plane tickets and we could get home to our real home, together. In our place, in Footscray.'

'No.'

'It's just that if we do it that way you'd wake up at home, so it'd be easy for you to fall into that routine, that life.'

I shook my head.

'Look, I know how hard those first weeks are. It's scary for you doing unfamiliar things.'

'No.' I got up from the chair and folded my arms across my chest.

'Okay, no problem,' she said. 'Perhaps we could set up this place for the two of us. It'd be easier if you just woke up here, together with me. We can work on bringing your other stuff over.'

'Julie—' I broke off, unsure how to say what needed to be said.

'What's going on? Why don't you want to do this? Is this about your dominoes? You want to finish them first. We can work that in.'

'It's not just that.'

'Then what is it?' She put down her coffee on the kitchen counter and planted her hands on her hips. 'You agreed we were right to fight. To do anything that needed to be done.'

'No.' I shook my head. 'I said I can understand why

you would fight. Why if that was me, I would fight. But I don't recognise the man in the photo. I don't know him. And I don't really know you either.'

'It's just us.'

'But it's not. It's not us at all.'

'You knew me well enough to kiss me.'

'Everything that I believed when I did that was a lie. I don't blame you for that. I hope I would've done the same as you. But a lie is still a lie.'

'But I'm telling the truth now.'

I leaned forward over the table. 'You're trying to get back something you once had. And I'm trying to hold on to what I have now. I don't think they are the same thing at all.'

'I don't understand. Tell me what you want. Explain it to me.'

'I want the same thing anyone wants. To survive. To be in control. For my choices and plans to push through into the future.'

'I can give you all that. I've done it before. We've survived this before. Together.'

We'd also failed to survive it before, by her own account. But there was nothing to gain from bringing that up again. 'Even if you can give it all to me, *would* you?' I scooped up the picture frame. 'What if, instead, you could bring this back? Recreate the man you married, with all his hopes and dreams? Nothing would remain of my time and my plans. All that would be left of me would be some lucky stranger, swept up on the sea of life, pushed about by choices not his own.'

'He would be happy. And loved.'

'But he would not be me, and he would not be mine.'

'It would just be you, babe. Just you, and just me, and that's all.'

'If you think that, then...' I shook my head sadly. 'You're the last person in the world I should be with at the forgetting.'

'Don't say that,' she snapped. 'Look, I can learn more about you. You can tell me what's important.'

'And how could I trust you to do that? You'd lie and build smoke bombs to get your life back. Why wouldn't you lie now, tell me what I want to hear, and then go back on everything the moment the forgetting hits, when you can do whatever you want.'

'I wouldn't do that.'

'Really?' I still had the photo in my hands. I held it up. 'Isn't this worth fighting for? What wouldn't you do, to get this back?'

She backed away from me, shaking her head. 'That's not fair.'

'Say it then. Look at the photo and tell me you wouldn't lie to get this back.'

'You know I would. *I would do anything.*' Her voice shook with frustration. 'And why shouldn't I? Why are your choices the only ones that get to count? What about me?' She pointed at the photo. 'What about him? What about everything we chose? Everything we promised each other.'

'So what does that mean for me? That I don't matter at all? I'm just a mistake you're going to fix?'

'All of this is a mistake I'm trying to fix.' She waved her hands in the air. 'You. Me. All of it.'

'I'm not just something that's in your way!' I yelled. 'I'm trying to live my life and make choices and survive. I'm not going to choose to stay with someone who doesn't care about my choices. That moment, when I forget everything, I'm gone. My mind is basically plasticine. And there is no way I'm going to give it to someone who thinks I'm just an aberration. Someone who wants to fix me and make me proper again.' My backpack was beside the couch. I went to grab it. 'I'm leaving. There's a word for people who just take what they want from another person, who trap them and keep them without caring about their consent.'

'But you did choose.' She stepped into my path. 'You

chose me. And you asked me to choose you.'

'This is my life. I'm entitled to protect it.'

'This is *our* life. And *I'm* entitled to protect it. I promised you all those years ago I'd be there for you. For better or worse. Well, this is worse. But I'm here. Just like I promised. Just like you chose.'

'They're words from another time. Another world. I don't want them.'

'You were there for me. You helped me through my drinking. Every day, every step. When I'd do anything to get a drink, you held firm until I was okay again. I can't walk away from that. The whole thing is my—'

'I release you from your promise, from any debt to me.'

'You can't release me. You can't just wish away a marriage.'

'Marriages end. It happens. Divorces happen.'

She flinched. Happy enough to throw around curses, but unable to face the D-word. 'Sometimes things happen, and two people grow apart. But that's not what's going on here.'

Funny, because that sounded like exactly what was going on here. Things happened. Two people grew apart.

Julie scowled, as if she'd read my mind. 'Our situation

is completely different. When people divorce they know each other, and they make a decision. This'—she gestured to the two of us—'is nothing like that. You don't know what we were like together. There's no decision here, just a car crash of a thing that smashed our lives apart.'

'There is a decision. I'm deciding, right now.' I pushed past her and towards the door.

I'd got my hand to the doorhandle by the time she spoke, her voice suddenly quiet. 'If you walk out that door, what do you think I will do?'

I stopped and slowly turned to face her.

'I don't need your agreement. I never did.' Her eyes grew dark. 'You think tossing a smoke bomb in a bin counts as extreme? If you leave me no other option, then on Sunday, I will tear down your door with a crowbar and take what's mine. What's ours. Get my Robbie back. And there's nothing you can do to stop me.'

'I could go extreme too,' I snapped. 'I could walk out that door and never go home. I could just jump on a train or bus to anywhere. The outback. It's a big country. You would never see me again. And I'd be free of you.'

'I would find you, just like I found you this time.' She advanced on me, her fists white-knuckled by her side.

'You can't afford for this to become a battle between us, Robbie. I know you. And I'm smarter than you. I'm harder than you. And I will never give up on you.'

Maybe so. But I had one power she didn't have. The power to destroy. 'None of that will matter, because you'd be too late for either of us.' I folded my arms. 'If I'm picked up on the street again, they'll put me into care. In an institution.'

Julie's advance clattered to a stop. 'What?'

'It's what the doctor said they'd have to do. If it happens again, the state would say it's too dangerous to leave me on my own. Doctor Varma said she wouldn't be able to stop them putting me away.'

'What, like in a hospital? In a ward?' She stepped back. 'They would institutionalise you?'

'She said it would be their duty of care.'

'Duty of *care*? You couldn't survive in such a place. Fuck, Robbie. It would kill you. You shouldn't even be outside on your own. I should have come to you this morning. I've been so busy thinking about what it's done to our lives that I never—'

'*Our* lives?' She spoke as if it happened to her as much as me. As if she faced the annihilation four days away.

'Yes, *our* lives. Look around you. Look what my

life has become.' Her hands waved, her eyes suddenly wet and shining. 'Uprooting myself, spending every moment of my life, every dollar I earn, planning, thinking, lying—to win back a man who doesn't know me. Do you cry yourself to sleep every night? Do you have to stand next to your one friend in the world, acting like he's a stranger, when every fibre of your body wants to just—' She broke off, wrapping her arms around her shoulders. For a moment, she didn't look fierce or conniving. She looked lost, and alone. 'And not because he'd decided it had to end, but because he'd forgotten it ever started.'

The tears broke their banks and streamed down her face. The urge to take her into my arms and comfort her almost overpowered me, but I kept my arms firmly folded. 'You understand it would kill me if they put me in a hospital ward?'

'Of course.'

'Why? Because without control of my life and my world, the forgetting would strip me of my self, maybe? Everything about me that makes me the person I am?'

'Sure.' She wiped at her tears, as if annoyed at them. 'But isn't that just what you'd do to me anyway?'

'No! I'm trying to rescue you. Bring you back.'

'I don't want to be back—I'm right here! This is why

I have to be on my own, and in my place. So I can be myself, and not something made up by someone else. You're smarter than me,' I echoed her bitterly. 'Harder than me. Better than me. What do you think would be left of me, in the face of you?'

'I didn't say "better".' She scowled. 'Never better.'

A tear escaped the corner of my eye. I hated appearing weak before her, but my face felt like it would crack in half under the strain.

'Oh, don't *you* cry too.'

'What do you care? You're the one doing this. You're the one keeping me trapped.'

'Don't say that. I would do anything for you.' She reached towards me.

'Don't touch me!' I recoiled.

Her hand went to her mouth as she stepped backwards. 'God, Robbie. I would cross mountains and the desert for you, but I cannot endure this, not even for your sake. This anger and fear. I signed up for everything else, for better or worse, but not to become something you fear.'

I breathed out slowly. 'It's not your fault. It's just what happened.'

She paused for a moment. When she spoke, her voice was quiet. 'I didn't tell you the truth earlier. Not the whole truth. I think the reason your past self didn't tell you about me in the letter was because he thought he had got rid of me.'

'What do you mean?'

'He sent me an application for divorce.' She went over to a box by the wall. The same place she'd looked when I asked her if we were married. She crouched down, rummaged and eventually pulled out a large brown envelope. It looked like the one I kept my letter in.

But when Julie sat down at the table and opened it, I could see its contents were nothing like the letter. It was a sheaf of forms, stapled together. A bunch of tiny red rectangular stickers poked out from the sides at various points.

'You—your predecessor—sent them to me eight or nine months ago, a few weeks after I'd first barged in on you.' She grimaced. 'I wanted to burn them. I could hardly imagine a world where I would give you up.'

I stood beside her, peering over her shoulder at the crisp official-looking pages. 'Why…?'

'I wanted to show you something you can trust.' She reached across the table for a pen, and then turned the pages to the first of the little red labels. It pointed to an empty box: a space for her signature. Just underneath was my name, written in my own hand. 'You're right. You should be able to decide what happens to you.' She picked up the pen. 'So if you tell me to, I will sign. And then you can post them, and we will no longer be married.'

She looked up at me. 'Please don't ask me to do this.'

'But you will, if I ask?'

'I never agreed to be something you'd fear. If that's what you see when you look at me, then…Yes, I will.' Her lips trembled. Her face was streaked with tears.

It hurt just to look at her, but I answered honestly. 'I do see something to fear.'

She made a tiny, painful sound, then turned to the document. Her pen poised above the paper. 'You loved me. So much.'

I reached out and gently stayed her hand. 'That's not all I see.'

'Then what?' Her hand trembled under mine like a captured butterfly. 'You have to tell me. Because I need something to hold on to.'

I saw something beautiful and lost. Something I could rescue and make right again. But I couldn't give voice to that thought. 'All I do—my journal, my dominoes, my exercising—is to help me stay who I am, despite what will happen in four days' time. You said before that you could do all that. That you'd held me together before. I believe you. So you're everything I most fear. And everything I need. And I can't tell which.'

'Where does that leave us?'

An idea tickled the back of my mind. 'What if I did know? What if I knew what it was and could be—full disclosure, like you said before—and then I decided?'

'But how could you know?' She shook her head. 'No photos or stories can get you back there.'

I bit my lip. 'Let me think. Let me just think for a moment.' Anything I chose at this point would be a risk. I looked around at the room, at all the life and history hanging on its walls and cluttering up its benchtops. No way you could get all this in a bag in five minutes. 'I can give us one day,' I said. 'From morning until night. As if we were together.'

'That's not enough. It's not even—'

'It's all I have. The forgetting is in four days. I need time to prepare. You know I can't be around you near the date, not if I haven't made the decision already. Because if it happens when you're there, I'll never get to decide.'

'But—'

'You said you'd try anything. Is this so much crazier than everything you've already tried?'

She turned her back on me. At first I thought she wanted to hide her face, but she walked through to another room. Her bedroom.

Shortly, she returned, a garment wrapped around her hands. Dark grey, soft material. A jacket, well worn. It looked way too big for Julie.

Mine, then.

She stood before me, twisting the jacket around her hand and wrists, until it looked less like a garment and more like a strange cloth binding. 'One condition. If I get only one day, you have to really try. You must be open to what we had. You can't keep these shields up against me. This fear. You'd be cheating yourself too, if you don't try. You deserve to choose what's best for you.'

I nodded.

'Okay, two conditions.' She corrected herself. 'I get to take you out in the evening. To dinner. Whatever I want. You can decide what we do during the day. But I get the night. They're my conditions.'

She held out the jacket to me.

I kept my hands at my side. 'And I need to trust you will be able to walk away, if that's my decision. One day is all we have. If I choose "no", then you sign.'

'If you really try, and you give me a day, then yes, I will sign.'

'And you can live with that?'

'If you know what it's like for us to be together, and you choose something else, then I can live with that. I'll sign your forms. I will release us both.'

I reached out to take the jacket.

Julie continued to grip it. 'You promise me. You promise to try. To be open.'

'I promise.'

She released the jacket. 'Well, then—'

'Your turn.' I cut off her words and her smile, leaving her holding the jacket between us. 'Once the day is done, you'll respect my decision. Either way.' I gritted my teeth. 'For better or worse.'

She nodded. 'When the day is done, I promise I'll respect your decision. Either way.'

Something had changed, when I promised her the night. Her voice sounded sombre, but her brow was furrowed in thought. As if she had a plan.

Of course she had a plan.

Apprehension gnawed at my stomach. Could I really fall so hard in a single day? What if the man who loved her for years still lay somewhere within me? I remembered the sudden euphoria when I first kissed her. 'If you don't sign, I'll call Doctor Varma and tell her what you've done, and that I need to be institutionalised. For protection from you. She can make that happen.'

'You don't need to make threats. I take my promises seriously. That's what I'm doing here.'

I took the jacket.

'Shall we begin?' she asked. She was smiling.

'Not today. Tomorrow.' She went to object, but I shook my head. 'If you want me to really try, it can't be today. I know it's only ten o'clock in the morning, but I have nothing left to give you. And you said shields down.'

'Fair enough. Tomorrow.'

I made to leave as soon as I could. With the divorce papers safely tucked away in my backpack, I wanted to get out before she started to have any doubts. But Julie insisted on walking me home. My earlier talk of being put away in an institution really seemed to have panicked her. With only days before the expected date, Julie insisted that it was an unnecessary risk for me to walk the streets alone.

Outside, the bright yellow sunshine and cool air showed it was still morning. I felt drained, as if my emotions and thoughts had been pushed too far, but Julie seemed content to accompany me mostly in silence. I stole a few glances at her as we walked. Occasionally she met my glance and smiled in return, but behind her eyes I could see her mind working. Strategising. Conniving. Growing more cheerful with each passing moment. By the time we arrived back at my apartment, a noticeable spring had crept into her step. But she kept her thoughts to herself, and our goodbyes were brief. We agreed she would arrive at my apartment at seven o'clock tomorrow morning.

A wave of relief washed over me the moment I secured myself safely back at home, the door locked and the envelope with the divorce application stashed in the mementoes box. For the second time in recent days, I found myself scouring the letter—this time for some hint of the divorce proceedings my predecessor had begun. Nothing—except one part where he stresses that I must follow through on everything he has planned out for me. I'd always thought that referred to the dominoes, and maybe the exercises. But now I wondered if it was meant to apply to other, less visible plans.

I shrugged my speculations away and turned to the dominoes. Tomorrow I'd be otherwise occupied, which meant that after today, I'd only have two full days left to complete the entire structure.

I threw myself into the work. After the second hour, I allowed myself a quick break. On a whim, I went to the corner store at the end of my block and brought myself a jar of coffee—the same brand Julie used. I didn't have a kettle so I boiled a saucepan of water on the stove. Meeting Julie had not resolved as many secrets of my past as I might have liked, but it had thrown some light on a few little things. White, no sugar, for example.

The coffee helped me focus. After each cup, the work felt a bit more manageable, and I whizzed through it. Hour after hour, more and more of my little standing stones stood to attention, spreading out across the landscape. I skipped lunch and had another cup of coffee instead. Eventually I decided it was possible to have too much of a good thing. My head buzzing, I stopped making coffee and put together a sandwich.

By the time the afternoon sun began to pour in through the windows, the maths looked better. I went through my little ritual of pulling another two cartons of dominoes out from the bed, leaving it with just a third of its original foundation.

Only a little over twelve thousand dominoes still to put down now. The dominoes room reflected that dwindling figure: on the floor only one large corner remained to be done, as well as a few of the platforms. This close to finishing, it looked more like a sculpture than ever before. A work of art—even if it was one only I could really appreciate.

A simple meal finished off the day. Julie had said I used to cook. If only I'd left myself some ingredients and utensils—I might have been able to pick it up again. On instinct, like my morning exercises.

My thoughts drifted towards tomorrow. One way or the other, I would have to decide, and then there would be closure. And not by building a new wall for Julie to bulldoze down, but by our own agreement. Set in legal stone.

Day Three

I whipped through the morning exercises. Julie had said she would be over at 7.00 a.m. for breakfast, so I had to move fast.

I CUT myself shaving in my haste, which of course wasted more time than if I'd been my normal careful self, and by the time I was done it was almost seven.

She better not try arriving before then, because I had things to do.

Every time I went outside I took precautions in case the forgetting struck early. Being alone with Julie posed a risk every bit as serious. If the forgetting happened to strike today, I had to be protected against any lies she would tell in those first moments, when I would be at my most vulnerable.

I wrote myself a little note.

Read this now. And read it by yourself. Without her.

You've probably already worked out you've forgotten everything again. It happens every six months, and it was due on Sunday. If you're reading this, it must have happened early, leaving you alone with Julie before I—before we—have made up our mind if she can be trusted. You have to find and read the journal. It's a blue book. It should be on the kitchen shelf. If you can find it, you'll understand our situation.

If you can't find it, then she has hidden it. That means she can't be trusted and that you'll have to get away from her: disappear completely.

I copied the note out again and put one in my jeans pocket, the other in my sock drawer.

Julie was smart, and I needed to be smart too.

Yesterday, I'd promised to be open. And I owed that to myself, as much as to Julie. But what did being 'open' mean exactly? Two days ago, I'd kissed her. My mouth still tingled as if part of me wanted that moment again. I gritted my teeth against the unwelcome urge, and put the divorce papers on the kitchen bench, where they'd remind me of my priorities.

Next I set out all the mementoes on the kitchen table: the wooden elephant, beaded bracelet, crystal vase, key, geode and copper medallion. I hadn't thought to ask Julie about them yesterday, but it wasn't an opportunity I intended to miss this time. The first two looked African. North African, if I had to guess: maybe Moroccan? That was the word my mind tumbled over as I fumbled the little carved elephant from one hand to the other. How had it come into my possession? Had I travelled? Or was it a gift? Or maybe—

Rat-tat-tat: 7.00 a.m. precisely. Of course Julie would be punctual. She only had a day. It struck me as I slipped the locks back that there's one fatal flaw in every lock on every door in every home: the person inside, who can't help but let the outside in.

I opened the door, and there she was.

'Hi,' I said.

Julie returned the greeting and slipped past me into the room. It turned out to be a bit of a squeeze. In addition to a well-stuffed leather satchel slung over one shoulder, she was loaded up with plastic bags. 'You brought groceries?'

'Everything will become clear.' She wove past me and

towards the kitchen. 'It's all part of a plan.'

'Of course it is.'

The corner of her mouth curled in a smile.

I followed her into the kitchen, curious. She busied herself unloading all her baggage onto the kitchen bench and I took in the full effect of what she was wearing. Comfortable-looking trackpants flopped around her legs. They matched the crumpled T-shirt she wore, its colour faded to a threadbare grey, several sizes too big. The neck line hung loose.

'If I'd known you were going to dress up,' I said, 'I would have worn a tie.'

'We said full disclosure.' She put the last of the bags down on the kitchen table. 'So in the spirit of brutal honesty, I thought I should present in the strict marriage uniform.' She held her arms up and spun neatly before my eyes. 'I call this the Saturday morning couch ensemble.'

As she twirled, the T-shirt slid away from her neck, revealing bare skin almost to the point of her shoulder. The thing wasn't just large, but stupidly large. No one could get the sizing that wrong. As my mind followed the evidence to the only possible answer—it was my old T-shirt draped so alluringly over her curves—a grim sigh escaped me. If she could get my heart pounding wearing a threadbare band T-shirt and a pair of old trackpants, then this was going to be a very long day.

'Your hair looks different.'

She ran a hand through it. 'It's not nearly back to natural, but I washed out as much of the rinse as I could.' Her eyes tracked me from top to bottom. 'You look good. You still work out?'

'Yes, push-ups, crunches...' I started to rattle off my current workout.

'...chin-ups, lunges, squats, calf-lifts, planks,' she chimed in. Clearly, the morning exercises had been part of my routine for a long time.

We turned to the bags she'd brought over, and the prospect of breakfast. 'Those are for me. I'm cooking us omelettes again.' Then she gestured towards the other plastic bags, while fishing around in her handbag. 'Those are for you. You're doing lunch.' She produced a small battered notebook. 'Here.'

I took it from her. No title, just a sturdy cloth cover, frayed at the corner and stained in several places. I flipped it open: a recipe book. *My* recipe book. The different pages discoloured with use and inked with different pens. The writing shifted from one recipe to the next, some printed carefully in blue pen, others scribbled in pencil, with cross-outs and edits. But each had the same handwriting. Mine.

I skimmed through page after page, my imagination firing so much it insisted it could create the memory of each one. It was a treasure to rival any of the mementoes. A user's guide for my own self.

Julie smiled as she looked on. 'I'll look through it all later,' I said. 'Let's get the groceries put away.' The little piece of history took its place among the collection on the table.

'What are those?' Julie nodded at the mementoes as she sorted her groceries.

'I thought you could tell me.' Odd she hadn't immediately recognised them. 'They're everything I have from the past—all the keepsakes from my life. The letter didn't explain anything about them, so...'

Julie came over to the table. 'I thought you'd lost everything from back then...' She frowned as she studied my treasures. 'What's this stuff?'

'Don't you know?'

'I don't recognise any of it.' She turned the objects over. 'It looks like someone walked into a gift shop and grabbed a handful of the first knick-knacks they saw. All except this.' She picked up the key. 'What's this open?'

I shrugged. 'No idea.'

'It's got a number on it.' She smeared the grime away.

'An apartment, maybe? It looks a bit big for a locker… maybe a post office box?'

'Two eight nine.' I'd memorised the number months ago, when the mementoes had loomed with great significance. In three days the proudly recalled number would be gone again. 'We never had one of those? A PO box?'

'No. This isn't from our time together.'

'From earlier then? Back before we met.'

'We've been together seven years. Why would you hold on to some useless key?' She ran her finger along it. 'Besides, it's not that old.'

'It looks old.'

She shook her head. 'It's just dirty. Feel it. The teeth are sharp. It's barely been used.'

Julie held the key out, and I ran my finger along its jagged edge. She was right.

She tossed it back with the other mementoes. 'I don't know. I guess it must have been important to your predecessor for some reason. But it's not from any earlier. Not from our time.'

'Maybe it was something you never knew about.'

She scoffed. 'You've never been a secrets kind of guy. Anyway, you weren't home when that forgetting struck. The third one, when we were separated. All you had was the clothes you were standing up in. You would have had no way of bringing things with you. I'm sorry, but if you want your history, it's up here.' She tapped her head. 'And in here.' She pointed to the recipe book. 'Anything you want to know, just ask.'

Disappointed, I put the mementoes back into their box. I couldn't think of any reason Julie would lie to me. Yet the letter described them as precious pieces of my history. It made no sense. I shunted the box back to its place in the bench of cartons.

Julie started on the omelette. I offered her a coffee.

'You don't have coffee.'

I gave her a look.

'Oh. In that case, white with two.'

Soon enough the smells and sounds of cooking filled the kitchen. It was kind of fun. We ate breakfast and drank our coffee as I leafed further through the recipe book. Julie had a story about every recipe. The pages were stained with use and life. A real prize.

I cleaned up the plates after breakfast with Julie's help. As she passed me her coffee cup, her other hand reached up to hold the top of my arm. The movement looked effortless and instinctual. It felt supportive, not sensual. 'You know, I'm—' She smiled, shaking her head. 'I just meant to say I'm glad you're here, and okay.' She dropped her hand. 'I got this panicked feeling yesterday on my way home that the forgetting had struck you on your way up the stairs. I wanted to call and check you were okay. You should never have gone out by yourself so close to the date. It's a medical condition, not a program. You can't be sure when it's going to strike.'

'I protect myself. I take a letter to myself and a map with me everywhere I go.'

'Good.' She smiled, approving. 'That's smart.' Coming from Julie, that was perhaps the ultimate compliment. 'Well, you won't have to worry about that in the future. Once we're back together I'm planning to use industrial staples to join us permanently at the hip.'

I shook my head as I wiped my soapy hands on a tea towel. 'Do you joke about everything?'

'Sorry.' She smiled ruefully. 'I once knew a guy who loved my sense of humour.'

'I know we're spending the day as husband and wife.' I hesitated, not sure of how the words were going to come out. 'I'm just not sure what exactly that means in terms of—' My voice trailed off, spluttering into a silence.

Julie frowned. We still stood a little too close. Realisation dawned, and she backed away. 'Oh. You mean...?' Her turn to avoid mentioning the unmentionable.

'Right.' Then it occurred to me she might be thinking I meant something else. 'Oh, not, you know, *that*,' I hastened to assure her. 'I just meant the way you'd see couples out in public when they're...holding hands, whatever.' Conversations about sex with parents were less awkward.

We both started speaking at once.

'I hadn't actually meant in any—' she began.

'It's just you'd said how I needed to make an honest effort—' I said.

'—physical sense. Not that I meant to rule it out. Or in. I mean—'

'—and of course I want to make the effort because you're right that I'd only be cheating myself if I didn't try but—'

Our babble stumbled to a halt.

The subsequent silence managed to be more excruciating than the prattle it replaced.

'Wow,' Julie said. 'I think between us we've managed to totally purge any possible spontaneity from—'

I kissed her, leaning forward and tilting my head to enter her space. For an exquisite moment her lips responded with the mix of life and desire from the last time I'd kissed her. But I felt her melting back. Her lips left mine and she stepped away.

What had I done?

'O-kay,' Julie said. 'First, that was the nicest weird awkward kiss I've ever had. Second, that was weird and awkward. When I said we should be open, I didn't mean we had to...' Her eyes looked up at me with a newfound vulnerability. And her vulnerability made sense. After all, how could she really know for sure if I was being open and keeping my promise? Come to that, how could *I* really tell if I was being open and keeping my promise?

'What is it?' asked Julie.

Total honesty. I could do this.

'Come with me.' I reached out to take her hand. No hesitation this time.

I led her into the dominoes room, and over the stepping stones until we arrived at one of the two incomplete platforms. Only about a quarter-filled with dominoes, it sat a fair way from the ground, but not too high for my purpose. Hand in hand, we stood before it. With my free hand, I reached out and plinked a domino on the outside corner. In a flash, the adjacent tiles started falling.

Julie stiffened, her fingers clenching against mine as the chain reaction accelerated. 'What are you doing?'

The platform had only one bridge spanning from

it. I plucked out a couple of standing dominoes and the racing cascade came to a stop almost as soon as they'd started. The whole thing was over within seconds. When dominoes fell, they fell fast.

'This platform's yours.' I turned to Julie. 'You set them up.'

'What? No.' She backed away, her feet feeling for the nearest foothold behind her. 'I'd just muck it up. It would interfere with everything you've done. Like you said. The flow and the timing.'

I shook my head. 'This is where it begins. You can do this platform however you want. Once it leaves this bridge, then it will be all mine.'

'It's meant to be all yours. You said that yesterday about the dominoes. That it's meant to show you who you are and what you've done.'

I nodded. 'Who I was, what I did, and what I wanted. And I want this.'

'What if we do it together? The two of us.' Trust Julie to come up with a strategic compromise.

'Done.'

We worked almost until lunch. Julie took the design seriously, quizzing me about different types of arrangements, and the speed and rhythm of their fall. Piece by piece the platform came together. If she had any continuing concerns, they faded away as we built together. We worked side by side, shoulders and hands occasionally bumping off one another. It felt comfortable. Happy even. Perhaps this was what she meant about showing me what it was like when we were together.

The tables turned as we moved back into the kitchen. Julie had suggested that I make lunch, and I was curious to attempt something from one of my old recipes. So now it became my turn to stumble through an unfamiliar job, with her occasional guidance. I didn't have ingredients for many of the recipes. Julie had just brought over what she could. But she insisted it didn't matter, and I should just improvise. That was how I used to do it, apparently.

I struggled to settle on one or another recipe. The book itself was too exciting. More than the journal, it felt like a living document. A how-to guide for survival. Or better yet, for living. Page by page, it reached back through time to forgotten skills and knowledge.

In the end, I opted for a stir-fry. Julie had brought over most of the ingredients, and the method seemed straightforward. The smells and sounds of cooking soon filled the kitchen. My hands and eyes seemed to half-remember how to cut and measure—islands of memory that had survived unnoticed when the forgetting swamped my mind—but much of my expertise was gone. At the start of cooking I let the oil overheat and Julie had to throw open all the windows to blow the smoke away.

'Not to worry,' she said with a grin. 'The fire brigade knows the address.'

By the time the meal was ready, the kitchen had become sticky with sweat and steam and smoke. We ate on the balcony. The breeze was hot, but dry. Julie sat in her normal spot in the sun. The stir-fry didn't taste too bad, since I'd tossed out the burnt oil and started again, and Julie seemed happy enough. I suppose she'd been on the receiving end of better cooking efforts on my part, though.

After we finished, Julie stayed out on the balcony to smoke while I cleaned up the kitchen. In all the bustle of cooking, the envelope on the bench had been half-buried. I brushed it off and put it back in clear view.

When Julie came in, I suggested a walk down to the river. Even though I was in charge of the day, it didn't feel right to just ask Julie to work inside with me on my project the whole time.

I pulled on my sneakers while Julie stepped into her thongs. Outside the sun was high and hot but the air freshened as we approached the river, and a few scudding clouds provided some relief.

Julie walked beside me. Her shorter steps should have had to almost double-time it to keep up. But instinctively my steps slowed and shortened. That was not the only instinct flickering back to life. Julie's hand almost brushed mine as we walked. My fingers itched to take it. How many miles had I walked beside her over the course of my life? And how often in those miles had I reached out and scooped her hand into mine?

For all I knew, Julie's hand felt the same itch.

Soon we arrived at the river. The water glistened in the sunlight, transforming the day's belting heat into a thousand sparkles. A green lawn sloped down to the rock wall at the water's edge, almost deserted, with few people around on a Thursday after lunch. A large fig tree offered some shade, and we sat down on the grass.

We must have looked for all the world like any other young couple enjoying each other's company. For a while, we sat in silence, enjoying the view and the breeze. Then Julie picked up her phone, plugged one earbud in her ear, and offered me the other. The music drove into my head, not tinny—as it sounded from a distance through those tiny speakers. Injected directly into the head, the music sounded rich and full.

Julie muttered something. A band name. I nodded. For once I didn't have to wonder if it was the sort of thing I should pretend to know. There were some benefits, at least, in being with a person who knew my secrets.

My foot started tapping along. Maybe it was the peacefulness of the water curving around us on its way out to the ocean, or the feel of the grass under my body and the shade on my face, but the music felt less intimidating than the time Julie had played it on her birthday.

Correction: not her real birthday.

Julie lounged back on the grass, looking out across the water, her chest rising and falling in rhythm with her breath. She had to lie close because of the earbud cord connecting us. We weren't touching, but I could feel all the places where we almost were. I took a deep breath. It was one thing to try to be open. Quite another to be in thrall. No wonder Julie seemed so confident she would convert me.

She took out a cigarette. 'I'd thought I wouldn't like the heat, coming up here into the summer.' She smiled. 'But it's not so bad.'

'Was this what it was like? The two of us, together?'

'Less close calls with fire alarms, as I recall.' She turned to look at me. 'Those days aren't gone. No matter what happens, we're always just a moment away from happiness. Look at us now. We're like we were on Monday, happy and together. You'll see. In no time, we'd be back squabbling like a married couple.'

Like we were on Monday? I smiled, but inside her words stung. Today I was aware and in control; back then I'd been her dupe. The two states were not comparable.

'I never asked you how you got the delivery job.'

'It wasn't my first choice.' Julie leaned back to rest on her elbows, her voice a little louder than usual, speaking over the music. 'My first plan was to get an apartment on your floor, or at least in your building. But there weren't any vacancies. I was scoping that out when I noticed your deliveries coming in every few days.' She turned to look at me. 'This wasn't Frank's fault at all.'

'You mean Mr Lester?' For some reason, it bugged me that she used his first name.

'Yeah. He just wanted to do the right thing. None of this is on him.'

'You got him to let you do his job? How?'

She shrugged. 'The truth.'

I must have looked sceptical, because she sat up and folded her arms defensively. 'I don't know why that's so hard to believe. If the situation becomes desperate enough, I'm altogether capable of resorting to honesty.'

A snort of laughter almost escaped me, but I pushed it down.

Julie glared at me. 'You will ultimately succumb to my sense of humour, you know. I have history on my side.'

I kept my lips pressed shut.

'Once Frank realised we were still married, and saw how much I wanted to get you back, he decided to help. He's old-school Catholic, so he took the marriage thing seriously. Also, he cares about you.' She smiled grimly. 'As it panned out, I had a lot more success convincing him we belonged together than convincing you. Once he was willing, I explained what I wanted and how it would all work. He's not on holidays, of course. He's servicing his other customers as normal.'

'But it wasn't just me. You knew Mrs Davis, too. The lady from the second floor. You had other deliveries.'

'Well, I had to take over the other two deliveries in your apartment block.' Julie shrugged. 'The jig would have been up if you'd seen him delivering to someone else while he was meant to be off on holiday.'

I stayed silent. The whole thing was beyond anything I could imagine. 'What did you plan to do next? If I hadn't panicked and kicked you out last Monday?'

'I don't know.' She lounged back on the grass. 'I just wanted to make you like me again. For you to remember how it felt when we were together. I hadn't thought much beyond that.'

'Here I was thinking you had every piece of this planned. You'll lose your reputation for deviousness.'

A smile tugged at the corners of her lips. She rested back on the grass, knitting her hands behind her head. The movement stretched the old T-shirt tight across her body, making it clear the Saturday morning couch ensemble did not include a bra.

I wrenched my eyes away, angry at the sudden rush of desire.

'You know,' she said, 'people always talk as if Machiavelli was this evil guy. But he wasn't. He just wanted peace for his country. He was devious, but not for himself. For the greater good.' Her eyelids flickered, almost closing.

'I guess if I had fallen for you, and asked you to stay in my life, there would have been no need to bring up the history at all. You wouldn't have had to go through any of this.'

'We would have been together.'

Heat burned my cheeks. 'Why dredge up the history so long as you've saved the future?'

There was a moment of silence, and then her eyes flashed open, suddenly suspicious. She flicked the earphone out of her ear. 'Where are you going with this?'

'You weren't planning to tell me. If I'd fallen for you, and hadn't pushed you away, you'd never have had to reveal the truth. Not until after the forgetting, when you could tell me whatever you wanted.'

She twisted to sit cross-legged, her eyes fixed on me. 'And you never would have got to choose.'

I met her gaze in silence.

'I know what it's like to forget. And to hate those parts of you getting torn away.' She tapped out a cigarette and lit it. 'It didn't happen at first, not until after I found you up here last time, all angry and scared. After that, it seemed like some part of my mind decided it was just too painful to live with all those happy memories. They started disappearing, like in some sort of unconscious self-defence. All these events I knew had happened, but stripped from my memory. Just gone.' She shifted her weight, until she sat on her knees before me. 'So I started to look over all the photos, every night, curled up with my head on your jacket. To keep the memories alive.'

She smiled bitterly. 'I'm not saying it's the same for me as for you. Just that I understand. I've felt that loss, or some of it, at least. I should have thought about how it must be for you, but I didn't. I've been too wrapped up in my own feelings.'

'That's why I need to know everything,' I said. 'When you said yesterday about knowing the good and the bad of it, about being able to make a decision—an informed decision—it made sense to me. That's why I promised.'

Silence fell. Julie's eyes searched my face. 'Okay,' she said. 'I understand.'

'If you really do understand, then you'll know there can't be any more secrets. Nothing left untold. If I can't make a real decision, with knowledge of all the good and all the bad, then everything we're doing here today is pointless.' I swallowed. 'If I know everything, then it's my choice—like the work you did on the dominoes this morning. If I choose it, then it's a part of me.'

'I get that now. I do.' She reached forward to clasp the top of my hand, fixing her eyes on mine. 'Knowledge of all the good and all the bad. That's what today is about. I promise.'

'The truth. All of it. Good and bad.'

'I promise.'

'Okay.'

She swallowed. 'There was something yesterday. Just a little thing, but if we're doing full disclosure then I guess it needs to be said. When we were talking about the smoke bomb, I told you I'd thought of everything. That wasn't completely true. Remember how the vibration from the alarm felt so strong that we checked the walls and floor to see if it might topple the dominoes? That possibility had never occurred to me. I really panicked then, for a moment, at what I might have done. What a disaster that would have been.'

'I guess no one can think of everything.'

'And poor Mrs Davis stranded there with her furniture delivery. I actually did feel a bit guilty about that.'

'Okay. Thanks for telling me.'

'Always.' She leaned back, releasing my hand. 'Do you want to go back now?'

'Not just yet.'

Julie seemed to have taken the message to heart, and that was all I could ask for. No need to spoil the afternoon.

Our spot of shade grew deeper as the sun shifted westward, and the breeze off the river strengthened. We sat in the quiet for a while. Normally, silences made me feel awkward, but this one was different. People walked by, and the boats and ferries shuttled across the river.

'I suppose you just used his uniform shirt,' I said. 'Mr Lester's.'

'He loaned it to me for the Tuesdays. It wasn't a great fit, was it?'

I smiled, remembering how it had hung sack-like across her shoulders when she arrived at my door.

'What are you smiling at, you jerk? Fine, so my disguise had one or two little wrinkles.' She snorted with laughter. 'One or two tiny, imperceptible flaws.'

Then we were both laughing. At Julie's ridiculously oversized disguise. At how completely I'd fallen for it. At everything.

Eventually, we pulled ourselves together and decided to head back home, and by the time we arrived at the apartment most of the afternoon had drifted by. Julie was in charge of the evening. She had plans to take us out, I knew that much, but she'd provided no details. I wasn't sure whether to feel anticipation or wariness.

I took the first shower and pulled on my nicest pair of pants, then let Julie take her turn. She hummed in that musical way of hers and let her gaze wander over my shirtless chest as she passed.

I felt my face flush, embarrassed that she might think I'd been showing off when in fact I was trying to work up the courage to put on *the* shirt. It was academic really: nothing else in my wardrobe of age-faded T-shirts was remotely suitable for a dinner date. The good shirt, with its rich crimson-purple sheen, looked as if I'd bought it yesterday. I sighed, pulled it on and felt it slip like warm liquid over my shoulders, down my arms.

Searching for something to keep me busy while Julie got ready, I went to put away the dishes in the kitchen. But doing chores just didn't seem right in the fancy shirt; it was as if I'd put on a new persona. I went into the dominoes room and began work on the remaining platform. The upper work on the platforms now looked almost complete. The end was approaching, in more ways than one.

I soon became engrossed and was unprepared when Julie appeared through the kitchen archway, dressed in a slim dark dress, her hair sculpted into a neat wave.

My eyes widened. 'Wow, you look—'

'Oh!' Her exclamation cut off my words. 'Of course.' She smiled wistfully in an I-should-have-known sort of way, and came over to me. Her hands reached to my collar, popping a button open, and then straightening it. 'I always liked that shirt on you.'

So the shirt did come from my earlier life. Perhaps I'd been wearing it when the third forgetting struck, and Julie and I were torn apart. That would make sense. But did that explain how different it was from the rest of my wardrobe? Or just make the difference more perplexing?

Julie had stepped back to survey me, smiling, but her eyes stopped at my shoes.

'Where are—' She broke off, shaking her head. 'Have you got some other shoes? Something with smooth soles?'

'No.'

'Nothing else at all?'

'No.'

Julie looked at her watch and stomped her foot in frustration.

I bit my lip. As much as I had no reason to buy nice shoes, it was hard not to feel a bit embarrassed. The sneakers were old and scuffed up. 'I guess they don't look too fancy.'

'What?' Julie frowned.

'The shoes. Is it a fancy restaurant? They do look a bit crap.'

'I don't care what they *look* like. Do they even fit you?'

'Sure,' I said. Not defensively at all.

Actually, they could have been a better fit. My predecessor must have just grabbed them at the local op shop or something. It had never mattered much before, though I had noticed it on the long walks I used to take. But it did seem a little strange they were my only pair. Wouldn't I have had shoes from my earlier life as well? Something that would go better with the shirt?

I shuffled my feet nervously. Maybe going out wasn't such a great idea.

'Let's not worry about it,' Julie said. 'You look great. Shall we go?'

I nodded, glad to see the back of the issue.

On our previous walk, we'd headed north towards the city. This time we turned west, following Dornoch Terrace as it snaked its way through the hills towards West End. The day darkened as we walked. This city didn't do twilight, especially in summer. Night fell like a theatre curtain.

Julie had picked a Greek restaurant near the end of the long street. Clean and friendly, but not at all fancy. No one noticed my shoes, as far as I could tell. It just wasn't that sort of place.

I breathed a little easier at the informal bustle and loud chatter. It was hard enough keeping my thoughts straight around Julie in unflattering daylight. Heaven help me if I'd had to face candlelight and ambience.

The food was great. Julie knew what I liked and she ordered confidently: souvlaki, haloumi with lemon,

Greek salad; lemonade for both of us. But as I ate, the looming decision weighed on my thoughts. Eventually the evening would end. I would have a choice to make.

Despite its occasional bumps—maybe in a strange way because of them—the day had been a delight. But the choice wasn't whether I'd want to live this day, or something like it, over and again for eternity. I would choose that in a heartbeat.

The question was what would happen to a new me—the infant me, devoid of any life knowledge—being brought up in Julie's world. What would happen to my ability to form my own hopes and plans in the face of hers? The day had brought some reassurances on that front. The fact that we worked and ate and talked together so well suggested that Julie wouldn't need to shape me radically in order to recreate the marriage she had lost.

I couldn't be a hundred per cent certain on that score, of course. She could have temporarily shelved any of her desires to change or improve me. And some questions still nagged at me. My predecessor hadn't just rejected her, he'd gone to all the trouble of getting a lawyer to start divorce proceedings. That seemed an overreaction. But Julie had looked me in the eye and insisted that she was telling me everything, and that she understood the importance of letting me choose with full information.

She smiled at me now, catching my thoughtful gaze. If a similar worry about my looming decision was gnawing at her too, she did a good job of hiding it. She looked pleased, enjoying the moment.

'You said earlier I could ask you about my past.'

'Sure, shoot.' She finished her mouthful. 'Oh—except what your job used to be. We'll get to that later.' Her smile was loaded. Mischievous. I hadn't been thinking about that question at all. But now I was, of course.

'How did we first meet?'

'You remember the story of the fire, the cigarette in the bed? All true. Except that I left out that I'd been drinking that night.'

'Okay.'

'Your workplace was just across the road, and I'd seen you there before. You were working late that night, and when my smoke alarm went off, you arrived first on the scene.' She grinned. 'You didn't kick the door down and charge into the burning building, if that's what you're thinking. The fire alarm had woken me, and I'd managed to stagger out onto the front lawn—half-awake but still half-drunk, and pretty shaken up. You put your arm around me and asked if I was okay.'

Her grin eased into a wistful smile. 'There's more than one way of rescuing someone.'

'So you thought you'd try it again. The whole fire-alarm rescue thing.'

'It worked once.'

'And that's what made you give up alcohol?'

'I wish.' Julie sipped her lemonade. 'But that was... the beginning of the end.'

'Because you nearly died from it?'

'More that I'd found something that tasted good without a splash of Jack.'

Her eyes pinned me like a rabbit in headlights. I squirmed. 'Was your drinking much of a problem back then? When we first met?'

'Apart from almost killing me in the fire, you mean? No. I had zero problem drinking.' She nursed her lemonade, holding it in both hands before her, elbows resting on the table. '*That* turned out to be my problem. I was a happy drunk. Everybody loved me. I could drink until sunrise and you'd still have to wrench me off the dance floor. The next day I'd be ready to go again. Shiny as.'

'What got you addicted in the first place?'

'Three words: bourbon is fucking awesome.' She paused. 'Four words.'

'That's it?'

'That's it.' She shrugged. 'There wasn't a part of it I didn't love. The taste. The buzz. The fucking colour of it. Like burnt amber. And that sound when you're pouring from a new bottle.' She did a musical *guck-guck-guck* from the back of her throat.

'Then why quit?'

'I didn't quit because of what I did when I was drinking.' She smiled at the thought. 'It was when I sobered up that was the problem. I wasn't functioning in normal life. I'd always done well at uni, but in the last year my marks began to suffer. And I'd started wanting it every day, itching for that first drink, as if there was no other way to have fun.' She bit her lip. 'It's frightening when you realise you've lost the ability to enjoy anything else—even a conversation over dinner.' She raised her glass. 'By the way, you're welcome to order a wine if you want. It's no problem.'

'Did I used to drink around you, while you were quitting?'

She sighed, shaking her head. 'You said you'd lost the taste for it. I got the impression that if you live with an alcoholic for long enough you start to see the bottle as the enemy.'

'Do you think—if it was you who had the forgetting

instead of me,' I wondered aloud, '—do you think you could leave all that behind? That you could stop being addicted by forgetting that you were addicted?'

'No. It's like wondering if a forest fire could burn away a volcano. I might get to forget a few of the stupid things I've done while drinking. That'd be nice.' She paused. 'But I think the urge would still be there, beneath it all.'

It was hard to trace her tone. Her words had started off regretful, but they finished almost hopeful. Which made no sense, given the topic.

Before I could puzzle it out, she began talking again. 'Maybe there'd be some things that would change. The part of me that wants to drink. It's not just an urge, it's like a person sometimes. And she thinks and plans and speaks and lies. You wonder why I'm so strategic? That's what it takes to beat her. The voice. So maybe the urge would still be there, but the little personality inside me might not be the same.'

'Would you miss that part of you, though, if it disappeared? After all, she's part of you. That voice in your head. She's what made you smart. Without her—'

'Fuck that. Erase the bitch.' Julie skewered a piece of haloumi with her fork. 'Maybe that seems harsh, but you don't know her like I do.'

I pasted a smile on my face. But it was hard not to wonder what parts of me might face the same fate, if Julie was in charge of the forgetting.

For the first time, I wondered if I would have to say no to her. Really wondered. I could scarcely imagine how to do it. It was one thing to react in shock and rage, as I'd done three days ago. It was another to reject her in cold blood. The food before me suddenly looked unappetising.

'Are you done?' Julie's voice pulled me out of my reverie. I wished she didn't sound so happy. It would only make things harder. 'We have somewhere to be.'

She insisted on paying, saying since she'd been put in charge of the evening, she had to cover the costs. I couldn't argue with her logic, but it grated a little. As always, she was the one with all the power.

Julie led us towards West End. This area was my favourite part of the city, with its random shops and boho cafes. The people walked with a bounce in their step, and dressed however they wanted. With my lustrous dress shirt and worn sneakers, I probably fitted right in. But Julie veered us down a side street before we hit the main nest of cafes and nightspots. She too had a noticeable spring in her step. Excitement buzzed from her whole body and shone from her eyes. Whatever she was planning, we were on the verge of it.

She drew to a sudden halt. I looked around, but there was little to see. Just an ordinary inner-city street with neat brick houses cluttered up close together.

'It's a surprise,' Julie said. 'So you need to shut your eyes.'

Suspicion warring with anticipation, I closed my eyes.

Julie hooked her hand around my arm. 'Forward,' she ordered, and we continued down the path. To guide me, she had to pin my arm tight to the side of her body. I tried not to focus on the soft warm press against my arm, but with my eyes closed, there wasn't much I could do to distract myself.

I took a deep breath. The nightly caterwauling of lorikeets in the nearby trees filled my ears. And something else.

A beat.

Beneath the birds' screeching, an ordered, steady thumping. With each step forward, the sound got louder and filled out in depth and strength, until it transformed into something more than a mere pulse. Rhythm. Music.

'No peeking.' Julie's grip on me tightened as she turned us around a corner, and towards the music. It didn't sound like her type of music—either the power riffs thundering from her earbuds or the ambient instrumentals she'd played over at her house. This was a bigger band sound, with brass and strings and more. Yet it still seemed somehow familiar.

'There's stairs.' Julie counted me up five of them, one by one.

After a few more steps, the music jumped in volume and the surface under my shoes became smoother. Polished wood, perhaps. My sneakers squeaked as they gripped it.

'Hi.' Julie greeted someone.

A female responded—an elderly voice. 'Twenty each.'

'I thought ten?' Julie queried.

'Only on Tuesdays.'

I moved to reach for my wallet, but Julie was already replying. 'Right, no worries.' She kept my arm pinned hard against her. 'I got it. My plan. My money.'

Julie leaned closer. 'Chasing lost husbands across the country is not as cheap a hobby as you might think,' she whispered.

We set off again. Julie manoeuvred me in front of her, and I had the sense we were navigating a doorway. As we passed the threshold, the music surged again. Meanwhile, a soft babble of voices issued from left and right, as if on either side of a large room. Was it a party?

A musical? If anyone was looking in our direction, we must have seemed a strange couple. A stunning woman in an elegant dress leading a tall guy with terrible shoes and tightly shut eyes. She navigated me over to the left side of the room—I was picturing it as a large hall—and guided me down into a chair.

Julie released me at last from the warm press of her body. That was a relief. Well, I felt something anyway, at the loss of her touch, and it stood to reason it was relief.

'Ready?' Julie's voice came from a little distance away. Across a small table perhaps. 'Three, two, one,' she counted down, her voice a whisper of enthusiasm. 'Eyes open!'

Colour, light and movement hit me all at once and... dancing.

In the centre of the room, couples glided and turned in rhythmic harmony. Women and men moving like cogs and wheels in a living clockwork of spinning perfection. Brilliant lights shone from a ceiling rack and a nearby mirrorball, sending shining circles of colour onto the dancers' dazzling clothes. There was no band—the music was coming from speakers mounted at the back of the room.

'Surprise!' Julie's eyes shone, catching the reflection of the coloured lights.

I soaked in the sight. The perfect set of a man's shoulders. The smooth snap of a spinning heel. The locked eyes of a twirling couple.

'It's not ideal.' Julie was talking, but I hardly heard her words, lost in the sounds and sights. 'But it's the best I could do with a limited budget. At short notice, in a new city.'

'I was a dancer.'

Julie's smile filled her face.

'A dancer.' I repeated. The dancers stepped and spun around each other with a hypnotic grace. Excitement built up inside me, to think I'd once been part of something so beautiful. It felt like I was free-falling into another world, tumbling within a child's kaleidoscope.

Somewhere in the back of my brain, a voice screamed against that giddy excitement, yelling that this was it: Julie's plan. Right here and right now. Her final strategy to sink her claws into my soul—the source of her optimism since we made our deal yesterday morning. I couldn't afford to get swept away and distracted from the decision at hand.

But that voice dissolved in the din of sound and light reverberating through every nerve in my body. 'This is crazy.' It jarred with everything I knew about myself, as unbelievable as if Julie had told me I used to be a fighter pilot or a treasure hunter.

Unbelievable—except for what my eyes and ears and heart told me. They recognised this place. It lay within me, in my mind's eye. I could see it all, the neat, quick steps of the young man in the yellow shirt, the cocked wrist position of his partner.

'Crazy?' Julie echoed. She surveyed the room. There were people whizzing about its centre, and a few couples loitering along the margins. 'There isn't a person in the room who couldn't find something crazy hidden in their history. Something beautiful. Something terrible.' She paused, and her smile dimmed.

'Was I…' I fumbled for the word. 'Famous?'

'Steady on, Baryshnikov.' She laughed. 'You earned a living doing what you love. That's success enough.' She cocked her head to one side, as if measuring her words. 'Occasionally you got in a major show. Mostly you got by on teaching, the local dance studio. And always working on your next performance.'

'I would have been as good as the dancers here?' I looked at the floaty way they glided across the floor.

'These dancers?' Julie snorted. 'You are so cute.' She leaned across the table, lowering her voice. 'Robbie, these are all amateurs.' She surveyed the dance floor with a clinical eye. 'A few of them are pretty good. I'm going to get us a drink. When I get back, you're going to tell me which is the best couple on the floor.'

'Me?' They all looked amazing. 'I wouldn't know what to look for.'

'Remember after the fire brigade showed up and we lifted that cabinet with Mrs Davis?' Her eyes drilled into mine. 'Do you remember what you said?'

Of course I did. The first time I'd ever snapped at anyone. 'Drop your weight. Widen your stance.'

'You taught me to dance with those very words.' She stood up. 'The memories are in there somewhere.'

'I thought you were upset because I'd been bossy.'

'No.' Julie shook her head. 'I mean, I was upset. But what got to me that day was the realisation you were still there. *You*. My Robbie. Your voice. Your words. All still there.'

Wow. I'd so totally misread that. I wondered what it would have been like for Julie, in the midst of all that noise and activity, to hear the language of my lost self tumbling out. The words of a ghost spilling from the mouth of a child.

'You play judge.' Julie redirected my attention to the dancers. 'I'll find us some juice.' With a quick pirouette, she set off towards the counter at the back of the hall.

A quick pirouette. How often had I seen her do just that? Noticing the dance move without knowing why it registered.

I turned my attention back to the movement and colour. The song finished, and for a moment the dancers held their position. Then they relaxed, and were just so many ordinary people. Music started again, and again they were transformed.

Time must have passed. Julie broke me from my trance, arriving back with two tall glasses of orange juice. She slid one across the table to me and raised her eyebrows expectantly.

'The couple in red.' I could hardly explain my reasons. Just the way they held themselves, delving in and out of each other's space, every movement polished to the point where each dancer looked an extension of the other.

'Right.' She nodded.

'*The guy especially.*' The two of us said it together.

'Ha!' cried Julie. 'See? You still have it. Perception.' She pointed her chin at the two. 'They're at competition level.' She leaned back in her seat, her eyes measuring, evaluating. 'Probably in training now. Three or four times a week they'd be going along to classes and getting taught.' She smiled. 'By someone like you.'

The couple flowed across the floor like liquid poetry.

'Point being,' she continued, 'you could wipe the floor with anyone out there.'

'Imagine that.'

Julie put her elbows on the table. 'I don't think we have to imagine.'

I shook my head. 'Just because I can see things doesn't mean I can still do them.'

'Two words. *Muscle memory*. You don't lose everything when you forget, you only lose specific ideas: people, places, events.'

'Yeah. The doctor had a word for it…'

'Episodic memory.' She nodded. 'You don't lose all the other types of memory. You don't forget what words mean. And you don't forget how to do things like eat, or speak, or walk—'

'Or dance,' I finished her thought.

'You won't remember where you first learned the dance, and maybe not the names of the positions and moves. But the muscles will remember.'

'Dancing is complicated, though. It's not like walking or talking.'

'It's actually the complex things you have the best hope of remembering. The ones where you've had to drum the movements into your muscles. They are the ones you'll still have in you.' Her eyes sparkled. 'Potentially,' she added. 'In theory.'

My hands shook with excitement. What if it were true—the body remembering when the mind could not? After all, how else had I teased out all of my morning exercises? The push-ups and crunches and planks and stretching had all been inside me, just waiting to be teased out. Maybe dance would be like that, just waiting for a connection to the music in my ears and the polished floor under my feet.

'Let's do it.'

'Right now?' Julie laughed and put down her juice. 'This is a rumba. I was thinking we should wait for something a bit easier, but sure. Let's go.'

She stood and offered her hand to me, palm up. I took it. 'You dance too, right?'

'I get by. This guy I dated once gave me a lesson or two.'

We weaved our way over to an uncrowded corner of the dance floor. It was good to have a little space to work in. At least I wouldn't stumble into anybody. My free hand clenched and unclenched. Excitement gave way to nervousness. It had taken days to work out the exercises. It hadn't happened all at once. Under pressure. In front of strangers.

Julie turned to face me, eyes radiant with hope.

Great. No expectations or anything. I gritted my teeth against the nerves.

'Right.' Julie began assembling me into a starting position, bumping and nudging my limbs and shoulders to her satisfaction. Fortunately, I was anxious enough that the touch of her hand didn't deliver its normal electricity. Eventually she stepped back and nodded. 'Wait for it.' She positioned herself beside me. 'We're going to step forward with the right. Let's see if anything comes back.' I could see the count going in her eyes, as she waited for the pattern to begin.

I fought the urge to grip her hand too hard, trying to leave my fingers loose and free. The way my nerves were jangling, I could have been standing on a precipice, preparing to jump off the edge.

'Now,' she said.

And off we stepped.

Memory fluttered, the beat of its wings brushing against the mind's edge. My foot landed and I glided forward. My back foot arched onto its toes, followed me forward, and then stopped.

Perfect.

I felt rather than saw Julie mirroring me. She turned to me as I swept towards her. In unison our feet swung through the air, turning in mid-stride to…

Clunk against one another. Julie stumbled and we bumped side-on, bouncing off each other like dodgem cars. She laughed, her eyes gleaming. There had been something in my movement she'd seen immediately.

'Let's go again.' She started setting me up again, arms and hips and wrists all in order. The process moved quicker. This time I counted down to the first step myself, feeling into the moment to join the music.

I repeated the step forward, the pause, the turn. My foot slid alongside hers, my tatty sneaker next to her slender black shoe.

Yes. I had this.

We turned away, as if folding ourselves outward to the world. Reflecting each other, we returned to facing forward. I skimmed my left foot forward, but my sneaker squeaked and gripped the floor.

No. Wrong.

I stumbled slightly and pulled myself to a halt.

'Again,' I said, and set about manoeuvring myself into position. But the song finished, leaving me standing like an oddly fashioned shop dummy.

Julie looked up at me, biting her lip in excitement. 'You see? It's still there.'

I buzzed with the same excitement. There was memory

here, within me, bursting to be used. An overpowering urge to take the forgotten and to see it made real in the world once more. She had been right, after all. Julie knew me better than I knew myself. There was something unnerving in that. When every sure-footed step pushed me further into a world I didn't know.

The next song started. 'Not sure I know this,' Julie said.

'Let's sit this one out.' I wanted a moment to breathe and get my head around this. My body seemed to be screaming at me: *This changes everything*. But my mind wanted to pause, to think, to work out what it changed and what it didn't. We retreated to our table and I slumped into my seat as if my legs had given out. Julie perched on the edge of her seat.

No words were spoken. We both knew what had happened. I just didn't know what it meant.

'I wonder why I never left myself any music,' I said. 'Not even a radio. Something to trigger these memories.'

Julie sipped her juice, watching me. 'It's not only about music. Haven't you ever found yourself standing in the centre of an empty room, and feeling all that space all around you, just waiting for you to take it and fill it with something new?'

'I don't think I've ever found myself in the centre

of an empty room. Full stop.' Not with that mountain of dominoes standing in the middle of my apartment. I reached for my drink, thirsty more from nerves than from exertion. Even now, I couldn't take my eyes off the dancers. What would it be like to belong out there, to be part of what they did?

Soon enough, the song finished and the opening bars of another began. Julie bounced to her feet. 'A waltz. You could do it in your sleep. It's the first dance you ever taught me. It's as simple as one, two, three.'

We headed back to our corner of the floor. Again, she arranged me, her hands professional as they moved me this way and that. I suppose I'd once done the same to her.

'This arm wraps around my back.' She demonstrated, moving in and letting my right arm close around her. 'And we hold these hands.' Our palms pressed snugly together, our fingers curling to hold them in place. The tips of my fingers tingled where they touched her.

My body felt more awkward and mechanical than the first time. Perhaps it was the greater expectation I had now. Or Julie being so close.

'You can pull me in quite tight if you like. A waltz can work either—*oh!*'

My arm knew what it was doing better than I did. It

scooped her in with effortless authority. All at once, I could feel the crush of her hips and the press of her hand against the small of my back. Her face came in close to mine, far too close for comfort. Wide eyes looked up at me, eager and gleaming, filling my field of vision. Her perfume assaulted my senses, blending with the scent of her hair and skin.

Sensory overload: my jangled nerves overwhelmed by her hips, her lips, her scent. Sweat prickled at the back of my neck. A sense of panic gripped my stomach.

'Perfect,' she said. 'Now up on your toes.' She raised herself up, and I followed her movement exactly, as if I'd known the command before she spoke it. Everything snapped into place. The music. My arms, shoulders, hips, feet. And Julie, fitting into my space, shaping around my body like a silhouette. Her words tumbled into the sound of the music and the swish of couples spinning past. 'So you start by stepping forward with your right foot, almost as if you're stepping into me. When you do, I'll...'

I barely heard her words. Some alien force had taken control, listening only to the music, feeling its lift and glide. Thought was gone; arms and legs held themselves poised, waiting for the moment, ready to pounce on the opening provided in the one-two-three, one-two-three—

Go.

My right leg swept forward, and Julie moved back, steps locked, legs melded in their synchronised sweep. As my foot touched the floor, it spun and elevated. Julie turned in my arms as I pulled her around. There was no effort, only momentum. I spun us forward, towards the centre, into the maelstrom of spinning, gliding dancers, Julie's face the only fixed object in the world. The room whirled behind her, lights and colours whizzing past: only her eyes and her smile held steady.

Everything was a rush with Julie at its centre. Her smile shone: this was what she'd been waiting for.

Muscle memory had given way to something deeper. A tumult of desire, will, perception. It felt like a drug racing through my blood, an intensity outside my control, as if the excitement and sensation were someone else's. Someone more important, more powerful; more alive.

This wasn't like the exercises, all muscle twitches and the resurrection of a few buried habits. This was intention and emotion programmed into the depths of the mind. The same sense of possession had gripped me the first time Julie played her music, but this time there wasn't that nauseous sense of moving-not-moving.

This time I could only follow its direction, the space

spread open before me, Julie, the sound, the group, the lights, all pushing me on the same trajectory as that internal force. Our every step, our instinctual flow into a new space, all seemed stepped out by someone else. An unseen puppeteer, perfecting every part of me through a thousand tiny strings. It felt like drowning, disappearing under the tide of a forgotten, alien will. This was what she'd wanted all along. This spell.

I pushed back at it; against its strange knowledge.

I pushed back at *her*.

Julie stumbled. There had been no force in my movement—more wrenching myself out of her arms than pushing her away. But it brought us to a shuddering halt, and relief flooded my body.

'Oops.' Julie still smiled. 'We got that one wrong. Let's blame the footwear.'

She thought my action had been a mistake. Unintentional. But it felt like the first intentional thing I'd done since stepping onto the dance floor.

Her arms opened in welcome again. 'You really had it there for a moment.'

'No. It wasn't me. I didn't know what I was doing.'

Around us, people stared.

Her smile faded. 'That's okay. It's not all going to come back in a rush.'

But that was *exactly* how it was coming back. This was the opposite of control. The opposite of choice.

'I can't do it.' I raised my hands like stop signs. 'I just...no. We shouldn't have come here.'

I stumbled off the dance floor, the waltzing couples veering out of my way.

Back at the table, I sank into the chair and cowered over my drink. Julie arrived, but I kept my eyes down. I didn't want to see the expression on her face. Whatever she was feeling—disappointed, upset, betrayed, embarrassed—I didn't want to know.

'We've got all night,' she said at last, her voice so tentative it sounded like a question.

I flinched and shook my head. 'No.' There were no other words.

The sound of the waltz was still going in the background, mixing with the buzz of chatter from those at the nearby tables, but the two of us were trapped in our own world of awkwardness. I could feel her staring at me.

'I might just go to the ladies for a moment.' Her voice sounded broken.

The black dress swished as she turned away. I looked up and watched her weave through the tables, her movements hasty and jerky. She almost stumbled into someone. I'd done that to her.

But what was the alternative? I'd promised I would try, and I had tried. To go another step further would be not to choose but to abandon myself.

Julie couldn't know all that: what it was like to feel a stranger taking control. It made me sick to the stomach. I stood up. I would go after her; apologise. Try to explain. But she had disappeared around the tables at the back of the hall.

I slumped down in the chair, wishing I was somewhere, anywhere else. I didn't know why the dancing wasn't like the morning exercises: a neat skill to be unearthed, then turned off or on as needed. But it wasn't. It was as if emotion and authority were hidden in every movement, urging me to just let go. To surrender.

Well, to hell with that.

I nursed my drink until Julie returned from the bathroom. She didn't sit down.

'This one's a waltz, too.' A forlorn hope sounded in her voice. 'Just a bit slower.'

She lifted her chin, but her lips were trembling, her eyes red where just moments earlier they had been shining in triumph. She shouldn't have looked beautiful. 'I think maybe the shoes aren't helping.' Her voice quavered, but she forced it onward. 'There's too much grip, in all the wrong places. I know it would seem weird to just try it in socks, but it—'

'No.'

'Okay.' Her voice broke on the second syllable. She sank into her chair. 'I'm sorry.' Her eyes were on the table, on our glasses of juice. Anywhere but me. There was no anger in her anymore. No strategy. She looked beaten.

'I didn't mean for this to be awkward for you.' Her hands were balled into fists on the table. They held her full attention. 'You remembered before. We got you back into the studio not long after the first time. You'd forgotten my name, forgotten all of us, but there was a world you still knew. In your arms and in your eyes, you knew the dance.' Her tone stayed even, but her fists squeezed hard as she spoke. 'It must have been too long away. Stupid idea.'

This had been her master plan all along. Now she'd played her trump and lost, it was as if she had lost everything. Looking at her, watching her try and fail to put a brave face on it, I didn't feel sorry. I didn't feel guilty.

I felt free, I realised—free to choose.

Water began to well in her eyes, but she just kept staring at her clenched fists. Sad because I wasn't him, the man I'd once been? Or because she felt she was losing me, the man sitting in front of her.

I knew which I wanted it to be.

'No,' I said slowly. 'We were right to try.' I reached across the table; wrapped my hand gently around her fist. Julie looked at it blankly.

Moments passed, and we stayed like that. Her hard white knuckles under my light caress, the tips of my fingers grazing the underside of her wrist. She frowned. She stared at my hand a moment longer, her jaw tightening. Anger?

'If you're trying to be comforting,' she said, 'you're not doing it right.'

'I'm not trying to be comforting.'

Her breath hitched, and her lips pressed together hard. But hope flickered in the red-rimmed eyes that searched my face. 'Oh.' She swallowed, and then nodded.

My other hand closed around her still-clenched fist. Her eyes fixed on mine. I felt her fingers relax, then uncurl. Slowly, deliberately, her hand rolled over, palm upward and open. My hand slipped into hers.

'We could walk along the river on the way back to my place,' I said.

The breath released from her body, shuddering. An almost imperceptible nod answered me.

Julie reached for her handbag with her free hand

and hooked it over her shoulder. We stood in unison, hands and eyes locked together. The grip of her hand was soft, almost yielding—like she was frightened to grasp too hard at something that might slip through her fingers—but every move kept open our line of physical touch and sight.

Wordless, we left the table. Everything else floated into the periphery. The cacophony of voice and music. The colours of dress and light. The shifting bodies and the solid walls that must have marked our exit. She didn't say anything at first. I had the sense she didn't want to break whatever spell was at work on me. Whatever was changing me.

We'd almost made it back to the bright lights of West End when Julie stopped short. She still had her hand in mine: now she gripped hard and pulled me to a stop.

'So…' she said. 'Um, so this is nice.' She looked down at our interlocked hands, then up at me. 'But Robbie, I have to know. If you've made a decision, you have to say the words. Because I'm dying here.'

'Yes,' I said.

'Yes, you've made a decision? Or yes to me?'

'Yes to everything.' Then my hands were on her hips, and hers were in my hair and we were kissing and it felt nothing like the other times. There wasn't a hint of hesitation or clumsiness: this was what it felt like to move with complete confidence.

After a while, we got to the main street. I stopped at the streetlights, unsure of my bearings. Tucked in the loop of the river, every direction led to water except the direct route back to the apartment.

'This way,' she said, her voice quiet. We drifted into the bright lights and hubbub where the restaurants and bars had spilled out onto the footpath in the warm evening air. Bodies brushed against us as we wove through, the noise and movement no more than a backdrop.

Past the last of the hotels the noise and people evaporated, leaving us to ourselves. The river appeared before us, inky black ripples reflecting the city lights and a cool breeze gusting over the water.

Somewhere along the way, we'd both started smiling too. Perhaps I'd been smiling ever since I reached my hand across the table to her clenched fist. But it was impossible not to notice it now. It seemed an effort just to keep my feet planted on the ground, as if the lightness deep in my chest had infected gravity itself.

The rest of the world carried on. On the bridge above our secluded path, cars roared back and forth. The red-on-red flash of a fire engine above us seemed distant. It shone on Julie's face, flashing its crimson across her pale skin. The second time this week I'd seen that sight.

'What?' she asked, marking my gaze.

'Nothing.'

Her eyes narrowed. 'I am not responsible for every fire alarm in this city.'

'I didn't say anything,' I objected. 'It's just you were out of sight for almost five minutes at the bathroom back there. Who knows what you got up to?'

'Oh. My. God.' She turned to face me. 'Was that a joke? An actual attempt at a joke? I'd given up all hope a sense of humour still survived in there.'

'Huh. I can see the funny side of felonies.'

'Well,' she sniffed, stepping backward, mirroring my own steps forward. Now that I knew about the dancing there seemed to be rhythm in her every movement. 'If you can think of a completely legal way to inject yourself into someone else's life, feel free to let me know.' Her crooked smile widened into open mischief. 'I'll use it next time.'

'*Next time?*' I should have been outraged, but it was impossible. 'If it comes to that I'll get your mugshot tattooed on my chest with the words "Here be dragons". Just to ramp up the difficulty level for your next attempted infiltration.'

'Here be dragons?' Her free hand shaped into a fist

and mock-punched my shoulder. 'You *jerk*.' She gripped my shirt at the shoulder. 'That's it. When you forget on Sunday, I'm not going to tell you you're a dancer. I'll say you're a performance artist working in the medium of, um, milk and toast. See how funny you are then!'

Our linked hands reset themselves, palms pressed, fingers interlaced. 'Well,' I grinned. 'I'd like to thank you for a truly forgettable evening—'

Julie pressed a finger hard up against my lips, cutting off my words. 'You know,' she said, lifting herself up onto her toes, pushing herself forward. 'I'm thinking I liked you better *before* we found where your sense of humour was buried.' Her finger slipped off my lips just in time to make space for her mouth.

Eventually we set off again, and the world flowed by us, slowing to a stall each time we circled into each other, and then rolling forward again when we turned homeward. At last the river retreated behind us, and our steps traced out paths I'd once taken long ago.

This did seem a particularly familiar stretch of walkway, come to think of it. 'Were you looking in on me three or four months ago?'

'Of course. I moved up well before that.'

'Did you notice I stopped going out so much about then?'

'Yeah.' She nodded. 'Absolutely I did.'

'Random fact. It's because of what happened right here. Just a stupid thing, but there was this jogger—'

'You *did* see me!' she exploded.

'What?'

'That was me!' She turned to confront me. 'I told you I'd tried everything.' Her hands flew up in the air. 'I thought I'd staged my fall wrong and you just hadn't seen me.'

'You were the jogger?'

'I took all my jewellery out, added the sunglasses and the running gear.'

I thought back, trying to paste Julie's face into my memory of the jogger. 'Your hair was different.'

'Right,' she said. 'That was the shoulder-length phase: dyed brown and pulled back in a ponytail. Each new disguise, I had to take a little more off the top.' She grinned. 'Lucky things are looking more promising this time. There's only one place left to go.' She pressed in closer to me. 'What's your feeling on the military look? Shaved head, uniform. Work for you?'

'Oh.' We had been in different worlds, she shedding her skin, again and again, while I built cathedrals in the sky, one tile at a time.

'Oh?' She mimicked my surprise, and punched me in

the arm. 'You just left me lying there.'

'I'm sorry, at the time I thought—' My mind took a moment to catch up with the rush of guilt, then sanity took hold. 'Hold on. Am I apologising for not falling for your ruse?'

'You damn well should apologise.' She pointed to one finger. 'A: I spent weeks working on that ruse. And B:' she moved to a second finger. 'Jerk.'

This really was the limit. The months I'd spent feeling guilty, thinking I'd been responsible for the whole thing. 'Is there nothing you didn't try?'

'Well…' She linked her arms around my neck. 'There was a plan involving chloroform and handcuffs, but it didn't come to that.'

We kissed again. The sharp edge of her teeth brushed against my tongue. She drew back. Not far, but just enough to speak. 'Sorry. I'm smiling too hard. It's a problem.' Her hand cupped behind my head. 'It's been so long.'

'Was it all so perfect?' Surely it wasn't always like this. Ordinary life would be impossible. 'That you'd fight for it so hard?'

'Not perfect at all.' Julie wrinkled her nose. She kept her arms linked around my neck. My hands circled her waist. Our feet shuffled together, spinning in slow motion in our corner of the park. 'We both had our careers. You in dance, me in theatre. One of us drank too much. That took some dealing with.' She smiled ruefully. 'Perfect? God, there were times when we'd drive each other crazy.'

'Why then? Why pursue this so hard, for all this time?'

She ran her hand through my hair, tousling it. 'Well, there were times when we'd drive each other crazy.'

'I'm serious.'

'*I'm* serious.'

'Ohhh…wait…' An awful thought surged into mind, like a thick hand crushing in on the butterflies inside. 'I've been so wrapped in my own little bubble I didn't think about what would be best for you.'

'What do you mean?'

'However good it once was, that's not what it could be now. That's not our future.' I held my hands firm on her hips, drawing our circling to a halt. 'We're not going back to those times when we first met. We're going back to me forgetting everything in three days' time. And then again every six months. Maybe for years.'

I ran my hand through her hair, shaking my head at how callous I'd been. How thoughtless. 'You saw me drowning and thought you could rescue me, but all I can do is claw you down with me.'

Julie shrugged. 'Well, you know my policy on that. One vice at a time.'

'No,' I said, annoyed. 'You've been so busy plotting how to get here, did you ever stop to think about whether this would make a good life for you?'

She smiled fondly. 'You always think too much. And always about all the right things.' But my eyes burrowed into hers, forcing an answer. She sighed. 'All right, no, I didn't, to be honest. The big-picture thinking was always more your suit. That's how we worked.' Her hand slapped gently against my cheek a couple of times. 'That's why I got one of you. You're the one choice I got right in my twenty-eight years. The one thing I really had sorted.'

'Sorted?'

'We fit together. Somehow our warped grooves and jagged edges lined up in all the right ways. It's like if you have one person staggering and contorted, it looks mad. But if you have two together, different maybe, but still in tune, in beat…' She thumped the heel of her palm against my chest. 'It becomes something else entirely.'

'Dance.'

She nodded. 'And that's worth holding on to. It's worth fighting for.'

'Maybe once. But now?' I squared my shoulders.

'You'd be condemned to a future building something over and over that just keeps falling down. That has to be my life. It doesn't have to be yours.'

Julie shrugged, but with gravity rather than her earlier nonchalance. 'That's what life is anyway. We'd have an argument. I'd stomp off to bed and we'd sleep on opposite edges. The next morning we'd wake up and you'd ask if I wanted a coffee and I'd grunt at you and you'd make us a coffee, and I'd manage a thanks. Then we'd start picking up the pieces. If I wasn't up for perpetual rebuilding I'd never have got married in the first place. Actually, I'd never have done anything worthwhile. I don't know how many times I made it to a week sober before having to reset the clock. Once I made it almost a year before falling off the wagon. And starting all over again at day zero. Everything falls. Everything is rebuilding.'

'This is different. You know it is.'

'Whatever *this* is, I signed up for it. For better or worse. I could never just walk away from you.'

'But that's just it,' I seized on her words. 'We're *already* "away". So you wouldn't be walking away. You'd just be...' I searched for the words that might convince her. 'Not walking back.'

She raised her eyebrows. 'I don't feel very away.'

She had a point there. Her lips were inches from mine. Our eyes could hardly pull away from the other's for more than a moment. Close? We were *entangled*.

I pushed the unhelpful thought aside. 'I've created a life here on my own. I'm okay.'

'You're facing all of this every day, alone,' she scoffed, 'without anyone to rely on and get you through it? Do you really believe you're okay here on your own?'

I looked away, unable to meet her eyes. I wasn't okay. Not anymore. Not after having been here with her, like this. No one would be okay after giving this up. But in three days' time, when the forgetting came, this feeling would be gone, and all memory of it. Only the journal would remain, a pale copy of something once complete. 'I'll be okay,' I not-quite-lied. 'It would have been different if we'd been together all along. But it's not like that. You have an opportunity to be free of this. To live your own life.' I took her hands. 'You wouldn't be leaving me. The leaving already happened, and it wasn't anyone's fault.'

'Robbie—'

'You said yesterday that you've suffered more from this than I have, and now I can see that's true. This is worse for you than for me. And for me, escape is impossible. But not for you.'

'I suffered because we were *apart*, not because we were together. Anyway, it's not like it will be forever. Your condition might just…stop tomorrow.'

'Said Doctor Varma. I thought you didn't like her.'

'I didn't like her because she was right about everything. About your condition. About me.'

I put my hands on her shoulders and spoke with something intended to sound a lot like honesty. 'I'll. Be. Okay.'

She shook her head. 'Look at me.' Her emerald eyes blazed into me from point-blank range. 'How do I make you feel?' Soft hands slid up to where my shoulders met my neck, thin fingers pressing into the muscle with sudden strength. Her face filled my vision. 'Don't think. Just answer. How do you feel right now?'

'*Alive.*' The answer tumbled out of its own accord.

The grip around my neck released. A small nod of satisfaction. 'There you are, then.'

I frowned, angry at my own admission. A betrayal, even if it was the truth. It would have been better to lie.

'Okay, look.' Her hands went from my shoulders to my hands, and she stepped back. 'Imagine we'd had long enough for you to fall for me. Really fall. Imagine you love me.'

'Okay.' I kept my voice level. 'I'm imagining.'

'Now I tell you I'm sick and that it's bad.' Her eyes searched my face. 'Does that change your mind? Does it change what you want or how you feel? Does it change what you will do for me?'

'No.'

'No.' She nodded.

'But that doesn't change what *I* should do,' I objected. 'I can't give you happiness or the life you deserve. I don't have that power. But I have the power to let you go, and to stop this sickness dragging both of us down.' My hands clasped hers in front of me. 'What sort of person would I be, condemning you to this life?'

She stepped back from me and drew herself up to her full height. 'What was it you said this afternoon? An informed decision, with knowledge of all the good and all the bad. You deserve that choice. But I do too.' Her fingers curled around the scruff of my shirt. 'I chose this then,' she whispered, her lips almost touching mine. 'And I choose it now.' Her mouth pressed hard against mine.

Beneath her kiss, I was defeated. However much I wanted to protect her from this, I could not deny her the same choice I'd demanded for myself.

'And you know what?' She broke off the kiss. 'We have *this*. Tonight.' She pulled away from me a little. 'You and I will grow old, but *we* will never get old. For as long as the forgetting keeps coming back, *this* will never get old. Every time you forget, I'll make you fall in love with me all over again. I'll get a lifetime of you falling for me.'

'You are impossible.' I smiled in the face of her irrepressible optimism. 'You would take lemons and make—'

'Whiskey sours.' Julie's cheer cut through mine. 'But I'm trying to break that habit, remember?'

I lifted her, my forearm scooping underneath her until she was almost seated on it. She seemed weightless, above me, her face bending down to meet mine.

'That was the other thing.' She licked her lips. 'You still taste good sober. That's true love right there. You could put that on a Hallmark card.'

~

Back home, Julie blinked at the white glare of the kitchen's fluorescent light. 'Where are your candles?'

'In the kitchen cupboard beneath the sink. How did you know I had...?'

She grinned and started to rummage, then raised a slender hand triumphantly holding four long white candles. '*Mwah-ha-ha*. You have no secrets from your grocery deliverer.'

She melted the bases of the candles with her lighter and stuck them on saucers. 'That's better,' she nodded as the candlelight kissed her face with its flickering glow. 'Now, where were we?'

She leaned back against the table's edge, pushing her hips forward. The dim light turned her eyes from emerald green to coal black. Our mouths met, and the rest of the world faded, trapped outside my locked door as I pressed her body against mine. Her feet had left the floor, but I barely felt my muscles flex.

The bedroom. The thought had hardly touched my mind and I was carrying her through the doorway, knees dipping at the edge of the bed. I lowered her onto the mattress and slid alongside her.

'Hold up,' she said. 'I haven't waited this long to fumble around in the dark.'

She rolled away from me and slipped into the darkness, then returned with the candles. Their butter-yellow light and dancing shadows washed the room with warmth and life. She turned to me.

'Do we need, um...'—the question had to be asked—'you know, protection?'

Julie shook her head. 'I'm on the pill.' A sigh. 'Have been all this time. Hope springs eternal, I guess.' She looked me up and down and grinned. 'You always stretch when you're nervous.'

I looked down at my arms. One hand had wrapped around the other wrist, its thumb pressing hard against the joint, twisting it anti-clockwise. I hadn't noticed I was doing it.

'It's a dancer's habit.' Julie walked over and sat beside me on the edge of the bed. Our knees bumped as we turned towards each other.

'Do you know everything about me?' I released the stretch, trying to keep a tinge of bitterness out of my voice.

Her crooked smile broadened. She grabbed my shoulders, gripping the shirt as leverage, and straddled me. 'You have no secrets from me. But that's a good thing, right?' Her hands left my shoulders, and she slipped off the straps of her dress. It tumbled about her waist.

A lace bra hugged her breasts, almost but not quite see-through in the dim light. 'Wow.' My voice had become no more than a husky whisper. 'Nice bra.'

'This one's your favourite.' A wry smile creased her lips. 'Not ideal for dancing, structurally, but it's important to plan for the possibility everything might go spectacularly well.' Her hands grazed over her sternum and began to track down and sideways. My eyes locked on her fingertips. The way they meandered across her breasts, and then pressed down hard on the soft lace, pulled tight by her arched back. 'You see what I mean? Sometimes it's good when someone knows all your secrets.'

She was right. This seized me, electrifying every nerve ending in my body, animating desires hidden from not just the world but my own mind. But she knew. She'd had years to learn. I lay exposed before her.

'Umm.' The harder I tried to grasp at rational thought, the faster it slipped away. 'I mean, stop, God, please…' I grabbed her wrists. 'This isn't fair. You know me completely and—'

'Isn't fair to *who* exactly?' Her fingers entangled mine.

'There's no balance between us. You know how to drive me crazy, but I don't know anything about you.'

'I'm crazy enough.' Her hips tilted forward, grinding us together. 'And I've been waiting a long time for this.'

The action going on below my waist only highlighted my point. Julie was playing me like an expert musician, sending a humming feeling all through my body.

'I'm serious.' I sat upright to keep myself out of range of her lips.

She sighed and drew back. 'Okay. How about this?' She reached up behind her to the clasp of her bra. 'How about you act like you've never seen me naked before?

Like you've never touched me before.' The bra slipped off. 'That's something I might like.'

I swallowed. 'I could work with that.' Maybe for once my lack of memories could serve us both. My hands met her skin, tracing the curves of her waist, the swell of her breasts. She wore a thin silver chain to replace the gold one she'd snapped on Monday. The wedding ring hung there, its green jewels dark and glittering in the candle-light. I folded my fist around it and Julie stiffened. Wide eyes locked on to mine, suddenly open and vulnerable as my hand twisted in a flash of movement and the thin chain snapped.

Julie's breath shuddered, and the broken chain spilled on to the bed.

I took her hand and slipped the ring on to her wedding finger, feeling it nestle back into the tiny groove she'd showed me only a few days ago.

As if it had tripped a switch, she brushed aside my grip and closed her fist around the scruff of my neck. 'I always liked that shirt off you,' she said as her arms flexed and the shirt tore open, its press-studs rattling.

Her mouth met mine and she tasted of heat and fire, and there was no surprise in any of it. The deepest parts of my soul knew this was how kisses should taste.

Her hands moved from my neck, by turns grazing and grasping their way down, past my chest to pause at the base of my stomach.

Her fingers scrambled at the top of my pants as my body arched towards the intolerable sweetness. I grasped her wrists and pinned them up and behind her, rolling my body on top of hers. Our lips seared to each other's mouth and neck as, piece by piece, the clothes somehow found their way off. Soon nothing remained between us, and everywhere skin pressed against skin.

Then she reared back, her gaze darker, suddenly serious. Eyes locked on mine, she reached down and brought us together. The taste of her mouth became the salt of the sweat on her neck. My hands ran through hair that sprang up under my fingers as if alive with electricity; a buzz of pleasure ran through my whole body. We twisted until I lay beside her, her hips angled towards me, my hands everywhere, and every movement smooth, effortless. I moved inside her. Her back arched and for a moment everything turned to heat.

Then something deeper and older took over. Back at the hall, I'd recoiled from the waltz but we were dancing now, each alternately taking the lead and feeling the other follow. The dance pulsed between us, capturing us in its beat, playing us like a melody.

How much was instinct? How much learned from long-forgotten encounters? And how much honed to Julie herself, to this singular person, through our years together?

This was muscle memory, a shaping of flesh. And Julie's body moved as if she was the mould that shaped me: what I was made for.

We drew closer again, our bodies moving harder and faster, arching above the bedsheets and a transcendent feeling swept over me. I felt, finally, completely safe. At that moment, in her arms, it was possible to feel like I had a place in the world. A life and a home in Julie.

We were kissing as we came, lips open and pressed hard together as every other part of our bodies convulsed and my mind was still.

I collapsed back onto the mattress, and—

Oh crap, the bed.

'Wow.' Julie sat up. 'I thought I felt the earth move.' The bed was destroyed, the mattress warped over a landscape of valleys and hills. 'I'm impressed. How is this possible?'

We must have popped the old ratchet strap: without its firm hold, all the bed's structural integrity had collapsed. The empty boxes were crushed. The solid ones remained, but askew. The two of us lounged among the wreckage, with the mattress draped across the whole structure, the empty boxes curving under our weight.

Julie rolled over, reached down and rummaged beside the bed. She flipped a cigarette into her mouth and her lithe curves stretched as she reached out to light her smoke from one of the bedside candles. Then she rested back, almost cupped in the strange glove of the bed.

I watched her throughout it all. Something had changed. As my limbs hummed, my gaze wandered over her body. It felt like looking at the sun in eclipse, the beauty unencumbered by the dazzle. How could the possibility of all this happiness lie within a single person?

She shifted to nestle in the crook of my arm with her head on my shoulder. Her fingers toyed with the thin hairs on my chest. The warmth of her breasts pressed against my skin.

'This is what you meant.' My voice sounded deep to my ear. Foreign. I ran the back of my fingers along her neck. 'When you spoke about knowing the good and the bad. This...' I searched for the word. 'This happiness.'

'I didn't necessarily have bed-crushing sex in mind, although a girl can dream.' She pushed herself up a little, and the cigarette flared as she took a long draw. 'It was more wanting you to know about our everyday life. You were my person. The one person in the world I could be around without feeling awkward, or lost, or caged.' She smiled. 'And I was yours. I knew if we could just be together long enough, then you'd feel that again.'

She'd bet everything on it. She'd gambled and won. The smoke from her cigarette etched whorls into the candlelight. 'Should we be smoking in here?' I asked.

'If a single cigarette could trigger one of these old alarms.' Her lips bent into a crooked smile. 'I would never have had to mess around with smoke bombs.'

My hand found hers, feeling the hard metal of her ring as our fingers folded together. 'I meant what I said earlier, about it not being fair. You know me better than I know myself. And no matter what I do—no matter what small words I record in my journal—it'll always be like that. It will all be stored in there.' I touched the side of her head. 'I'll always be in your power.' Just for a moment, it was possible to admit it and not be scared.

For a while she didn't say anything. She just smoked in silence. I began to wonder if she'd heard me at all.

Then she spoke. 'There's something you don't see.'

She leaned away to crush out the butt on a saucer. 'The first person to fall in love loses all the power.' She pulled herself up on her elbows and brushed my hair back from my face. Our eyes met. She looked grave. 'I love you.' She shrugged. 'That's the awful, unmoving truth in all of this. I loved you long before you unlocked that door and I told you my name.'

My lips moved to say something but her free hand cupped over my mouth. 'You don't have to say it back. That's my point. My life with you is one where I lose all the power, over and over again. Forever being the first one in love.'

'It's not the same. Everything I can *be* lies in your hands.'

'I think if you knew what it was like to be in love—to be in love with someone who doesn't love you back—you'd see it differently.' She dropped back down into the crook of my arms, her head on my shoulder.

We lay for a while, neither asleep nor awake, but in some other state. One of the candles burned low, spluttering as the wick drowned in liquid wax. The shadows it spilled around the room started to flicker.

Julie roused as the light finally fizzled out. 'I don't want to be tired.' Her grumble carried a heaviness, almost a low growl, vibrating through her body and into mine. 'I tossed and turned all last night. It's not fair. It's tonight I want to be awake. For the first time, I don't have to think about anything. I can just be with you.'

She sounded at once victorious and unguarded.

'What was it like,' I asked. 'Having to think up all those plans and put them in action over all those months?'

'Lonely.' I'd thought she'd almost drifted off to sleep when she spoke again. 'Scary sometimes, when it all threatened to unravel.'

'It's not scary anymore. You can sleep. I'm right here. You've got me.'

Her breath trembled in relief. 'Goodnight, Robbie.'

'Goodnight.'

'I've been whispering that to my pillow each night, almost like a prayer, imagining your head hitting the pillow here on this bed, as I lay there at home. The two of us, alone and alone. Wishing I could keep you safe and happy when you were so far away from me. Every night for the last…' She paused, and I felt her eyelashes tickle the top of my chest. 'Three-hundred and fifty-six nights. Goodnight, Robbie.'

~

But who's counting?

The words tumbled over in my mind in the dark,

gnawing away at any hope of sleep.

Julie lay cuddled up in the crook of my shoulder. After her last words, all the effort and thought seemed to be released from her body and soon she was asleep. An arm lay across my chest, a leg on top of my hip, and the soft warmth of her skin pressed into my side. Every inch of me that touched her purred with life. It was no longer desire, but something more like contentment. I nestled in Julie's arms, as natural a fit as the ring I'd slipped on to her finger.

The universe could just stay like this forever, and it would be perfect.

One by one, the candles burned down and the room flickered into blackness. But only for a moment. As my eyes adjusted, the lights of the outside world sneaked through the curtains. And those three words rattled around inside my skull, tensing my relaxed muscles. Three hundred and fifty-six nights of goodnight prayer. Almost a year: just shy of two forgettings. The amount of time since we had said 'goodnight' to one another, from pillow to pillow.

But who's counting?

My body stiffened. Other conversations at other times. Jumbled memories from days ago. About the length of time since she'd had a drink.

I needed to remember it right. I disentangled myself from Julie's sleeping form, pulled on some clothes and padded to the kitchen. To the journal, and the entry for Day Seven. Was it really just four days ago? I skimmed through the entry, memory fluttering as the pages flipped, and found it soon enough. The conversation when she'd talked about how many days she'd got back. Of course, I hadn't recorded the exact number she'd said. Just that we'd been out on the balcony, and that she'd shown me the medallion.

The medallion.

Her handbag lay discarded on the kitchen floor. I grabbed it without a second thought, rifling through it until I found the hard metal disk. Then I was at the wall calendar, counting back six months from the date engraved on the medallion. And then counting back 179 days from the last forgetting. The dates lined up exactly. On the day of my third forgetting, when we were separated, she'd been drinking. *She'd been drunk*. Alcoholics don't fall off the wagon with a single drink. And they don't give up the next day, with renewed determination, because of a single drink. She'd been drunk.

What did it mean? This required serious thought—for once, I needed to be the clever one. I returned Julie's handbag to its place and lowered myself into the chair.

Time slipped and thoughts rolled over in my mind. Piece by piece, a story tumbled into position.

At last I went back into the room. Julie lay where I'd left her, in the middle of a crumpled bed, like an angel who'd fallen so hard to earth she lay splayed in the crater of her impact. The dim light spilling through the kitchen door cast more shadows than light over her, but she was still beautiful.

I was in no doubt about what the numbers meant. What they had to mean. But I could have these last few moments. I padded softly across the room, pulled on a T-shirt and slid in beside her. The haphazard mattress folded under my weight, tipping Julie towards me. Her body rolled over, warm flesh pressing on to me. She half-woke at the involuntary movement, smiling as her lithe arms folded around me, a movement so easy she could have done it in her sleep.

My skin tingled at her touch. She was a drug, and I was an addict. For a moment I thought she'd fallen back asleep, but then she spoke.

'Why are you wearing clothes?' Julie's murmur was heavy with sleep, playfully disapproving. She pushed at the thin cotton of my T-shirt. 'Your body's all tense.'

'You should probably wake up.' I sighed. 'I'll get the light.'

By the time I'd got up and hit the switch, Julie had sat up cross-legged in the bed. Wide eyes looked up at me, blinking in the light.

'Here.' I held out a T-shirt. This was going to be a train wreck, but at least we could go about it with some dignity.

She reached out and took it. I could see her waking up before my eyes, as the great clockwork mechanism behind her eyes began grinding its gears. It didn't matter. We were past strategy.

Her gaze measured me up and down, the T-shirt lying limp in her grip. 'What's going on?'

I took a deep breath. 'When you said goodnight to me, you said it was the first time in three hundred and fifty-six nights. But on Sunday you were counting the days since your last drink. Three hundred and fifty-one.'

'I don't see—'

'I can read a calendar, you know.'

She stopped short as my voice cut over hers. Her jaw clenched. For a long moment, her eyes drilled into me. Then she pulled the T-shirt over her head and slipped her arms through it.

'The last time you drank was when the forgetting struck, time before last.' I tossed the medallion on to the bed beside her. 'The dates match up.'

For a moment she looked like she was about to make some angry retort, but then her mouth clamped shut.

'It stands to reason you wouldn't have been drinking afterwards,' I continued. 'Not with me still lost in the system. So you were drinking when it happened.' I folded my arms. 'You were drunk when it happened.'

Inside me a voice screamed at her to deny it. I had all my reasons at the ready. Her being drunk explained everything. It explained why we weren't together at that fateful moment. Why I got lost in the system with her out of contact. Why she'd given up drinking from that moment. And why, this time, she'd managed to stick with it.

Despite all the logic, all the sense, my heart still wanted her to deny it. Yet she stayed silent. Flint-hard eyes glared up at me, but her lips remained shut.

'And I think maybe I knew. Somehow, I learned you hadn't been there for me. Maybe in that first day when you were nowhere to be found, Doctor Varma told me why my wife wasn't there for me. And that's why I was so angry with you when you first showed up here. Last time. That's why I wanted the divorce, and why I never mentioned you in the letter. You hadn't been there for me, and I wanted you out of my life.'

She wasn't glaring at me anymore. The worse my

accusations had got, the more her expression became something else. Imploring. She went to speak but I cut in before she had a chance. 'Don't lie to me.'

Her teeth bit down on her lip. 'Robbie, I made a terrible mistake.'

The strength went from my body, my shoulders slumping into the wall behind me.

'But I'm not that person anymore.' She sat up straighter. 'I went back to the program. And no matter how hard and lonely it got, I've never once fallen. Because I knew you needed me, and I had to do better.' She stumbled to her feet and padded towards me, until she stood within arm's reach, wide eyes looking up at me. 'I fucked up, Robbie. And you can blame me for failing to be there then, when you needed me. But don't blame me for being here now. This is me doing the right thing. Fixing what I broke.'

Her hand reached out, but I flinched from it, my back pressing hard into the wall behind me. 'How did it happen?'

She let her hand fall back, clasping it in front of her. 'I was weak.' She shook her head in anguish. 'Let's leave it at that. You don't want a history lesson. And I've changed since then. Grown.'

'Informed choice, remember?'

'Right.' She didn't look happy about it, but she seemed resigned. 'I need a cigarette.'

'Okay. Let's go outside.'

I went out to the balcony as Julie got dressed. Trapped under the starless sky, the warm breeze felt heavy, like a storm was coming.

When she came out she'd pulled on a pair of shorts under my old T-shirt. Even in the ugly orange light spilling up from the streetlights below, she was beautiful. It would be so easy to let this whole thing slide, to just give in to her.

Our eyes met for the briefest of moments. Hers looked serious and sad—but beyond that she was impossible to read. She went to the balcony rail and tapped out a cigarette.

She lit it and sighed out a stream of smoke. 'You know most of the story already. We didn't know about the timing. It had already happened twice so we knew it might happen again, but we didn't know when.'

She turned to look at me. I nodded, and a hint of hope flickered in her eyes. She still didn't understand.

'We were doing okay. You were planning your new show. I was doing great at AA. A year dry, and I was sponsoring—I told you about Jazi. But what I didn't say was that the more I worked with her, the more all these old memories flooded back about how I used to be.' Her gaze flashed to me. 'Sometimes I think you don't realise how lucky you are, not to be haunted by history. The rest of us are slaves to it.'

I returned her gaze evenly. She was dead wrong. History still haunted me. It was standing right in front of me, dragging on a cigarette in the thick night air.

Julie turned away, looking back to the city lights. 'Jazi didn't have someone like you lifting her up and the program wasn't working for her. Despite all the problems it caused, drinking still felt good. I thought I could reach her.' Julie shrugged with a grimace. 'She reached me instead.'

The words came out in broken puffs of smoke, her rueful smile twisting into bitterness. 'It wasn't her fault. I should've had the resources to stop me from falling back into that world.' She stubbed out the last of the dying cigarette, twisting it into the top of the metal railing.

'Go on.'

'I found out later why my defences didn't work.' She flicked the dead cigarette away off the balcony. 'You remember I told you about muscle memory? The thing is, the body only remembers properly when it's in the same situation where it actually learned the lesson. When you're in those same shoes again, with those people, that music, that smell—that's when you remember.'

'That's why you took me to the dance tonight.'

She nodded. 'It's the same with all memory. All the lessons I'd drummed into my head only worked so long as I was sober, and in a sober place. Once I followed Jazi into her world and risked the first drink, I fell right back into my old ways. Pfft.' She flicked her hand: a magician's flourish.

'And that was when it happened. When you were out with her.'

'I went to a party with her. The plan was to show her she could be dry and still enjoy life. I made it for about two hours before that message twisted in my mind, and I convinced myself I could show her how you could drink responsibly and still enjoy life. I don't remember much after that. There's just a gap until the next afternoon, when I'm in hospital myself, having my stomach pumped.' She turned to face me. 'I was a wreck, I was sick—and I knew how badly I'd let both of us down. You hadn't called my mobile at all and you weren't answering my texts. I later found out you didn't have your phone on you anymore. But in my muddled head, I somehow convinced myself you knew, and were angry.'

'Would I have been? Angry?'

She shook her head. 'Disappointed.' She slid down against the railing, until she sat on the balcony floor. 'When I finally made it home, more than a day later, there were all the messages on the home phone, and I realised what had happened. I raced to find you, but by then you'd moved hospitals. I was hysterical. The knowledge of what I'd done just kept playing on repeat through my head. Everything you're feeling about me right now—anger, disappointment—'

Betrayal.

'—multiply that by a thousand and that's where I was at. By the time I had my head together, it was too late.' She looked up at me. 'I think you were right that Doctor Varma knew. I don't know if doctors can search hospital records, but one way or another, she knew. She never approved of me even before that. She knew about my drinking problem, and I'd just confirmed all her worst fears. After we'd finally got in touch, she blocked me at every turn. As if you were better off without me.' Julie's voice cracked, and she fumbled for another cigarette. 'I shouldn't hate her. Everything she did was to protect you.' She swallowed hard, as if choking down a bitter pill. 'I don't hate her for being wrong about me.'

'You hate her for being right.'

She nodded. 'She was right. *Was*. I was different back then. Stupid and arrogant. I should have known my limitations. I should have known all my precious strategies weren't foolproof.'

'Of course you should.' Julie blinked at my words. 'You should have known because it's important, and if it's important it's worth being smart about.'

'Right.'

'Just like you were being smart in not telling me about this.' I kept my tone neutral. 'In keeping it hidden. Because that's what you do when things are important. You get smart about them.'

'But that's how I beat it.' She pulled herself to her feet. 'By being smart. I put in the work and I beat it. For us.'

'I believe you.'

Julie gasped with relief. She stepped forward, holding out her hand. She still didn't understand. I turned my back and made for the door.

'Robbie? What are you doing?'

I retreated into the cool of the kitchen, the sterile white light.

'Where are you going?' I could hear Julie's footfalls following me into the cool. Her hand closed on my shoulder, wrenching me around to face her. 'I know I let you down. But please believe me when I say I've paid for it.'

'Me too.' The words were out of my mouth before my mind had formed them.

'But you don't have to *keep on* paying.' She stepped forward, grasping my hands before I could back further away. 'That's the point of everything I've done. To make it right again. That's why I could never give up. So you wouldn't have to pay anymore for my weakness.'

'You don't understand. This is not about what you did a year ago. It's what you did today.'

Julie looked at me in surprise. She drew back, and her grip on my hands loosened. 'What—'

'*You weren't going to tell me.*' I pulled my hands from her grasp. 'If I hadn't figured it out myself, I would never have known.'

'I didn't lie to you. Not directly. I just—'

'You said you were away in the country. You said that's why it took you days to get back.'

She glared at me.

And I glared back: 'I told you no more secrets. I told you why it was important. You said you understood.'

'I do understand.' She was almost pleading, her eyes red-rimmed. 'But I'm hanging on to all this by my fingertips. It took me a year just to get you talking to me again. Just to hear you say my name. A *year*, Robbie, of silence and loneliness. I couldn't just throw all that away.'

'You couldn't risk letting me decide.'

She didn't know what to say. I could see her mind racing behind her eyes, but she just looked up at me, dumbstruck, wringing her hands.

'You were never going to let me make an informed choice, knowing the good and bad.' I folded my arms across my chest. 'Why let me choose when I might make the wrong choice?'

'There's more at stake here than you having some perfect choice over everything.' Her hands balled into fists as sorrow gave way to frustration.

'No, Julie. There isn't. In two days, that decision will be the only thing left to me. It was the one thing I asked from you. That you let me make a choice that would be my own, and not somebody else's.' I tried to keep my voice calm. And mostly failed. 'You had to tell me.'

'How could I?' She seemed on the verge of screaming. 'How could anyone? Nobody tells the person they love their worst failings. How do you think it would have gone? "Oh, you know what? I betrayed you in the one moment you needed me. Just by the way, you know. FYI."' Her voice cracked in rage. 'It's impossible to ask that of anybody. Nobody does that. Nobody *can* do that!'

'No one *has to*. I see that now. So I'm never going to ask it again. Of you. Of anybody.'

'You can't mean...' Her voice trailed off.

I held my silence. She knew what I meant.

'Don't throw this away, Robbie. Not after we've come so far,' she pleaded. 'Look, I understand now how it is for you. You need to be able to trust whoever is there when you wake. They are your memory. They are your...'—she fumbled for the word—'your life raft. I can do that. I will do that.' She looked around, grabbing my journal and holding it out to me. 'We can document it. All this history can go in your journal. Then it's there forever. The good and the bad.'

'You're being smart about this.'

'Yes.' She nodded vigorously. 'And you need to be smart about this too. Right here and right now. This is your future.'

I took the journal from her hands. Her eyes blazed with hope. I set it back in its place, and picked up my pen and the yellow envelope on the bench, with the divorce papers in it. I put the envelope down on the table.

'The important things in your life aren't what you should be smart about.' I extended my hand, offering the pen to her. 'They're what you should be honest about.'

Julie shook her head in horror, backing away. 'How can you pull this now? After everything?'

'I told you yesterday what I needed.' My voice sounded loud. 'And then again this afternoon. It's only happening *now*, after everything, because it's only now that I see the truth you hid.' My fingers shook as they held out the pen.

'Why are *you* angry?' Her voice rose to meet mine. 'I'm the one getting dumped.'

'I'm angry because I *want* this,' I yelled. 'This life you've shown me. But I didn't ask for dancing, or dinner, or anything else. I just asked for the one thing you wouldn't give me. The truth. And so now I have to walk away from it all, despite—' I clamped down on whatever word was coming, slamming my jaws so hard together my teeth clacked.

'Despite what?'

'It doesn't matter. It doesn't matter what I want, or how I feel. Because in two days I'll forget everything, and what I'll need then is someone I can fucking *trust*.'

I stepped forward, holding the pen out to her again.

'I can't do it.' She flinched from it, her eyes welling. 'Not after...' She pointed at me in anger. 'You put my ring on...on my...'

Wedding finger.

She couldn't say the words. Sheer force of will had held back her tears at the dance, but nothing could hold them back now.

As angry as I was, it killed me to see her like this. It wasn't her fault—I just needed something impossible.

Deep breath. 'We made an agreement. You would show me how it could be, and in the end, I would decide. You promised.'

'You promised, too!' she raged. 'All those years ago. You said it'd be safe for me to fall for you, because you'd always be there for me. I would never have let you in otherwise.'

'That promise was from another world. Yours was from just a few hours ago.' Fear tugged at my heart. What if she refused to honour it?

'Stop talking. Just stop!' Her hands went to her head, almost wrapping around it, as if she could block her ears.

I wiped a tear from my eye in frustration. Not the time to show weakness.

A shuddering breath shook her body, and she lowered her hands to her sides. The emotion that seemed to have twisted her body released it. The prim posture returned.

Step by slow step, she walked over to the table, and

slipped down onto the chair. She slid the papers out of the yellow envelope.

I put the pen down beside the paper. The hand that picked it up shook, but no hint of emotion flickered across her face. She looked like a queen being led to the block, determined to leave with dignity.

The pen paused, poised above the document. I watched it hover in place. She still had all the power. In two days I would forget, and she would remain. She could still come at me with lawyers and crowbars.

'Let's be free of this.' My voice was a whisper. 'Both of us.'

The pen closed on the paper, she signed her name and flipped to the next marking. Page by page she worked her way through the document. Then she shuffled the pages together and placed them neatly on the envelope.

'I'll get my stuff.' Her voice was small.

I stepped out of her way. As soon as she left the kitchen, I scooped up the pages and slipped them into the envelope. Then I put it up on top of the fridge where it would be safe from any sudden changes of mind. Guilt gripped me. It felt wrong to doubt her. Whatever her failings, Julie had kept her word in this at least.

I waited for her in the dominoes room. Standing there should have made me feel better. This work could now return to its purpose, free from the haphazard interventions of past lives—past wives. Just a few words more and I would shut the door. Safe and alone again.

Julie emerged from the bedroom into the kitchen wearing her party dress. Her shoes clicked across the kitchen floor. The fridge door squeaked open.

'I'm taking my birthday present.' She entered the dominoes room, stuffing the champagne bottle into her bag.

'Don't do that. Don't be like that.'

'Fuck you.' She strode past me without a second look. 'One vice at a time.'

One vice at a time. Worst vice first. That was what I'd become for her.

I tried to think of a decent goodbye. Everything she'd done to work herself into my life, all the years of marriage we'd spent together deserved something. But I stood there, mute, watching her leave.

Her hand closed around the doorknob. 'This isn't what they were for, you know.' Her voice sounded flat, indifferent. 'The dominoes. The ramps and platforms.' She half-turned, and gestured at my work with her free hand. 'They aren't here for you to show your achievement, or carry on your identity, or whatever your bullshit letter said.'

She kept her gaze fixed on the work, as if studying it with a scientific detachment, dark lips on her pale face curling in contempt. 'You wanted full disclosure.'

'What are you talking about?'

'Eighty-three thousand isn't a record. The world record is ten times that or something ridiculous. You can look it up in five seconds online.' She turned to face me, folding her arms across her chest. 'The dominoes didn't come from the author of your precious letter. They came from *my* Robbie. And he wouldn't have cared less about some stupid record.' Scorn dripped from her voice.

'What are they for, then?' I tried to muster some strength in my voice, but there was nothing left inside. Whatever final barbs of stings and lies—or of pain and truth—she wanted to plant under my skin, I had no resistance to offer them.

'Eighty-three thousand was the number we calculated to fit the stage at the Box Theatre. It had to be there, because we needed the raised seating. He'd hit on the idea after the second forgetting, ordering all the boxes, and the equipment and extra tools we'd need. But then it happened again. The third forgetting. When the time came for delivery, it was after I'd tracked you down. So I altered the delivery address and sent them here, hoping—' Her scowl deepened. 'I don't know what I was hoping. But one day, all the boxes must have just arrived.' She shrugged again, almost a scoff. 'Then your precious letter-writer apparently decided to make it sound like he'd come up with a special project for you.' She squared her shoulders, putting her hands on her hips, and her voice found a firmer edge. 'But none of this was his. It just landed on his doorstep.'

She lashed this history across my raw, exposed mind, targeting the letter and the task. Everything I'd been holding sacred. 'What were they for, then?' I moved to stand in front of her. I kept my voice flat like hers. Not defensive. Not vulnerable. 'If they weren't to break a record, then why did he want them?'

She faced me in silence. Maybe she regretted opening the topic. 'One show only,' she said at last. 'It would take weeks for us to set it all up, and then just eight minutes for the whole routine, lights up to curtain down. One song. No photos. No recording. That was the idea.' As she spoke, something approaching a smile danced on her lips. For a moment, all the defensiveness and scorn left her. 'The first few minutes he would dance, skimming over their surface, his feet gliding above them, touching only the stepping stones.' She looked around the room with new eyes, as if conjuring a long-lost memory into this new setting.

Not that it could be real memory, of course, since it had never happened. Or perhaps her words recalled some past speech, where an earlier Robbie—her Robbie—had spoken of his vision.

'His hands would fly through the air as he spun,' she continued, 'missing the dominoes on the platforms and ramps framing the stage by millimetres. Then he would leap and—' Her voice stumbled, her words grinding to a sudden stop, her eyes losing their wistfulness. A sigh followed, and she ploughed on. 'One of the tiles would be struck, and the first lines would begin to cascade, falling in time with the dance. And the wave's crest would flow out from his steps, racing ahead and then curling to wait as he spun across the stones towards them. All of it building to a climax as the final wave would approach him centre stage, and they would crash together.' Her gaze shifted from the room around us, from memory and imagination, and to my eyes. 'Eight minutes long. One show only. Just the single event, living only in the moment, and only in memory.' She spread her arms, gesturing to the structure around her, and managed a small smile. 'Imagine it.'

As crazy as it sounded, part of me could imagine it. Each footfall like a splash into water, dominoes rippling out from it, each twist tracked by waves flowing out to every corner of the room, and then flooding back in, chasing the dance.

'That's what they're for,' she shrugged. 'That's the history.'

I didn't doubt she spoke the truth. No one could just make up a story like that. Besides, it fitted all the facts. But I hardly had any idea how I was supposed to respond. 'That sounds...' I searched for the word, but nothing quite right came to mind. 'Weird.'

Julie blinked. '*Weird?*'

'I don't mean I don't believe you. I just meant the idea for the dance itself. It's strange, right? That's all I was saying. Not normal.'

Her head started to shake, rotating side to side. But her eyes were fixed on mine. Her hands were trembling.

'What?' I asked. To think just a minute ago she'd had her hand on the doorknob. If only she'd left then. None of this was helpful.

'I've been so fucking blind. I held on and on to the belief that the man I loved, and who loved me, would be strong enough to endure. I made myself believe there must be something, some splinter of soul, deep down that survives.' She laughed bitterly, throwing her head back. 'I thought I saw it in you. That day when you spoke about the beautiful fall and what you were planning with the dominoes, it felt like he still lived in there.' Her eyes looked me up and down, her top lip curling into a sneer. 'And even now, his fingerprints are all over you.' Her body seemed crouched, poised in anger. 'Look at your feet. Even now.'

I looked down. 'What about them?'

'No wonder you had me fooled for so long.' She shook her head. 'It's perfect. Always perfect.'

My feet shuffled backwards involuntarily. She laughed and pointed down at them. 'And again! From third to fourth! Perfect. Every fucking time.'

I looked down at my feet again. Their position, the back foot not quite in line with the front one, the balance distributed between them.

Now I could see it. She was right. It was perfect.

With my gaze downcast, I caught the flurry of movement only out of the corner of my eye. Julie's two palms slammed into my chest, knocking me backwards.

She laughed and pointed again at my feet. The stance had changed, the back foot planted deep to catch my momentum and brace against her force.

'And now! Perfect. Do you know how long it takes to imprint that on the body? How many years of dedication it took him? *My Robbie.*' The name was a term of open scorn now. 'When he was just cooking in the kitchen, going from the fridge to the stovetop, opening cupboards. Every moment a perfection of poise and posture, as he practised and practised.' She put her hands to her head. 'I've been falling for a ghost all this time, an after-image of something so perfect its shadow is beautiful.' Her eyes scoured me, top to bottom. 'Even now, you're a work of art.' She drew herself up to her full height. 'Someone else's art.' Her words dripped venom. '*Someone else's work*.'

Silence fell. She seemed to be daring me to respond, but I could hardly think of a word to say.

She shook her head. 'The Robbie I knew deserved a better funeral than this.' The tears were pouring down her cheeks. '*Weird*.' She repeated my word again. 'You're not fit to wear his reflection.'

I swallowed nervously. I should be glad she'd realised it wasn't me she loved, just some relic she'd seen in my face and feet. This would make it easier for her.

But the words cut.

'So you win,' she said, and her right hand wrapped around the ring on her wedding finger. 'I give up on this crazy, stupid dream.' She started to twist it off but it wouldn't yield. 'Fuck.' She spat hard on her hand, smearing it on her finger. 'I refused to believe the forgetting could beat us. But it has.' She tried tearing the ring off again, twisting it as she pulled, and this time it gave way. 'You *are* vanilla.' She flung the ring into my face.

I didn't have time to flinch. It struck me on the cheek—a tiny stab of pain—and ricocheted away.

Julie stopped short. She seemed surprised at what she had done. Perhaps she hadn't meant to actually hit me with the ring. One hand drifted in something like an apologetic wave. Tears still shone on her cheeks, but they weren't for me. Or for her. She mourned the loss of someone else entirely. I was just an uninvited stranger who had shown up at his wake.

She hitched the bag over her shoulder and turned from me. The door opened to her touch. I hadn't thought to lock it.

'Sorry,' she said, her head down and facing away from me, her hand steadying herself against the half-open door. 'You shouldn't have had to hear all that. It wasn't fair.' She sighed. 'None of it is your fault. I'm just tired, that's all. At long last, I'm finally tired.'

She left, and the door swung shut behind her.

The strength that had been holding me up evaporated and I slumped to my knees. Her anger was hardly unexpected. I'd been prepared for that. But not for her scorn, or at the end, her tired pity. Her words still bounced around the walls of my mind, echoing.

Vanilla.

Someone else's art.

Someone else's work.

Each phrase bit into me in a way I could hardly understand. It should feel good that Julie had seen me for what I was. Good that she'd left me of her own will. Yet the words still burned.

I struggled to my feet. I made it over to the door and slid the locks home, one by one. My chest felt like it was caving in on itself. I struggled just to breathe. Only a little over a week ago, I'd swung back this door to open my life to her. When our eyes met, she already loved me. Every day since that moment, she'd got to know me more and more, until finally we could part as strangers.

I turned back from the door, and to the room. It all still stood there, the ranks of dominoes vulnerable but undisturbed. Through all the worlds and words and wars crashing above them, my little soldiers stood serene. As far as I could see, nothing had changed.

As far as I could see, everything had changed.

Just minutes ago, I hadn't questioned what the dominoes stood for. Now, I could feel nothing of their significance. The beauty I had seen in them paled before the extraordinary performance Julie had evoked. No one had touched them, yet they lay toppled.

Something glinted in the shadows, just to the side of the path. Julie's ring. I took a deep breath. The little metal band made an incongruous fit with its surroundings. My cheek must have taken all the force of Julie's throw. Impetus spent, its tiny weight hadn't been enough to dislodge a single tile.

I picked it up, edging it carefully so as not to disturb the nearby dominoes. It felt almost like paying respect to another person's project. To someone else's hopes and dreams. Small as it was, the ring felt heavy in my hand. Julie had every right to be angry.

My fist clenched on it. *I* had every right to be mad. This was her fault for piling betrayal on betrayal. It didn't have to be this way. If she'd only been honest with me, everything might have been different. I felt like howling in frustration. Free of her? Right now, I felt more bound to her than I'd ever been.

My hand tightened around the ring. I pulled myself to my feet and strode across the stepping stones to the platform Julie had set up this morning. Despite all her agonising, the work looked amateurish. The spacing of the dominoes was uneven, the curves clumsy. Her fingerprint in my sculpture.

I plucked out the dominoes that connected the platform to the larger structure and swept my clenched fist through her work. Dominoes tumbled in every direction; in an instant, the entire platform was flattened.

It took me a moment to realise the angry heat in my fist was actually pain. I watched a trickle of blood seep out between my fingers and drip onto the fallen tiles, moving like a live thing. I let go my grip: the ring gleamed at me through a film of blood. With the force I'd been squeezing, the claw that held the stone had cut through my skin and left a gash. It looked as if I'd been stabbed by a tiny dagger.

Here was her real fingerprint.

I rushed from the room and onto the balcony; held my fist outstretched above the rail. All of the pain and humiliation burning in my blood—I could destroy it all. Erasing every part of her from my life was as easy as opening my hand. Already her precious platform of dominoes inside had been destroyed. Now the ring. Next would be the pictures on the phone—hell, the phone itself, smashed to oblivion on the footpath below. And the scent of her, still smeared over my body: I could scrub it away. Everything could be destroyed and the slate wiped clean for the next chapter. Even the journal could be revised. I could eradicate her utterly. It was within my power.

I breathed deep the hot, humid air and opened my

hand up to the night, as if in offering. It wouldn't do for my future self to be seduced by the ring, or by the captivating smile in the phone picture. How easy it would be for that future self to wonder what might have been; to try to return to this spot. He deserved to be protected. *Julie* deserved to be protected. She'd been through enough without having to fend off future Robbies who'd forgotten this bitterness, who had not lived through the barbs of her sadness and scorn.

My palm tilted, rotating. For a moment, the ring held fast, stuck in the blood, until it finally slipped and tumbled out into space.

No.

My free hand flashed out as the ring fell, a dancer's reflexes plucking it cleanly from the air. It would not be forgotten. Not one atom of it. The ring. The picture. The phone. And definitely not the journal. None of it would be touched. It was all my history, and my future deserved every part of it. No doubt the raw pain of this night would be forgotten in two days. I couldn't do anything about that. But I could still pass on what remained of that life. Whether the memory of happiness or humiliation was worse as an inheritance, I didn't know. But I didn't have the luxury of such decisions.

I stepped back from the brink and slipped the ring into

my pocket. It would become another of my mementoes. In time it might fade in meaning along with them, until it seemed as inscrutable as the little wooden elephant.

One last look into the dark, hot night. Somewhere out there, Julie was walking home, carrying her own memento of this disaster. The chilled bottle in her hand. If only she'd thrown that into my face instead of the ring. I'd gladly have worn the bruise.

I thought about the impossible happiness she'd awoken in me hours earlier. I couldn't explain it then, except to fumble at the thought that once upon a time we'd grown to fit one another. Nothing was any clearer now she'd gone. We had grown to fit; now each of us would have to grieve a lost half and learn to grow on our own.

The eastern sky was still black, looming clouds blotting out the stars, when I went inside, pulled the mattress from the crumpled boxes onto the flat floor and collapsed.

Day Two

I woke late. For a moment my mind remained blissfully empty, rinsed clean. But then the memories washed in, and the pain stung as fiercely as before.

JULIE HAD left for good, and that left me free—and this was what freedom felt like. My mouth tasted of acid. The scent of her clung to me. A shower did not remove it.

There was nothing left to the day. Nothing worth remembering. Just nothing. Exercise happened, or something that had the shape of exercise. Coffee had lost its magic. My stomach twisted after half a cup, and I poured the rest down the sink. Putting food in my dry mouth just made the acidic taste worse. The remaining detritus of Julie's visit was purged: the silver chain nestled like a tiny snake in my bedclothes, the two little notes I'd left for myself in my jeans and sock drawer, now redundant. Dominoes were laid and arranged, hands moving slowly through the work, clunking together clumsily. The nerves in my fingers seemed dull. Time crawled—grudgingly, as if it too had lost momentum.

Julie's claims about the purpose of the dominoes gnawed at me. But the letter had not actually lied. I checked: I could see how easily it had been misread. My former self had explained the task he'd developed, but the letter said nothing about how he'd acquired the dominoes. That was my mistake. Probably the dominoes had turned up unannounced on his doorstep, just as Julie said, and my predecessor had seized on a use for them. No one had lied. Still, the fact remained that 83,790 dominoes did not represent a record of any sort.

But so what? It was still an achievement. I tucked the letter back in its envelope. Resisting a brief temptation to squirrel Julie's ring away somewhere else, somewhere more obscure, I slipped it into the envelope beside the letter.

The day passed and I kept working. By the time evening came, the ache in my head and the acid burning in my gut started to recede, as if some larger power had turned down the dial on everything. I was tired. I plonked down another line of dominoes and called it a day. There were only two cartons left now—just a little under forty-five hundred dominoes, plus the thousand or so piled in the dominoes room.

And so the day passed. It was unmemorable. Which was appropriate, given the situation. Once, I'd feared the final day and what it would be like waiting for the end. Now the forgetting felt almost like an act of mercy.

Day One

Enough.

I WOKE to bedsheets tangled tight around my legs. It shouldn't have felt painful, but somehow it did.

Grief gnawed at every cell in my body. I deserved the pain, I supposed, but my future self didn't. It was the toxic burn of my choices and my wrongs, not his. I would leach them out of me with sweat and work. Things remained to be done before the new life could be born.

It was early. Light glimmered through the curtains, but the morning sun had not risen far enough to attain its full force. I pushed away the weakness in my limbs and forced them through a double dose of my regimen, as if the burn of lactic acid and exhaustion could wash away the sting of losing her. Of sending her away. But I would do what had to be done. The end and then the beginning would probably happen tomorrow, and the final pieces had yet to be put in place.

I dragged the two cartons of dominoes out into the kitchen and got to work flattening the crumpled mass of cardboard that had once been my bed, until it was all folded neatly against the wall. As I tidied up the kitchen—filing the recipe book away with the rest of the mementoes—I reached on top of the fridge and found myself holding a document that needed a different sort of filing. The yellow envelope with the divorce papers, yet to be posted. The bridges were burnt but the legal process had not yet happened.

It was Day One, so going outside was a risk. The forgetting, and with it the threat of institutionalisation, could strike at any time. But with so much already done to leave my future self a fresh start, I could hardly kick this can down the road. The documents must be sent today.

I'd have to prepare as best I could. I piled everything of significance into the backpack. Alongside the precious document itself went the map home, the journal, the mementoes and the letter. If the forgetting struck before I made it back to safety, at least I'd be equipped to handle it.

It was too early to go out yet. Saturday—the post office wouldn't be open yet. I invested a few hours in the dominoes and then set out. The sooner this last task could be ticked off, the sooner I could return home, safe within my little cocoon.

Outside, the clouds hung low and heavy. Still no rain, but the persistent cloud cover had finally mitigated the heat. The air smelled crystal clear, almost humming with electricity.

The nearest post office was scarcely four blocks away. If I walked briskly the return trip should take about twenty minutes. The dark clouds overhead looked forbidding, and I didn't fancy getting caught in it when the storm finally broke. Note to future self: buy an umbrella.

Up ahead, as the post office came into view, I reflected that, this one last time, memory had served: the next time these feet walked these streets, it would all be new.

Come to think of it, the same thing must have happened before. My past self would surely have taken this route when he went to post Julie the divorce papers. Just as I was now, he would have passed the shoe store, the charity shop, the bank, the gift shop…

I stopped short, looking at the shopfront, taking in the display of figurines and tapestries, dreamcatchers, clocks and carvings. The hairs on the back of my neck shivered. The cool breeze had become a cold wind, whispering words from another life.

It looks like someone walked into a gift shop and grabbed a handful of the first knick-knacks they saw. Julie had said that as she tossed aside the mementoes with a disappointed shrug.

A little bell above the door tinkled as I entered. It sounded crisp in the quiet shop, like a discreet wake-up call. Perfume and spice, the quarrelling smells of too many scented candles and musky weavings. A young woman sat on a stool behind the counter. She smiled up at me in greeting, but I looked past her, to a little carved elephant figurine on a display stand near the entry. It looked African. Moroccan, maybe. If I had to guess.

My heart started to hammer in my chest. I dropped to my knees and fumbled the mementoes out of my backpack. In fact, the comparison was unnecessary. I would have recognised the carving anywhere. But some part of me screamed denial: they couldn't be the same. I held the memento beside the shop's version. Identical.

I lifted my gaze. Hundreds of items were arranged

on the display counters, resting against the walls, suspended from the ceiling. But I knew what I was looking for—the beaded bracelet, and not far behind it, the thimble-sized crystal vase. I scrabbled over to them, still on my haunches, and fished out their counterparts from the backpack. Exactly the same.

I set mine down alongside the others on their display shelves, starting with the vase and then back to the African figurine. Standing side by side, absolute carbon copies, the mementoes seemed to lose their personality. There could be no denying it. Julie's throwaway remark had been dead right.

'Um.' The shop assistant behind me cleared her throat. 'Are you buying something, mate?'

'No.' I shook my head, unsure if I was answering her or myself. 'No. I'm not buying any of it.'

There were geodes on a display cabinet just below my eyeline. On this one at least, the match was less than perfect. Still, my little piece of past volcano fitted seamlessly among the ones on display. Not far away, hanging from a ceiling rack, were a group of the copper medallions on thick leather cords. Even the foreign script engraved on it was the same. I raised myself up and deposited my copy on the shelf next to them.

One memento left.

'Do you sell keys here at all?' My voice was loud in the quiet little shop.

'Keys? No.' The shopkeeper sounded surprised. 'Are you returning all these?'

'Yes.' I nodded slowly. 'Yes, I am.'

Stuffing the key back into my pocket, I turned on my heel and left. My brain buzzed with impossible questions. The mementoes were junk. No memory, no history: just grabbed at random from a nearby shop.

But why?

The cold, wet wind blew at my face, reminding me that whatever had possessed my past self to pass off a bunch of useless crap as meaningful mementoes, that question would have to wait.

Envelope in hand, I entered the post office. On a rainy Saturday morning, the place was deserted. There was a bright red mailbox on its far wall; beside it, orderly rows of black PO boxes.

If I hadn't just had the key in my hand only a moment before, I probably would never have noticed. But it struck me that I made regular payments each month to the post office. *This* post office, presumably. The letter itself had mentioned the payments, along with those for my groceries and electricity.

I tucked the envelope under my arm, and fished the

key from my jeans pocket. My fingers pressed against its sharp edges as I plucked it out. *Almost unused.* The number etched in the key's bow could just be made out in the glaring fluorescent light. Two-Eight-Nine. Julie had been right about the other mementoes. Pointless collectibles pointlessly collected. *Except this one*, she'd said, studying the number. A numbered apartment, she'd thought. A locker number.

Or a post office box.

I stood before the wall of boxes, looking them up and down. It made no sense. Why would you put something away in a box, and then give someone the key to it without telling them what it opened? Why would you toss the key in with a bunch of stupid knick-knacks?

But maybe I already knew. Hadn't I felt the same temptation only last night, when I'd almost let Julie's ring fall into the dark? The urge to shape the future by retelling the past. There are things, like rings, that cannot be bequeathed to the future without pain and risk. And there are things like rings that the future deserves to know about.

What if my past self was brave enough to resist throwing away the real records of my past—but not brave enough to hand them to me directly? You hide them in an easily accessible box, and you lock it with a key. And then you pass the key on down the line, staying silent about what it opens. And then, for good measure, you conceal it among a bunch of meaningless knick-knacks. Where better to hide a tree than in a forest?

I scanned the boxes. The numbers began at the top left, running sideways and down in three columns. 289. The box stood high in the final column, top row, almost in my eye-line. I pushed the key into the lock. It slid in smoothly. Everything turned on the key…

And the key turned.

I swung open the tiny door to reveal the long, rectangular space behind it. Its four sides were gun-metal black, casting the space into shadow. Even so, the little object within caught the light, glinting back at me. A circle of metal, shiny and smooth.

Things like rings.

I slid it out of its hiding place. It was a larger and plainer version of Julie's ring, which I now pulled out of my backpack. The two rings lay across each other in my palm, making a wonky infinity symbol. Made for each other.

There was no escaping the truth. My past self had hidden the history from me. Julie's words echoed through my mind: *no one can be honest like that*. No one can tell the full story of the past without fearing for how it might shape the future. We all hide, protect and forget. I'd believed those words when she said them. I just hadn't realised they included me too. And my past self. No one can be honest like that. *Least of all ourselves.*

Anger welled in my gut. My past self hadn't had the courage to throw away everything he didn't want me to know. He'd just hidden it.

I swallowed hard, burying the emotion. There were more significant matters pressing. Something else lay further back in the shadows. I shoved the matching rings in my pocket, and reached in, my fingers closed on a tumble of objects and cords. I slid them towards me and they all came out together.

A pair of black shoes loosely wound in a white cable. Dragging behind them, attached to the cable, came a slim object. A music player—I knew what it was for, whether through memory or deduction I couldn't tell.

What the hell? The ring I understood. My predecessor had feared I wouldn't choose the path the letter laid out for me, but would instead follow the gleaming white-gold ring to the sparkling green eyes. An unnecessary risk. So he'd sent Julie packing with divorce papers, already signed with my hand. To leave the ring would have been to leave the shiniest of clues behind. But a pair of shoes and a music player?

I disentangled the cord from the shoes which, on first impression, looked quite new. Closer inspection revealed they were just well kept. The size looked right. My shoes, then.

I sat down on the floor, kicked off my grubby old sneakers and pulled on the new shoes. Yes: perfect fit. I laced them up, and bounced to my feet. Standing in the shoes felt weird. Elevated. I seemed to float above the floor.

I snapped one shoe down on the floor and it clacked hard, echoing in the empty room. I felt a smile grow on my face. I snapped the foot down again, faster this time. *Clack!* The sound reverberated around the room, and the smile broadened. The rush coming over me felt at once alien and personal—and familiar. I'd felt the same on the night of the dance.

This was why my predecessor hadn't passed the shoes on to me. He feared what I would make of them. And more, he feared what they would make of me. They didn't fit in the life he had crafted. Better to keep control, not open the possibility that I'd veer in a direction opposite to the one he'd carved out.

He. Not *me*. Not even 'my past self'. It no longer made sense to think of the letter-writer that way. It presumed an alliance of sorts, a harmony of interests.

Anger burned inside me, stronger than before. This went beyond hiding the wedding ring. Whether or not such subterfuge could be forgiven, it was at least understandable. But the shoes were another matter. They led back only to my own history. To what I'd achieved and become.

I reached out to the music player and turned it over. When I thumbed the button on its side it flashed to life. I knew how to use it. Of course I did. It was mine, after all.

Flickering fingers brought up the song list. Nothing had proper song names or artists. The song at the top was titled JEZDmnsMxFnl15Apr. All the others followed similarly: unintelligible strings of alphanumeric characters.

Except they weren't. They weren't unintelligible at all. Their meaning danced on the tip of my mind. This wasn't about memory, it was *perception*. My flawed memory forgot facts, but not skills and not meanings. I could read this. I took a deep breath and reread the title. This time it was as clear as day and the words in the centre set my heart racing: *Dominoes mix. Final.*

My legs gave way as that hit home, and I dropped to sit cross-legged on the floor. I held in my hand the soundtrack to the show Julie had talked about. The one-off performance with the dominoes that I'd been working on. For all I knew, I'd been listening to it as the forgetting struck. Maybe I'd been working on the dance itself at that very moment.

The thought at once chilled and excited me. I snaked the little cables up to my ears and inserted them.

Not here.

The urge to tear off the blindfold and learn what had been hidden from me was fierce—but I didn't want to hear a single note without the freedom to respond. I wanted to be moved.

I swept up all my goods into my backpack, including the divorce papers. Best not to take any irreversible actions until all the relevant information was in. And I was increasingly sure that all the relevant information was not in.

The key stayed behind in its place, its work done, the PO box door swinging wide to the world.

The wind whipped at my shirt as I strode off, every step feeling sharp and strong in my new shoes. Halfway down the block, I tossed my old sneakers into a bin: they didn't fit me anymore. They never had, really.

Rain dusted my cheeks as I hurried on. Home seemed too far away. My feet—the shoes—itched for something more than walking, and I wanted to see what they might do for me. Almost out of sight, in the far corner of the park across the road, I spotted a basketball court. Perfect.

When I reached the court, its surface felt smooth beneath my steps. I parked my backpack down on a bench and made my way to the centre circle, and the little coloured lines seemed to coalesce around me: so many footlights marking centre stage.

The music player sprang to life at the touch of my fingers. The screen displayed the last song—the Dominoes Mix—as if it was poised for this moment.

My finger hovered over the play button. I had the same sense of stepping off a cliff that had gripped me two evenings ago. But this wasn't like the dance, Julie playing my history like a puppeteer with dozens of eyes looking on. This time I stood alone. No one in the world knew or cared. I was beyond Julie, beyond even the letter-writer.

My eyes closed and I stood tall, feeling myself in the centre of the space. House lights down. Breath coursed in, filling my chest and diaphragm. My eyes flicked open. I punched play and clipped the music player on to my jeans.

The merest hint of noise hummed in my ears. A pulse started; the pitch sharpened. From noise, music. From clamour, rhythm. The music moved through me as if at my command. I could breathe the beat into my lungs. My mouth tasted the guitar, rolling over my tongue and across my teeth. The boundary between where the music ended and I began trembled and disappeared and without consciousness or intention, I stepped forward.

The basketball court was slick with rain, almost slippery. My smooth soles slid across it; my arms and wrists and hips mirrored my steps. I spun, and water splashed. Every rotation, every angle, snapped into its new home. No muscle could be moved in isolation, the entire body carried with it. This was mine. I owned it.

Until I didn't, and momentum faltered and everything stumbled to a halt. The music ploughed on irrespective. One tiny mistake multiplying uncorrected until the whole thing came crashing down.

Again.

I returned to the centre, reset the music and stepped forward into the dance.

This time I got it right…

Almost.

Again the music barrelled on, leaving me lurching in its wake. I returned to the centre. The dance could not be expected to arrive all at once. It would take time.

Step by step, I worked my way forward, sometimes sure and flowing with ease into the unknown, sometimes lost and returning to centre to begin again. Each time I progressed further, flowing from one move to the next.

Slowly a new force started coursing through my movements. Intention and desire uniting with instinct, gathering behind each move and driving it forward. With every sweep of my arms, the world gave way before me, as if I'd tapped into harmony with it, gliding along its ley lines with the smooth momentum of inevitability. My mouth tingled from the tip of my tongue to the back of my throat, a taste like nothing I'd experienced before.

The taste of *power*.

I had no doubt this was the dance Julie had spoken of, to be done on a stage filled with dominoes and stepping stones. Each foot anchored in a specific location, and as the dance progressed, each new step returned to the same set of points on the surface. I tried to mark the relevant locations on the ground, to keep the pattern clear in my mind's eye. But the smooth wet floor of the court defied my attempts to scuff its surface.

Still, I carried on. With each repetition the last stumble would be smoothed over, and my limbs would find their way forward. Moment by moment, beat by beat, history yielded its buried secrets.

All of it felt deserved. Maybe Julie would disagree;

maybe she'd say this was all someone else's art, someone else's work. But I had discovered it. It had been hidden from me, and now it lay in my hands. Finders keepers.

Halfway through a glorious spin, the music stopped, and for the first time I was the one continuing on while the accompaniment faltered. I peered at the music player, and a blank screen stared back at me. Dead battery—and no wonder. The thing had probably been leaching charge over the months it had spent hidden away.

A band of pressure tightened about my chest. What if I couldn't recharge it? The player looked like the same brand as the phone Julie had given me. I flipped it over—same charge port. With luck, the charger Julie had given me would work for this as well, and...

Duh.

It had nothing to do with luck. Julie hadn't given me *her* old phone. She'd given me *my* old phone. She'd told me as much. Relief washed over me as I scooped up my backpack and headed home.

I quickstepped through the building's main doors and took the fire escape steps two at a time. Inside the apartment, I almost sprinted across the dominoes room and into the kitchen to get to the phone charger. Success! The cord plugged neatly into the new device and its screen hummed to life. I looked around. Cleared of furniture, the kitchen should be big enough. This would work.

I lugged the table to the bedroom doorway, tipped it on to its side, and angled it through the gap, my damp shirt clinging to my shoulders. I stripped it off, and my sodden shoes as well. I towel-dried the shoes as best I could and then jury-rigged a little platform in the bathroom/laundry so the clothes dryer would blast warm air on to them.

A hot shower drove the chill out of my skin and soon enough I was dressed in my exercise gear and back in the kitchen, where the music player seemed to be charging at a slow trickle with no regard for my rapidly diminishing minutes.

An unfamiliar sight tugged the corner of my eye. Across the apartment, the front door was hanging open. I'd neglected not only to lock the door behind me, but even to close it properly. I went over and shut the door, turned the locks and fastened the chain—for the last time in current memory. Then I did something I'd never done before.

I pulled the deadlock key from the door. Now the key would lie beside my journal.

My predecessor had placed the apartment keys in the same envelope as the letter, ensuring I didn't wander off without first getting my bearings. I looked down at the key in my hand. It had never really struck me before. The locks on the door were not only to keep others out. More fundamentally, they were to keep me in.

I looked at the room around me with new eyes. Bridges, platforms and dominoes surrounded me, their filigree beauty smeared in the shadows. If Julie had been telling the truth—and I had no reason to doubt her on this matter—the dance should take place not on a deserted basketball court or a kitchen floor but here, in the midst of all this fragility. This was the setting envisaged by my former self, the one before the letter-writer—the dancer: the Robbie of Julie's heart. He'd planned to build these very dominoes into a platform to launch something alive and beautiful.

But what was I building? A memento, nothing more. A cage, nothing less.

I'd been managed. Controlled by keys and letters. That was the truth of it. My predecessor had hidden the past to seize the future. In the face of his anger at Julie, and the horror of being left on his own for those first frightening days, he'd built a small, secluded life that prioritised safety. But how could he make that choice rule over an unknown future?

I clenched my fists. His reasons were not so different

from Julie's—but her sin was only of omission. My predecessor's was deliberate. Proactive. Calculated. Hell, it was *strategic*. Maybe the anger surging through me was unfair. Maybe Julie was right, and no one could do what I demanded, not even my own self. I'd raged against her for falling short of standards I myself had failed, but this time my fury had no target: my predecessor was long gone. Only I remained, still clinging to the life he'd fashioned for me and fuming in useless anger.

Maybe not completely useless. The stepping stones weren't welded down, after all. It was too late at this point to revise the whole structure, but with some tinkering, it could be bent to a different purpose. I had some time to kill anyway. The player was still charging, my shoes still drying.

I fetched my tools from the bedroom and began pulling up the stones. Moving them required resetting a heap of dominoes. It stung a little to disrupt the fall I'd planned and built so carefully, but the new idea would make for a fresh pattern of movement, putting the stepping stones themselves to purpose. No longer were they just for walks around the prison yard.

The drill whirred in my hand, and I threw myself into the work like a man possessed. Or perhaps dispossessed.

The work filled my attention for the best part of an

hour. At that point, I went and checked on the music player. The battery was still low, but it would do if I kept it plugged in. In the laundry, my shoes were still damp. I found some thick socks and pulled them on anyway. When I stood in them, my posture changed. It became alert. Sharp.

I left the player lying on the kitchen bench, charging. I could hear the music through its tiny speakers rather than the headphones. The sound was thin, but loud enough for my purposes. I pressed play and strode to the centre of the room. The music swelled, and I moved with it. Around me, the walls were no longer boundaries constraining the space. They were a frame creating it.

I progressed up to the point I'd reached in the park, and then began breaking new ground. The exhilaration of unlocking each new step felt like a revenge on my predecessor for his lies and subterfuge. He'd tried so hard to control me, to make me his clone. The letter. The dominoes. The key. The meaningless bloody mementoes. This very apartment. Yet all those shackles now lay in pieces. With every breath of my life I'd journeyed further and further from the path he'd laid out. Everything I would call a victory in my life must be recorded for him as a failure.

My feet landed wrong from a leap, and I clattered to a halt. Damn. Three times now I'd come unstuck at this same spot, a glorious moment where I launched myself into the air, feet tucked under me. But every time I landed, my feet came down in the wrong spot, nowhere near the stepping stones I'd mentally marked out on the kitchen floor.

Faster, try it faster.

There was a thought. Accelerate the whole thing. Take my stupid forgetful mind out of the equation and let my body work it out for itself. I cut off the music and amped up the speed. But no luck. The leap still felt perfect, the landing anything but. All the rest of my occasional missteps had felt like honest mistakes, but everything about this landing felt wrong. I flexed and unflexed my hands as I searched for a way forward. Frustration gripped me, along with some grumbles from my stomach. Come to think of it, I hadn't eaten anything since breakfast. No wonder I was struggling.

I ate a sandwich while doing some more work on the dominoes. Julie would love this, creating something to a crazy new plan.

Stupid thought. Julie no longer had any love for anything in this place. But once upon a time, in some yesterdays or yesteryears, she would have loved this.

That word she had seized on with such rage. *Weird.*

I was still capable of being weird. There was comfort in that. Even if all the links between Julie and me had been destroyed, some connection remained between me and her Robbie.

Between the dancing and the building, the day grew late. Time no longer passed in seconds but in tiny jobs and cups of coffee. The shadows deepened and I had to switch on the overhead lights. I turned back to doing the dominoes, hoping that a break from the dancing might refresh my mind enough for it to puzzle through the leap and the landing. I completed one more corner section, and then a patch by the wall. Unthinkingly, I pulled up its barrier and turned to the next one.

Except there was no 'next one'. The floor was done. I'd been so engrossed I'd stopped monitoring my overall progress, and now all of the changes had been made. The small pile of dominoes sitting in what had once been the central pathway were all the remaining tiles. The only space still to be filled was the patch of floor under them, a craggy island in a sea of frozen order.

After all the months of planning, the weeks of building and assembling, and these final hours of rebuilding, bare minutes were left. I assembled the final little batch. No room for any last spurt of creativity. This last group fitted into the larger mosaic like the final puzzle piece into a huge jigsaw, where the moment of triumph requires none of the thought that went before it.

I had done it.

I slowly spun around, taking it all in. The thousands and thousands of tiny standing stones. The strange little spirals. The magnificent platforms and the neat lines spanning the bridges. Without the cardboard grids overlaying the work, it looked naked. Fragile. A single bump of a single tile could now trigger a wave of beautiful destruction, tumbling every one of the eighty-three thousand, seven hundred and ninety dominoes assembled before me.

Afternoon had become evening. I made myself a light dinner and another coffee. Time to tackle the dance, and my mind was strangely relaxed. The threat of the forgetting had never felt so distant. It seemed almost impossible that it would strike tomorrow and all this would come to an end.

My hours of practice had not been in vain. I sailed through the dance's opening. My body itched for it, emotion and poetry flowing through every moment. Right up to the puzzling landing from that leap. Once again, everything about the leap felt all right, and everything about the landing felt all wrong.

I paced around the room, searching for a solution. Perhaps I could start from the moment of the landing and work forward from there. Maybe then I'd be able to work backwards to see how it all linked together.

The first part of this idea worked fine. Setting the music to begin just before the leap, I puzzled through the next steps using the same process that had unearthed the earlier movements. First placement, then power, then poetry.

But there was a problem. None of the new steps used the previously existing stepping stones. Every foot-placing after the leap seemed to require a brand-new stepping stone. It struck me that maybe the leap's landing was the moment I smashed the dominoes, which would explain why my steps could now take me off the stepping stones.

But no—that couldn't be right. None of the choreography of the dominoes' fall could survive me stomping and crashing around everywhere.

Frustration built within me with every step, clutching at my gut. The more my confidence grew in the dance's later sections, the more the clash with the earlier sections grew more inexplicable.

Julie would know the answer. Another useless thought. Gritting my teeth against it, I pushed further through the dance. But soon enough, two more minutes into the routine, the exact same problem reappeared. Another step landed me in the wrong spot. Everything felt fine until halfway through the move—a slow spin with one outstretched leg. But as soon as I set off, I found myself totally wrong-footed.

I killed the music and took a deep breath. The clock said eight. Only a matter of hours before all of this unravelled. Surely it wasn't asking too much to just get this one thing right. In his final days, my past self had been building towards one ultimate performance, in the spotlights and before an enraptured crowd. My ambitions were much smaller—to nail it just once. Here, alone, in my kitchen.

My forehead began to ache from the frown I'd worn over the last half-hour. I took a few slow steady breaths and tried to rub away the sore muscles.

Was it possible I'd got this all wrong, and this wasn't the same dance Julie had told me about? That made no sense. For one thing, all the footfalls fell on specific parts of the floor. For another, the movements always placed my feet directly down into position, never sliding them to their mark, or grazing the floor. Both clearly marked the dance as made for stepping stones. Made for the dominoes.

I squared my shoulders. I retraced my steps through the opening stages from memory, marking the stepping stones out on the floor with a pencil. This gave me a permanent map of how they would be arranged on the stage and it was just as I'd thought: from the moment I landed from the leap, the subsequent footfalls were all wrong, crisscrossing and landing outside my pencilled circles.

Fine. Time to get strategic. If it was important, it was worth being smart about. I retrieved all the flattened cartons and covered the kitchen floor with them, like so many pieces of a big jigsaw puzzle. I joined the pieces together with some screws from my toolbox.

This time I worked through the second stage, after the leap. Once again I marked all the places where my feet landed on the cardboard. But every time I landed or spun, the cardboard shifted. So I cut holes in the cardboard to mark the foot-placings. Now when I danced I didn't have to actually stand on the cardboard.

Yes: the foot-placings were different. The holes in the cardboard didn't match up with the pencil markings on the floor. I plonked myself down in a corner of the room. How to unpick this puzzle? It just didn't make sense.

Unless.

I slid the mat across the floor until the nearest hole lined up with the nearest pencil-mark on the floor. The other holes didn't match up. No surprise there. Still, some of the nearer ones were not far off: I'd just have to swivel things a little. Gripping two edges of the cardboard mat, I rotated it clockwise.

The breath drained from my lungs. Everything lined up. A dozen round holes perfectly eclipsed a dozen pencilled suns.

What did *that* mean?

A simple solution sprang to mind. As I suspended myself in mid-air during the dance, the entire floor—dominoes, stepping stones and all—simply spun and shifted under me, ensuring I landed perfectly on the newly positioned stepping stones.

Except that was stupid.

I rotated the cardboard map back and forth, watching the circles line up in clockwork perfection. It really looked as if some force pushed the whole thing around and made it rotate by the same—

No! The force didn't move the floor under me. The force moved *me*.

The dance was a duet. At the critical moment, I would jump into the air, catastrophically wrong-placed, about to crash down on the fragile sea of dominoes.

And then the other dancer would impact me in mid-air somehow, spinning me round to land safe on the stepping stones after all.

No prizes for guessing my partner: it had to be her. It was always her.

Earlier I'd wondered if Julie might know the answer. But she *was* the answer. And that meant the dance would never be completed.

Despair washed over me. After all the revelations of the last twelve hours, what was I left with? Nothing. The dominoes were complete. But the dance would never be.

It was late. I prepared for bed and switched out the lights, all except for the little lamp by the kitchen table. In its small pool of light, I sat down to write the day's journal entry. My last ever. Unless maybe I found a moment tomorrow to say a few words about how it felt to wait for impending doom. Perhaps that was a bad idea. It might be kinder to my future not to record such things.

As I sat, the cool of the air conditioning wore away at my earlier exertion. My muscles tightened and ached, and my skin prickled into goosebumps. I wrote and wrote, and the more I did, the stranger it all seemed. Everything had changed. The mementoes were gone, replaced with rings and shoes. And what had I been doing? Walking the streets. Dancing outside in the rain. Fuming at the letter. Leaving my door open to the world.

What had I become?

Something new. Something unplanned. Bit by bit, step by step, I'd left behind the man the letter-writer had hoped to create. I looked back at his designs with anger, with sadness. The two of us seemed to scowl at one another across time, each disappointed in our expectations for the other. Earlier in the day I'd felt proud about freeing myself from his cage. Yet what was I doing? Wasn't I trying the very same strategy?

The very same failed strategy.

The knowledge knotted my gut. What was I doing except trying to shackle my future self, to bend him to my will? And what could I expect in response? I might hold him for a while, then something beautiful would turn his head. A dance. A woman. At that moment, all my words would be bars on a paper cage. He would push them aside and turn into something new.

As I had.

I was the living proof that my own plan would not work. And if it wouldn't work, if there was no way of hurling my self past tomorrow, then tomorrow I would die. Despite the exercises, the dominoes, the journal—everything. My throat tightened, my breath grew short. But I picked up the pen, determined to write it down and at least pass on this one final lesson.

I'd failed.

> There was no way forward. Nothing I could do would matter. Nothing would change even if I stopped writing right

Day Zero

Now it hit me. I had the whole thing backwards.

I HAD to call her: Julie.

The room was still dark as I pulled myself out of bed. On the balcony the air felt thick and heavy, the humidity trapped in by the storm clouds above. Red light stained a corner of the dark sky away to the east. My final dawn. I sipped coffee and thought about the foolishness, the futility of sending her away.

Despite myself, I'd turned away from the path my past self had planned. So too my future self would be drawn by the same loves and lures as me. The *same* loves and lures. That was the thing. There, and only there, lay any hope of survival.

Julie was the future. The lifeline.

It was impossible, of course. I hadn't just sent her away, I'd made her realise the man she loved was lost to history. Except now I wondered about that. I'd changed. I'd become something new. Or perhaps something old—maybe something Julie would recognise.

Would she care? Things had been said that could not be unsaid. Still, if I could convince her to come over I could show her the dance. Perhaps, between the dance and the new design for the dominoes, she'd see something of her old Robbie still alive in me. She deserved to have the choice anyway, and to make it with full knowledge.

It was too early to call, so I threw myself into practising. If there was any hope of Julie seeing the old Robbie in me, the dance had to be as perfect as possible. Not actually perfect, of course. There was the not-so-small matter of the sharp changes in direction triggered by the absent dance partner. I'd have to simply ignore those, and continue on from wherever my leaps landed.

I worked my way through the dance as best I could. But despite my exertions, the clock slowed to a crawl. Every time I looked up and saw that mere minutes had passed, my impatience to phone Julie ratcheted up another notch.

Screw it.

It was still only six-thirty, but I couldn't wait another second. The forgetting could strike at any moment and if I left it much longer there might not be anything to see. Either way, Julie would understand why I'd called so early on this of all days. I didn't plan my words. I punched the numbers and bit my lip as the phone rang.

And rang.

It was ringing too long. A frenzy of what-ifs buzzed at my mind. I took a deep, shuddering breath and waited. Give the lady time to wake up, at least.

Nothing.

And nothing. The phone rang and rang with no answer. Surely she would have had time to wake up. Even if she'd gone out, she always had the thing on her. Perhaps she'd decided not to take my call. I couldn't really blame her for that.

I hit redial and waited while it rang. I flexed my free arm, reaching down behind the back of my head. A dancer's habit, she'd said, to stretch when you're nervous.

The phone rang until it rang out.

Wait. Julie had written her landline number on the back of her card. Fumbling, I punched the wrong numbers, hung up and tried again, pressing the numbers deliberately one by one. The number rang. And rang. And rang out.

No need to panic. She might be in the shower or... something. I tried her again. Both phones. Nothing. Perhaps she'd gone out and left her mobile at home on the charge.

Gone out at six-thirty in the morning into a city dark with storm clouds? Please. She just didn't want to pick up.

That was the best of the two possible explanations. The other didn't bear thinking about. But try as I might, my mind kept returning to fingers gripped hard around the green neck of a champagne bottle. That single bottle might have been the start of an unravelling. For all I knew, she could have been drinking nonstop since she walked out my door.

I put down the phone and wiped my hands on my shirt. They felt slimy. Despite the cool, sweat prickled at my shoulders and chest as I paced the room. Julie might be passed out in a drunken stupor on her bathroom floor. Driven to despair by what I'd said.

I'd try again in half an hour. That was all I could think to do. If she still didn't answer at that point then, well, more drastic action would be needed.

Sticking to that plan almost killed me. I ate breakfast

and washed up and the clock barely moved. A few other chores and at last the moment came. I tried both her numbers twice, with no luck.

I would have to go to her apartment. Maybe she wouldn't be there. Maybe she wasn't even in the state anymore, but there was no other alternative. I didn't know if I could help her, or if she'd let me help her. But at least I could show her she had been right about me. If she turned me away, it would be her choice. I owed her that much.

Having made the decision, I prepared as best I could. The forgetting could happen at any moment and going outside was certifiably crazy. But that didn't mean I couldn't be smart about it. I changed clothes: pulled on my purple shirt and laced up the black shoes. Not the time for half measures. Given the threat of the thunderstorm, I wrapped the journal, the phone and the letter in a plastic bag, along with the map home. It didn't feel right to just stuff the two rings in with them. My finger itched to at least try on my wedding band—to feel it slip into the niche it had worn into my flesh. Just to see how it felt. But I had no right to it. I pulled a piece of string from the kitchen drawer, looped the two rings on to it and slipped it around my neck.

A sprinkling of rain cooled my face as I set out. I

walked fast, more spooked by worries about Julie than being caught outside when the forgetting struck. When I made it to her place, I strode up the hall and rapped on her door.

Nothing.

Rapping turned to thumping, and I called louder. Was she standing inside the apartment, arms obstinately crossed? Or lying unconscious on the bathroom floor? I pounded harder. I jiggled the doorknob in desperation. The door stayed locked.

I considered just waiting here on her doorstep. But there was no guarantee she'd return any time soon—or at all. And even if she did, the forgetting might strike long before then, leaving me lost in the world and useless to her. I thumped on the door, harder now. If she was passed out drunk, maybe she was in danger. Enough alcohol could kill a person.

I called her name, then yelled it. Part of me hoped that one of her neighbours would come out to see what the ruckus was all about. Then I could ask them if they knew anything about where she was. But there was nothing. No sound or movement except my own frantic knocking and calling.

Finally, out of ideas, I backed away down the dark hallway, blood pounding in my head, and my legs buckled under my weight. I crumpled to my knees. *I'd tell a thousand lies, light a thousand fires, break a thousand laws*, she'd said. *What wouldn't you do?* I looked back at the door. I'd seen it from the inside. The lock sat just above the doorknob with the bolt sliding into a screwed-on bracket, not into the doorway itself.

I shut my eyes, flexing my body into a crouch. I could feel the distance to the door, not in metres or inches but in steps and breaths. My mind spanned the distance in a dozen different ways, working out how to take my body's force and drive it into one small square of wood at the end of the hall.

I took off down the hall like a sprinter at the starting gate and launched myself off one foot, twisting as I hurled myself into the air. Spin, muscle and velocity came together as my foot struck the target, and with a surprising crunch the door burst open. Splinters flew everywhere. I hit the floor and bounced back to my feet almost in the same motion.

'Julie?'

I would have settled for anything, an angry retort, a drunken groan. But the only sound was the rain unleashing against her apartment window. The storm had hit at last. I raised my voice. 'Julie? Are you here?'

The whole apartment was trashed, not just the

door. Furniture overturned, her little desk swept clean, the floor strewn with the shrapnel of a life exploded. Shattered glass crunched into the carpet under my shoes and I tried not to notice it looked like the broken pieces of the champagne bottle I'd given her. This was the violence of a life being forcibly reset. One vice at a time.

I went into the bedroom and then the bathroom. Maybe I'd find her lying passed out on the tiles in a pool of her own vomit, but at least she'd be alive. At least she'd be here.

Nothing. The apartment was empty and silent. The only noise was the storm raging outside.

My legs felt like lead. I sat myself down on the edge of Julie's bed next to an open suitcase and a large canvas bag. She'd emptied out her wardrobe by the looks of it, but most of the contents just lay in haphazard piles. The two travelling bags were barely half-packed.

She hadn't left town for good, then. Not yet, at least. But that meant she was outside somewhere. I wandered through the apartment, scanning the wreckage around me, not knowing what I hoped to find. Nothing in the livingroom. But in the kitchenette—a bottle on the floor in a corner.

Bourbon: empty.

Thunder cracked; my skin shuddered into goosebumps.

Rain splattered in through the bottom of the livingroom window. The spot where Julie had sat and smoked. I slammed it down and the rain lashed the glass. Julie was out there in this storm, almost certainly with a bottle of bourbon or more in her. So where could she be? There had to be something, anything, that would hint at her whereabouts.

I paced through the wreckage, lifting, moving, uncovering. On the floor, half-hidden behind the couch I found her phone. Jagged splinters webbed its screen. I stabbed at the home button, but it was dead. That was why she hadn't been answering my calls.

A little rubbish bin sat beside her desk, incongruously still upright. I upended it, and a used tissue tumbled out along with her six-months-dry medallion. Given everything else appeared to have been hurled around in fury, it felt significant that this had found its way into the trash. Wherever she was, she wasn't on Day 356 anymore.

Out of ideas, I slumped against the desk. Despite everything, I was no better off than I'd been on the other side of the door. Perhaps I should just wait here for her. She'd have to return eventually, but that might be hours, days. Time I didn't have.

I put the medallion back in the bin. Stuck in the

bottom was a scrunched brown paper bag, the type used by bottle shops. I tore it open. Inside was a crushed receipt for a bottle of Jack Daniels with a name at the top in faded print. South Brisbane RSL: I knew it from my neighbourhood walks. A huge building with dark booths and poker machines. A bottle shop on one corner. The date was from yesterday morning.

Maybe she'd gone back there when the bourbon ran out. Or maybe not, but it was the only lead I had. I leapt into action, racing around her apartment, grabbing anything I thought might be helpful. The one thing I didn't find was an umbrella. Given the way the rain was belting against the window, my backpack would be soaked through in minutes. I took off my jacket and wrapped it around the plastic bag, then made a stab at closing the apartment door. The latch was smashed, so it wouldn't shut properly, but it felt better than leaving the place wide open to the world.

Outside on the doorstep, the rain made me pause. Despite the awning I was getting drenched, and I shivered. The right side of my torso was freezing, pallid wet skin exposed to the world. My shirt was split beneath the arm; I must have torn it as I kicked Julie's door down. I pushed aside a last moment of hesitation and stepped into the downpour. Before I'd reached the end of the block, my shirt and the front of my jeans were soaked through. If it kept up like this, the journal, buried deep in my backpack, wrapped in two plastic bags and my jacket, might be in danger.

I shielded my eyes and ploughed on. The rain poured into tiny rivers down my neck and inside my collar; my too-long fringe kept falling across my eyes. Heart in mouth, I turned the final corner. The RSL's lights gleamed like a beacon. Within hours, perhaps minutes, all the memories that had got me here would be gone—but at least they'd survived long enough to find this place.

I pushed my way into the bright, dry warmth. The place was huge. One enormous room filled with black tables and seats led into a larger one with rows of poker machines. There weren't many people—it was still only early morning—which would make Julie easier to find. Flicking the water from my hair, I searched through the place at double time. No Julie.

Gritting my teeth against the possibility she might not be here, I ploughed on into the adjacent room. The light was dimmer here, lit mainly by the glow of the pokies. I searched the ranks of the machines: row after row yielded nothing after nothing.

My breath laboured and my mouth felt dry. My chest seemed to be collapsing in on itself. Maybe this wasn't disappointment or cold or exhaustion, maybe this was the first stage of the forgetting. I wouldn't know, after all. Whatever happened to me when it struck was by its very nature hidden from future knowledge.

I pushed it aside. I had to get home, and before that, I had to find Julie.

The bartender was a woman. In her fifties, maybe. She looked at me with narrowed eyes.

'Hi,' I said.

'How can I help you, love?'

'I'm looking for someone.' I pulled off my backpack and rummaged through it. Cocooned inside my jacket and the plastic bag, the journal and mementoes were dry. Small mercies. I pulled out the phone, and showed her the picture of Julie and me. 'Has she been here?'

She took the phone from my hands and looked down at the picture, then back up to me. 'Who's she to you?'

'She's my best friend. She's not home. Or answering her phone. I haven't heard from her since Friday, and I'm worried.' My mind was racing. Julie would know what to say. 'When we took that photo she was three hundred and fifty-one days dry.'

The woman pursed her lips. 'Well, it's back to zero now.'

'She was here? This morning?'

'I had to move her on.' She gestured to a sign behind the bar: *Patrons will not be served if visibly intoxicated.*

'Where would I find the nearest pub? The nearest place to get a drink.'

'That's what she wanted to know.' The woman handed my phone back to me. 'I told her maybe she should give it a bit of a rest.'

I wanted to scream at her to tell me something, anything, but I kept my voice as steady as I could. 'Please.'

'There's a club at the end of Musgrave Street? Charmers. It'd be open now. Take a right outside, then right again at the crossing. Three blocks down.'

'Thanks,' I called, already making my way to the exit, stuffing everything back in my backpack. I shoved the phone into my back pocket. Maybe the picture would come in handy again.

Outside, the rain thundered down in full force. I was shivering again, worse than before. It didn't feel right. I took a deep breath. Just a little longer, I prayed. Give me this last shot at seeing her. I shielded my eyes and pushed forward into the maelstrom. By the time I saw the place, my shoes were squelching with every stride. If this kept up, the only thing I'd be passing on to my future self would be pneumonia.

Inside, the club was dark: mood lighting only. There

was a dance floor and sunken booths. Music throbbed softly. I scanned the room urgently as my eyes adjusted to the low light. My eyes went from one stranger to another with a growing dread. This was my last chance. She had to be here.

There. Near the bar, a glimpse of cropped-short hair. She was sitting on a tall stool at a high table. Her pale neck and shoulders shone against her black dress in the dim light. A stranger sat beside her. Male. Close, almost in her space. Julie seemed oblivious. She was leaning forward, cradling a tall glass on the table.

'Julie!' Relief flooded me.

She looked up, her gaze drifting from my face down to my soaking shirt, then back up to my face again. She didn't speak.

'Who're you?' The guy beside her was older, in his forties. Thickset. He too looked me up and down, and I realised how I looked. Drenched to the bone, shirt torn, skin flushed, eyes wild.

'I'm her husband.' I kept my eyes fixed on her. 'Well, I'm her—'

'I'm not married.' Julie's voice sounded slurred, thick with alcohol.

'Divorced?' the guy asked her.

'Widowed.' Her eyes met mine.

'Yeah, about that,' I said. 'I need to tell you something.' I took a deep breath. If only we could have had this discussion back at her place, or mine. Everything felt out of place. Her drink. The guy next to her. The distant beat of generic music. But this place and time was all I had.

'I lied to you,' I said. 'At the dance when I said I didn't remember. I promised you I'd try, and I didn't. Not truly.'

'So you lied.' She shrugged. 'Now you can live with the consequences. Alone.'

'Fuck that.'

Julie blinked as the word rolled off my tongue. She couldn't have done better herself.

'Come back with me,' I said. 'I've got something to show you. Something you wanted to know. I can show you now.'

She glared at me, her glazed eyes hardening. Maybe a little anger was a good thing. Better anything than indifference. 'So show.'

'What, here?'

She shrugged.

'I need to show you at home, back at the apartment.'

'Then forget it. I don't care anymore. That's what I'm doing here. Not caring.' With her eyes still fixed on me, she put the glass to her lips and swallowed two mouthfuls.

'Fine,' I said. '*Here.*'

I turned and strode to the bar. Perhaps it was better this way anyway—to do it here, rather than at home. My past self would have done it this way.

'Can I have two large glasses of water and a song request?' The bartender didn't look particularly open to the idea, but I pushed on. 'There's a tip in it. I've got—' I emptied the contents of my sodden wallet on the bar. 'One hundred bucks and…some change. For one song.' One more thing I could bequeath to my future self: destitution.

The bartender stared at me.

'Please,' I said. 'This is life or death for me right now.'

'We don't normally do requests.' He looked around the room briefly, then shrugged. 'But if it's life or death.' He scooped the pile of cash off the counter and I breathed a sigh of relief.

Julie had turned herself away, shifting a little towards her companion.

I plonked the two glasses of iced water down on the table in front of her. Her eyes moved from the water to me. 'Your shirt's torn.'

'You were right about the letter,' I said. 'And right to be angry. But you need to know the whole truth, because you can't make a proper decision without knowing how things really stand. It's late, but you deserve to know.'

'Late?' Julie sat up straight. 'Wait. What's the day today? What's the date?' She punched at her companion's phone, sitting on the table near her drink. 'The twenty-fourth. *Fuck*. This is the day.'

The words sounded like an accusation. She reached for the water glass and took a slug, looked at me again, and sculled the rest. 'Okay. First, for the record, I cannot wait to get you out of my life. But second, Robbie, what the fuck? You can't be out on the streets now. Of all days.' She stretched her legs to the floor, pulling herself clumsily to her feet. 'I have to get you home.'

'I don't think that's important right at this minute.'

'That is the only thing that's important. This is not going to be some repeat disaster ending with you in a fucking hospital.' She turned to the guy next to her. 'Listen…Pete, right?' She placed a hand on his shoulder. 'I have to get this guy off the streets. It's a medical thing. You don't want to know. Honestly, I wish *I* didn't.'

She wobbled a little and leaned on the table. A few more mouthfuls of ice water and she glared at me over the top of the glass. 'What the hell were you thinking? You spend half a year alone in your room and then on the one day—*the one day*—when you really need to be at home with the door locked, you take to the streets?'

She took another slug, and then poured the rest of the water into her hand and splashed it on her cheeks. It slopped over the table and down her dress.

'If you'd spent half a year living in fear, is that how you'd spend the one day you had left?'

She shook her head and stretched out her hand to me, like an exasperated mother demanding the hand of a naughty child. 'Come on. We're going.'

I stepped forward, slipping down onto one knee and taking Julie's hand in mine. She stopped in her tracks.

Well, I had her attention.

'I love you,' I said, looking up at her. 'I love how you chose what you wanted and went after it with everything you have. I love your conniving mind and its twisted sense of humour. I have no idea how I could once have been worthy of you, but I love you anyway. Part of me loved you the moment you arrived at my door.'

I pressed her hand. 'There. Now you have all the power.'

Julie looked down at me. About five different emotions seemed to flash across her face. She blinked and swallowed. 'Are those new shoes?'

Not the words I'd been hoping for. But perhaps not the worst response possible. I raised my hand slightly: *listen.*

The song had started, its slow opening pulse just audible. Julie looked down at me in surprise. 'How do you know this song?'

'I know more than this song.'

Releasing her hand, I backed away from her, towards the empty dance floor. My shoes were still damp but the soles had dried out: they glided nicely on the smooth floor. I set myself, poised and centred, feeling the dance floor's symmetry around me. The music began to take hold, and the coloured lights shone down on me. In my mind's eye, I could see the stepping stones. I searched for one last glimpse of Julie, but the lights around me made shadows of everything else.

The beat began almost before I was ready, but the reflexes formed by practice took hold. My body swooped forward, my leg striding out in search of the safe footfall.

For a moment, everything else fell away—the apprehension and exhaustion, the chill of the wet silk shirt clinging to my chest, and the forgetting itself. All of it disappeared, leaving me alone on my little stage, accompanied only by the lights above and the music around me. The sound swelled, and I flowed into it. My body sang through the steps and turns. All the months of strain and stretching, the hours of practice over the last day, focused into this present moment.

I could sense eyes on me, but all that mattered was the audience of one, and whether she'd see something in the man before her of what she'd once loved.

The jump approached. I needed to concentrate if I was to get the landing right. As soon as my feet hit the floor, I would have to reimagine the space around me, rotating my mental map of the stepping stones.

But just as I prepared myself, a sudden flurry of activity came from outside the dance. All I could do was to concentrate harder. Control the dance before me.

I leapt into the air and—

A burst of movement, a swish of black cotton, a shock as Julie's knee slammed into mine. I spun in mid-air, past full circle, until my feet slammed down onto the floor. Onto the little circles of safety carved into my mind.

Perfect.

There it was: the force that could move the world.

Julie had landed safely, too, one knee dipped so low the hem of her dress almost brushed the floor. In that one movement, the dance transformed and I could see *her*. The water she'd splashed on her face and hair shone in the coloured light. Her eyes met mine, almost in challenge. As if daring me to know this dance. To know how it ended.

The music pulsed and we flowed with it, our movements locked in time. The future faded into irrelevance and there was only the dance. When our bodies touched and brushed and held, something new appeared in Julie's eyes. Wonder; disbelief at what I could do—what we could do.

My arm stretched out and Julie's hand met it, fingers wrapping around wrists. Her other arm stretched high, her body buoyed by my strength. Then she twisted, and her hand became a fist, plummeting downwards. My muscles screamed as I halted her plunge, just in time for her knuckles to kiss the floor.

There it was. The moment when it would begin.

The beautiful fall.

A new partner seemed to join us in the dance. I felt I could almost see the dominoes cascading around our every step, and racing ahead with waves and ripples.

When the time came for the next leap, there was no longer any doubt. I could see her movement before it happened. I could feel the impact bunting me backwards and downwards, into a new and perfect path and—

No.

Julie's knee smashed into my inside thigh and a bolt of pain tore up my leg as my body twisted in mid-air and I tumbled to the floor. She came down on top of me.

An audible *ohhhh*, a sigh of disappointment, sounded from outside the dance floor.

I must have misstepped.

I reached for Julie in sudden panic. 'I'm sorry, I'm sorry; are you okay?'

'Shit.' Her body shuddered beneath my hands: laughter. 'Given my bloodstream is ten per cent bourbon, I think we should all be impressed I made it that far.'

She rolled towards me and grabbed a fistful of my shirt at the shoulder, pulling herself into a seating position, her eyes meeting mine.

'What happened? How did you know about the song?'

I pulled myself upright. Our legs were still half-entwined, our faces close. Under her eyes, heavy shadows and the lines of too much drink. The heat of exertion flushed her cheeks, and a sheen of sweat glistened on her skin. She looked perfect.

'I found where I'd hidden everything from myself—the music, the shoes—and the dance turned out to be buried in my muscles and my mind, just like you thought. But then I realised it was a duet. Without you, I didn't know how it finished.'

'With us going splat on the floor.' She grinned.

'I thought if I showed you the dance, you might…

see something in me. Something of him, the old Robbie. Your Robbie.'

'Why do you care what I see? Last time I saw you...' She shook her head.

'I was so scared of my love for you. I thought it was a trap, a...a lure that would pull me away from who I am.' My hand went to her face, brushing her cheek with the back of my fingers. 'I had it the wrong way round. The only way I have to save myself is to hold on to what I love, and hold it so tight—so hard—that it can remake me. Today and every day.'

'Hmph.' She pulled herself up, half-sitting and half-kneeling, and reached for the cord around my neck, clearly visible now that my shirt was shredded. She studied the two rings for a moment, and then turned her gaze to my face.

'Julie,' I said. 'He's still in here.'

'No, I don't see him.'

Her hand reached up to mine, pressing it against her cheek. 'I see you.' She pulled my face to hers.

Somewhere outside the footlights, there came a sound like applause. Our kiss broke off, and Julie reached again to the cord where the rings hung.

She smiled, and the cord snapped from my neck.

We ran home, through the streets and through
the rain.

Julie said she loved what I'd done with the dominoes, seeing them complete at last, in all their glory and without any of the barriers. She saw straightaway that I'd changed the stepping stones. I'd set them up for the waltz I still owed her from that night at the dance hall.

Right now, she's getting changed into a white dress I stole from her apartment this morning. I told her it's important to plan for the possibility everything might go spectacularly well, but she just laughed and called me a stalker.

Soon we will dance, and perhaps I will forget. And if I do, then you will be born into the beauty of this falling world, held in the arms of someone whose love stretches beyond your every horizon.

Acknowledgments

Thanks to all those who helped bring this book to life: Mandy Brett, Dianne Blacklock, Kylie Scott, Kath FitzHywel and Alex Adsett.